GHOST MUSIC

Ghost Music

Candida Clark

review

First published in 2003
by REVIEW

An imprint of Headline Book Publishing

10 9 8 7 6 5 4 3 2 1

Cataloguing in Publication Data is available from the British Library

ISBN 0 7553 0102 1

Typeset in Perpetua, Janson and Centurybook Condensed
by Avon DataSet Ltd, Bidford-on-Avon, Warwickshire

Printed and bound in Great Britain by
Clays Ltd, St Ives plc

HEADLINE BOOK PUBLISHING
A division of Hodder Headline
338 Euston Road
London NW1 3BH

www.reviewbooks.co.uk
www.hodderheadline.com

For Dominic, once again, with love

I

*I remember thinking how wise a man was H.C. Andersen.
The king told his secrets down a well, and his secrets were
safe.*

John Steinbeck, *The Winter of Our Discontent*

1

Late June, with thunder imminent in the ending day. Jack watches the boy running towards him down the hillside made vivid by last night's fall of rain. He sees him long before he can hear him. But it does not matter. He is certain what he will say, as though he's waited a lifetime just to hear it, as though the last fifty years have in one moment been eclipsed.

The greenhouse door is open and there's a warm breeze rising along the surface of the land. With it comes the freshness of rain-wet meadowgrass. He breathes it all in, remembering.

He imagines the moment, more than the boy, travelling at speed towards him. His body braces itself involuntarily, as though the news the boy carries were a spark, burning its way through dry tinder. He can see that soon enough the fire will reach him and everything will start again. Nothing has died, he thinks, it has simply waited, quiet as a buried seed.

He bunches his hands inside the tray of soil before him. A whole life diminished to one small point of revelation. He watches the boy approaching, and feels the faded light on his head like a gentle hand in remonstration: did you think you could keep your secret safe for ever? He had known this day would come. No time is so light that it can be held off absolutely. He had known that one day it would fall, and he would feel the full stone weight of it again.

Now the boy's legs are cutting a shadowed wake down the hillside, slantways from the top, where only moments earlier he appeared, paused, and, seeing the station house set on the limits of the small town, had seemed to fall down like a flag being lowered from that high point of visibility.

Jack rubs his forehead and feels the thunder there. His breath comes hard and high. The boy is still running downhill towards him. Take your time, he wants to tell him. I've waited long enough for you not to bother with all that hurrying. It makes no difference now. It's much too late for endings.

In the air there's the murmur of wood-pigeons, descending. Bees are worrying at the honeysuckle, and he listens with his head tilted to snare these delicacies of sound. He watches a red admiral. Its gaping wings tremble where the breeze catches them, stretching wide as though waiting for the air's rich residue of pollen.

But when is waiting merely stubbornness? Jack shuts his eyes and sees his father poking at a rotten plant with an angry stick, his shoulders raised in outrage at the thing's refusal to flourish for his sake.

When he opens his eyes he is surprised to see the boy right there in front of him, panting on the gravel. He does not move. His hands are still finger-deep in peat. Later, when he has gone, he will notice that he crushed an entire tray of seedlings in those few moments of listening.

The boy – a young man, really, in his twenties – is out of breath. He leans forward like a marathon runner, resting his hands on his thighs, gulping in air. His face is flushed with effort, and when he speaks his voice is ragged. Behind him, on the hillside, the route forged through the grass by his descent looks like an ancient pathway, finally revealed. It is as though all the boy did was follow a course set out for him long years before.

A wasp is smashing itself against the glass roof of the greenhouse while Jack waits for the boy to speak. It smashes itself as though in disbelief at the limits set out for it. To see it do this, he feels almost calm, thinking that messages are written everywhere, and through everything – you only have to look – and that that wasp's persistence in its anger might've been a lesson in defeat for him, if only he'd had his eyes as wide open as they are at this moment. Jack rolls his shoulders, settles himself in readiness for what the boy will say.

The wind has gathered, picked itself up as though it had been only temporarily at rest. Beyond the rim of the hillside, the green of meadowgrass is replaced by the darkening moor. For some miles – around fifteen, travelling straight – the moorland runs on uninterrupted to the coast, and when there's a westerly strong as this one, the scent of sea is delivered here along with the peatiness of moorland, the rich tang of ryegrass and damp verdure.

Between the meadow and the town there's a small coppice of thirty or so trees, well tended. Further behind this, to the north, the hotel stands hidden by a sloping pinewood, the treetops undulant as a high spring tide. In the coppice, larches, a few birch trees, alders, hazels, beeches, and one large horse-chestnut are caught up in the motion of wind grown stronger by degrees all afternoon, so that he knows what it'll mean, would've known even with his eyes shut. He can tell a storm by smelling. And in his body's hidden marrow he's a weathervane. His limbs grow stiff and burdensome in such hours as these, before a storm.

He looks again at the hilltop where the boy descended, and it's true: in the space of perhaps three minutes, the sky has turned to louring, the afternoon already heavy with the nearness of the rain.

His hands, like a pair of moles slain in the night, are still set out before him in the peat. His fingernails are black with the stuff. It has worked its way also into his skin, which is purplish, as though he's held his hands inside that earth for years, until through the force of time it has bled into his flesh in proof of past and future – both to be revealed. And here they are etched plain upon his skin. He stares at his hands, looks away fast as the boy begins to speak.

He tells him that he's come from up on the moor, that he's one of the archaeologists who have been working there through the summer. Jack looks at him: he has seen them going up there, orange oilskins against the green. The boy asks to use the telephone. When Jack does not immediately answer, he introduces himself as 'David', as though his name were a calling-card to verify his credentials. He says that it's urgent, squinting back at the shadowing hilltop. Rooks rise from the coppice, blackening the blue that's clouding in the west. 'It'll only hold off for another hour at most,' Jack tells him, nodding at the sky.

The wasp smashes itself so loud it sounds like the first of the rainfall, and the force of its weight on glass seems to propel it backwards, away at last into the open air.

David looks back up at the hillside, tipping dark hair from his brow, frowning and apprehensive. Jack follows his gaze. What has he seen? But there is nothing. Only the day growing each moment more dusky with the approaching storm.

When he speaks again, Jack is watching the hillside, the way the lush skin of green covers the earth's deep secrets, so long held in check now that he can understand perfectly that line about green thoughts in green shades. It makes perfect sense to him. It's the weight of what's outside those lines that'll drown us all, he thinks – the red moments before and after whatever pause might come in such a meadowful of green. And it is more true of that field, he tells himself, than that boy will ever know.

He sees again the pathway he himself so often cut, on his way to the hotel to meet her. And he sees himself with her, stumbling through the meadow, walking together beneath the full June trees.

His hands are shaking, still screwed tight inside the soil. His heart contracts. He has the thought of strong fingers pressing round his throat, and perhaps it's this, he asks himself, that is making his eyes smart?

'I must use the phone,' David is saying. 'There's a body—' But beyond these words Jack cannot hear a thing. He tells him where the telephone is, just inside the doorway on the hall table, tells him he can go in there himself to use it, please will he just do that? And when the first large thunder comes, echoing through the distance, the sound it makes is nothing like so loud, in his mind's eye, as the sound his grief makes, fathoming out the hidden places of his love.

He covers his face with his hands. He can remember everything.

They are wading upwards through the knee-high grass, laughing, breathless with effort. Jack is yards ahead of Elena now, and she uses this excuse for not hearing his 'Take off your shoes!' as through a sense of secret dignity she counts shoelessness as something someone in her position ought never to contemplate – not even now, being as they are to one another, intimate as children, separated by nothing of consequence beyond matrimony: hers, to another man.

But no, shoelessness would be the very end, the last thing on earth she'd be likely to let go hang. Thinking this, she straightens the seams of her stockings with a tweak of instinct, bending into the hillside slightly to do it as she follows him, her hands lingering in the depths of green that rush and whisper about her knees and calves as she stumbles unevenly after his departing back.

He turns to her at this moment, his face darkened by the approaching storm so that she cannot quite make out his expression, although from the way he pauses she is certain that he is smiling. 'Darling,' he calls out to her as she steps beside him, holding her close against him with the wind rising, quickening up the hillside so that even the grass is loud with that sound of weather.

Her head fits snug inside his strong neck's curve, his hand pressing down her hair which flashes by his face, tickling his lips so that he longs to run them free across her where he wills, and tells her so, so that she smiles, unseen, in that secret place where she nestles. 'My cave,' she calls it. 'My nook and hollow, perfect for me to hide away from the world, as though that's just what it was made for.'

'But why do you doubt that that's true?' he asks her, him the greater believer of the two in fate, and history's having a sense and purpose expressly engineered to bring her to him. 'How else would I have found you,' he asks, 'if it hadn't been meant?'

And they stop just short there, neither needing, still less wanting, to spell out all the facts and points of circumstance keeping them apart.

'But what if you go back?' He holds her closer. 'Return to the other world you came from?'

'Wouldn't you come to get me?' She kisses him, but he draws away, and tries to joke.

'Where would I find you? Bel-Air or at the Marmont? The Eden Roc, perhaps? Some Fifth Avenue heiress's fancy little *soirée*, or a Radio City première? There'd be a man there with epaulettes, can't you see him now? He wouldn't let me through.'

When he talks to her this way, she knows that he is no longer seeing her, and for her this is the worst form of exclusion – he can see only the celluloid patina that the world can have, as far as she's concerned: it means nothing to her. 'Don't believe the pictures, believe me, look, here I am.' She has the urge to shout at him until he understands. Although shouting, like shoelessness, is another thing she counts undignified, and will not do, especially not with him, her love.

'Oh yes,' she pulls a face, 'I'm so grand, so imposing,' and holds him tighter. But here they go no further, as though both are looking out upon the landscape of her life, seeing in unison how very plainly it excludes him.

His eyes slide from her, and her body grows rigid in his arms, a statue full of secrets that he hopes to learn. They make plans. But both worry that their time spent planning is a form of waiting – for which they have no time. In all their plans there is a stranger: her husband, the reason for her being there at all.

'Really, I'm here because of the novel that was set here, more than him,' she had insisted to him the first time. They were in the town square, and had met there as though by accident: the spectacle of market-day gave them an alibi. 'He's set on turning it into a movie, and he sent me here to look around.' She had tried to change the subject. But he wanted to know more. 'He's in pictures, a very powerful man. He made me, I suppose you'd say.' She touched her hair. 'I'm really a brunette. But my eyes. These were what saved me. Very highly prized.' She lowered her voice, pretending to smile. 'A pretty young Jewish girl from a small town in Germany. That's all. An actress!'

He started to turn from her then, so she took hold of his arm and forced him to look at her. 'All this is nonsense. Only believe me. You know the story in that novel?' She blushed: two runaway lovers escaping to their island by the sea. 'It was written by another Yank,' she carried on, talking to elude the vision, conscious of his eyes upon her, 'and was something of a hit – top of the *New York Times* bestseller lists three years ago, right through the summer months of 1935. It put the place on the map.' She had quoted her husband.

'For sure it did something of that nature,' Jack replied, running his hands along the passing undulations of a building, standing on that spot, as he pointed out with a nod to the date carved there upon the cornerstone, since 1689. She smiled, and secretly he touched her, a fragile brush against her waist where no one else would notice.

'You're not expecting me to be grateful that you have a husband, since that's the reason for your being here?' He had tried to laugh but could not, and she took his hand and kissed it – openly, for anyone to see.

Now there's the rumble of bad weather almost overhead, and he takes her by the wrist. 'Come on.' He has to shout now that the wind has grown so loud. 'Not much further.'

But she wants him to turn back. She is afraid. The storm is reflected in his eyes. Blue turned black and unreadable. She winces slightly when he pulls her alongside him, up towards the brow of the hill, away from town. She has heard what lies beyond – the moorland stretching for miles, uninterrupted, to the sea. Before, when Jack described the view, he laughed. It's almost a point of myth. He smiled. A sea view no one here has ever seen.

Yet there's a saltiness about the air right now, she thinks, as though a layer has ripped its way in one clean breath right off the ocean's skin to deliver it to this place. She imagines how it will fall, how it will try to drown them both.

He tugs at Elena's wrist, grazing her where her watch presses against her skin, a gesture rough and unexpected that draws a drop of blood. She is startled, and she doubts him — suddenly doubts that he is who she thinks he is. The worry rests there in the thunder running swift across the land towards them. She cannot shake it off.

She is on the hillside. The day is ending, and she is afraid. The rain comes sudden and peremptory, drenching her absolutely. When she calls out to him, telling him that she has lost a shoe, that it was whipped off somewhere a few steps behind her in the long grass, that she must go back for it, so let her go, he grins at her, his teeth polished bone in the dazzle of lightning, and he laughs as though she must be crazy to think about her shoe at such a moment, and he will not let her go back to retrieve it.

'Damn it, listen to me,' she shouts. My God, these things I never thought I'd know. Shoelessness and shouting. And here I am in this foreign place, with no witness or even any chance of help.

She looks back at the way she has come but the path is in darkness and the town is completely hidden now beneath the crest of the hill. Looking ahead at him, it would be impossible to say for sure that he is anyone she knows. Just as she is concealed by secrecy, his face is hidden by the night.

'Will you not stop?' she calls out to him. But he does not seem to hear. He walks ahead of her, out on to the open moorland, his back a black cameo against the silvered green.

David is swearing beneath his breath, damning the fact that he can't go faster. The long grass catches against his flying limbs. He sees himself already at the station house, asking to use the phone. He wants to overtake himself and catch up with himself there. He feels caught in a too-slow loop of time, as though he is being pulled steadily backwards, his legs whirling in hopeless retrograde.

Even in this last part of the day, just past dusk, the sun is still fat with all the heat of a fierce midsummer. But up beyond the rim of the hilltop the clouds are falling, gathering low with the weight of rain – and it's this that he has to beat, although the reason for his haste is something else entirely. He cannot unfix his mind from it. He just wants to tell the others and get straight back to it, to see if it can be true.

He can see the body taking shape beneath his hands, the outline of the skull and torso, the right arm wrapped around the pelvis, the left flung wide as though reaching out to take hold of someone long since lost. If the body is what he thinks it is, it will change everything. But it still seems too close even to name, the image appearing to prosper in his distance from the fact that inspired it, so that with every hurtle and stumble forwards, it settles closer and more vivid there. He half expects to find it at the bottom of the hill.

He is caught between exhilaration and fear, as though danger has always been a hair's breadth away from him, running in tight parallel, and he has only just noticed – like a man walking along a nocturnal clifftop, confronted with the drop only at sun-up. He imagines the discovery itself as a kind of light. Flat colours spring into life when it shines upon them.

But with illumination, he feels the vertigo, too, the immense drop of past and future. Even that morning seems to be set at an impossible distance now. He can see himself, setting out to the dig, humming with a carefree idleness that now he marvels at. Is he even the same person? The young man on the hilltop, wondering which route to take, seems remote as a story, only just overheard.

And yet the meadowgrass is still flattened, his wake still visible in places: it was him, sure enough, but he is not the same.

He catches his running stride on hidden rocks, finding an uneven rhythm of descent - running, falling, rolling on and downwards.

If I can just get ahead of these moments, he thinks, then I'll be fine. He imagines himself slipping out ahead of the past's great weight that otherwise might overwhelm him. He feels as though his discovery is starting to rewrite everything he knows.

His chest tightens at the sound of sudden thunder, not yet loud, but seeming to run close to the ground and start up vibrations there, the wind hissing through the long grass. But no rain falls, and the emptiness is a threat, as though the day has drawn its breath before a shout. He can see a light, gleaming blue in one of the old station buildings, and a figure, just visible, in a chair inside the greenhouse.

He runs now to catch up with himself. He does not dare to look back.

Anna is woken from sleep by the sound of thunder. She opens her eyes to find her bedroom dazzling, bathed in a brilliance of storm-light cast down broken from the sky. Beneath a thin Egyptian cotton sheet, her body feels electrified by the force of noise and lightning, and when she sits up she sees the city rooftops gleaming pale beneath the opening cut of storm.

Soft beneath her breath she curses, realising, at the sound of an erratic drip of rainwater, that she must have left the kitchen window open. She slips out of bed, pads barefoot through the unlit flat. The walls, pale blue by daylight, appear to be streaming torrents of rain running down and away to nowhere. The books lining her bedroom walls gleam slick as bullion along the shelves, their spines reflecting starlight.

The kitchen floor is awash. She has to paddle to reach the window, the sash raised high to catch the last of the late June light. Anna leans across the sink to run the window back into its casing, pausing for a moment to stretch her hands and forearms out into the wetness of the night, gathering up a dish of rainwater in her cupped palms. But when she breathes in its scent it seems to her to bear little of the day within it. It is a shallow pool, reflecting nothing but the streets below.

She shuts the window against the storm, and goes back to bed, her skin dampish now with smatterings of raindrops as she settles down beneath the sheets.

The dream is ready for her once again and she returns to it, smiling as she falls asleep.

In the wide bed, she takes on the appearance of an ink-haired Chinese doll, snug in a silk-lined box. Her body occupies a tiny space, small even for someone so small as she - as though in sleep she sheds the outer layer of herself, leaving for day the nacreous sheen of a life she doesn't really own. In sleep, she has no name. She belongs to no skein of time or circumstance. She becomes weightless. Her history dissolves. Her memory is not entirely her own. The daylight facts of her life – the effort and fuss, the gravity of her recent illness, barely overcome – all are fallen silent.

In sleep, lives run through her, and she wakes to find herself written through with stories. She glimpses generations of exertion, overhears discarded scraps of kindness. Daylight fragments sink into the silt of memory, re-emerge by night. Nothing is lost. Everything is lodged there, waiting, and each night she feels more definitely shaped by the flutter and hum of all that touches her by day.

Only when she wakes does the worry return, as though she is in possession of a very definite kind of emptiness – the dreamless part of her where no stories can go but her own; and she has so few. She supposes that her illness has opened up this space inside her, brinking death, though of course she cannot say for sure. Yet by night that same emptiness is a comfort. It invites so much to live inside her; and dreaming, she is full of riches.

The novel lies beside her on the bedside table. She had been reading it just before she went to sleep that night. Now, with the storm beside her window and the story resurfacing once more, she speculates about her shape, nudging out its soft dimensions. Her lips flicker with faint smiles of wondering about herself, and when sleep enters her at last, she sighs, and all her loneliness is set aside.

In the novel's story, the plot works like a mirror. It reflects from a central point both forwards and back. The two main characters, the lovers, are, as it were, standing back to back. He looks ahead. She looks behind. He is thinking about everything he imagines they might do and be; she is concerned, for the most part, with everything they've reneged upon by being together. Both are vivified by the levity that comes of being transfixed on precisely that point of simultaneous expectation and forgetting.

Together, they're the thunderbolt that splits the tree, rending it from its roots, leaving nothing there upon the landscape but that pale and fragile point of brightness - a warning and an encouragement to eager travellers; the moment on the crossroads: you can but choose.

Anna found the novel by no real serendipity: it had been referred to in another of her favourite books; the title had intrigued her, and she'd written it down on a scrap of paper. It had lain in her bag for weeks, along with a quantity of receipts, lists, programmes, train tickets, cinema stubs, matchbooks - most of them scrawled upon in varying degrees.

Every couple of months, she would tip the contents of her bag out on to the floor of her flat, and spend an hour going through what she found there.

It was a kind of system that presented her, across time, with a shadowy map of how her days were spent. Often, she would find herself wondering whether certain annotated intentions had ever, in fact, been carried through. Had she seen that movie, or did she only ever mean to? Did she read that novel, or is her memory of it only second-hand, gathered through a review or friend's description? To look backwards over her life gave her a fragmented picture, as though she was not staring but glancing, seeing only the flashing half-image of what had happened – a fast-vanished view from a train.

In this way, the things of most significance to her were often either imagined or misremembered; she moved forward with an unsteady point of fixity to guide her; and as tonight, sinking once more towards another person's dream (but was it the author's, or one of his character's?), she was conscious of wading through papery layers of illusion – and it troubled her. That her life might be the sum of other people's imagined parts, and not her own, filled her with sadness. It made her miss lives that she had never even known, still less lived.

It was as though she conducted her life in pencil, and, unsuperstitious, none the less she saw her illness as a warning, or loud reminder: set your dreams out in the daylight, even if they vanish in that exposure, otherwise – she would shudder to think this far, and feel the oddness of her haunting. The ghost was her future self, her life unlived.

How had it happened? It felt like a very gradual kind of fading: a photograph left too long paling in the sun. Because when she was a small child, people would look at her face in surprise and faint worry, jangling the ice-cubes in their glasses as they turned quickly from her as though caught out, pronouncing, 'She's been here before!' or 'Have you ever seen such a wise-looking child?' or 'She's got us all taped, that one!' She would look at herself in dismay: what could they see? It was as though they were pointing to her invisible twin – a person with whom she would one day coincide. The impatience made her wide-eyed, full of nerves.

Glancing about her in this way, with an aimless kind of

hunger, she would seem often to catch glimpses of herself reflected piecemeal in unexpected places – staring out at her suddenly from a newspaper, passing her in a busy street, in the crowded background of a film. But she was always mistaken, of course, and felt cheated by her own credulity, as though it were a nostalgia to which she had no right: she had not lived the lives that she was looking out for.

But still she looked. And that was how, following the thread of one of her pencilled notes, she found the book, and recognised herself there – the self she'd chased since childhood, dodging ahead of her, always a few paces too far for her to catch up. It revealed her to herself, not like a mirror but like a painting that articulates the buried sense she would have been too dulled by habit to perceive.

She told no one about it. She had no desire at all to share her discovery. And anyway, she told herself, it's so hard to find that it would only be a nuisance to mention.

The day she discovered it – a day of rare heat towards the end of April – impressed itself upon her, so that book and day were ever after bound up in her mind. She could not think of one without the other, and both were full of promise. They made her think of days drawn out of light, as though anything were possible in the next gradation of the sun. The world was kept away throughout the plot, and for the duration of its reading.

The book was long since out of print and, from time to time, she had looked for it in the Charing Cross Road. In the end, she found it quite by chance in the second-hand section of Foyles. It was a Penguin paperback edition, dated 1977, though the book was first published in America in 1935. The bookseller had raised his eyebrows at the darkened pages: 'Should get more of a discount in this condition.'

She read it in one go. She started it in the park two streets away from her flat, read it until the light had gone and the swallows were whistling through the darkened beech trees and she had turned for home, reading it badly as she walked, so then rereading the barely read chapter inside with lamplight beside the open window, and by the time she had finished it there was a faint lift of colour that meant dawn, softening the start of a day she had feared for weeks: she was due at the hospital for 6.30 a.m.

The book had held off her fear. When the fear came to her, covering her, she had already rolled way ahead of it – the waves were parted, she went through. Reading the book had been her way of waiting for the right moment to come so she could slip inside it like slipping inside a shell, and listen to the fear rumble by around her.

She had smiled, before, at the extravagance of people saying that books 'changed' or 'saved' their lives. She had not understood what that might mean. But for the months of her chemotherapy, she was conscious of the book the way someone is conscious of a talisman, pressing for charm against their collarbone, swinging past their heart as they step out into a busy road.

In its totality, the story would come to her in half-sleeping, broken moments, or during the violent boredom of drawn-out pain. It felt essential to her. It reminded her of that childhood fable of the princess and the pea. She could feel it through however many mattresses of numbness were stacked beneath her.

The book was just like that for her. The reassurance it had given her lay beneath everything. It gave her a hook on which to hang her longing. In this way, it tipped her towards a future that otherwise she would not have had the strength to fall to. Leaving hospital, being told that the prognosis was good, that she was free of danger now, she wondered if she would overhear herself, in some future time of health, exclaiming to a friend how a book once saved her life.

Had he been alive, she would have written to the author with her gratitude and admiration. But checking the flyleaf she saw that he had died in 1972, the year that she was born. It saddened her more than she could understand, the fact that she would not be able to write to him, even one short line – just a note. She even knew the tone she would take, almost whimsical, to hide the seriousness of her emotion. The cover carried a quotation excised from a personal letter to the author's editor, discovered after his death. It was a remark that gave his reason for writing the novel as 'to stave off heartbreak'.

But the story had so much joy in it: it puzzled Anna that it had been born out of any kind of unhappiness or proximity to defeat. She worried at this thought as at an equation that would yield no answer. Each number she tried to pare down seemed instead to break up to a greater complication. She felt as though she had looked through the book as through a prism. Beyond, there she was, through her illness suffering in a way her body's heartbreak. And nearby, as though sitting a little way downstream of the same deep flood of anguish, there was the author, writing to 'stave off heartbreak'.

She remembers feeling like a spy when she had read that this had been his secret reason in writing it – or as though her presence there, in reading the book, had set something new in motion, or exposed a long-hidden secret, not entirely meant to be revealed. 'Hidden', because the reviews quoted on the back described the book as a kind of modern pastoral, all trouble kept distant from the breezy garden atmosphere of pleasure. But had no one noticed the fragility of it? This thought troubled her, as though only through her illness could she see the ghost; and she thought of how so seldom any story is in fact entirely told.

It took place between the wars, in a small provincial town not far from the sea. It was a love story. According to the cover, it had been a great success. People had read the book and flocked to the town where it was set, lit it for a time with that reflection of celebrity. Anna could imagine the place perfectly. She had only to shut her eyes and she could feel it draw near so that she could no longer hear the traffic, smell the bad air of the city, and the scene beyond her window became a view of meadows humming with beesong, and beyond, the moor, stretching out beneath the dusty light of perpetual summer, rich with stories.

She decided to go there. She was curious to see how much the place might resemble the book, and if there was any truth in the author's descriptions of the town and the surrounding countryside. There's no harm in looking, she told herself. I've been a reader, now I'll be a tourist.

2

Jack watches her as she steps off the train on to the busy platform. She is small, not showy, and very self-contained. But people turn their heads as she passes, and he wonders who she is.

It is the last week of June 1938, with a number of holidaymakers still drawn, in the heat, to this small spa town. Jack looks up at the sky and wonders how soon the good weather will break.

He guesses, rightly – although he doesn't discover this until later – that she is an actress, though he thinks this not through any clue given in her clothes or manners. It is his presumption. Something to do with the way other people look at her. They can see something in her that he would have been slow to spot. He tries not to stare. He doesn't want to be part of the gaping throng. But it is hard, he has to admit – and this thought makes him smile. Yes, she must be an actress. Probably American. People maybe recognise her from the pictures, matching her up in their minds to that gleam of fantasy. He has a sudden urge to protect her. He feels his feet shift involuntarily, as though he's just about to stride over to her and pretend to be the person sent to meet her, just so that he can whisk her off fast before they take another look.

Apart from the feet-twitching, he stays still, of course, although he watches her out of the corner of his eye, pretending to scan the headlines of the evening papers delivered with her on the train from London.

Often, as a child, he would sit out on the station platform at this time of day, waiting for the papers to arrive on the six eighteen. Even now, news and the approach of darkness sit closely in his mind. Before, when the bundles were cut, he would beg to be allowed to keep the string. Now he thanks the deliveryman for his newspaper, which still feels hot from the press, as though it has been kept warm in the belly of the train.

His father is the station-master; their house stands back only a few yards from the tracks. Father and son live there alone; his mother died before he knew her. At night, if he raises the mottled bathroom window to look out, he can just see the freight trains glistening furiously by, like a flow of cooling lava rushing through the land.

But it is for more than this that he feels at home here. The flow of familiar people around him is a kind of family. Even after years at university in a different town, he recognises so many of them, as though their motion homeward was uninterrupted, the pattern of faces unbroken. He wishes he had sketched them all in in pencil before he left, so that he could work the impression up again now, overlay their younger selves with the people they've become. That'd be the only way to render them properly, he thinks, because still they all seem so young, as though in a change of light their younger selves might actually return. He cannot quite believe in their ageing. It seems like a trick of some kind. Just as she seems like an act of conjuring, he thinks, as though the only way to capture her would be to cut a hole out of the paper to let the sunlight shine right through.

He straightens the newspaper, raises it so that she is concealed. He tries not to think of her in isolation, but as part of the crowd, that way making it easier to ignore her. But he cannot do it, and is quietly proud of this fact. It was a secret test and he is happy to have failed. He sets the paper aside, and wonders why she has come. He is surprised that she has travelled here alone.

Usually, such women travel accompanied, or in groups – young women with vivid eyes that alight on objects of beauty with relief. They are a familiar sight here, since the American's novel. They have prettified a place once drab with relics of Victorian industry and leisure, the old spa buildings standing empty. Blowing here like pollen or spores, he thinks, some of them have even taken root and stayed. The Georgian crescent, and the stucco villas on the far side of town beside the river, slowly all have been acquired and given back some measure of their former lives.

But she has arrived alone, and her separation makes her appear vulnerable. He decides to wait to see that she is collected – any moment now, he is quite sure. She does not seem to be the kind of person anyone would wish to keep waiting. And he cannot imagine her depending on anyone's favour.

She touches her hat, adjusts its pin, her fingers fluttering against the pearl. Her movements are quiet and gentle, as with a habit of caring for others. But by seeming to want to draw attention away from herself in this way, she somehow lights up the act of care performed, and so the attention loops straight back round to her – a clever trick, he thinks. I wonder where she learnt it?

He tries to look away from her. But grace magnifies her, makes her seem luminous, self-sustaining. When she walks behind the glass wall of the waiting room, he misses her, and his breath halts at what this means. As she steps out from behind the glass it seems that the air sparks around her.

A door slams shut inside the house. They both look up, and he notices that her step falters at the sound. The station is emptying. No one has come to meet her.

Windless, the day is full of late June heat. The scent of crisping cow-parsley makes the air soporific. The station clock shows a little after half past six. She glances from her wristwatch to the clock and raises her eyebrows slightly, although she does not seem annoyed at being made to wait. She walks away from him to the far end of the platform where it slopes down towards the sidings and beyond, where the countryside opens up into meadowlands, with three chestnut dray horses grazing in the sun, their docked tails switching flies.

She stands in the open sunlight with her back to him. He wonders what she can be thinking. He wishes he knew. It makes him yearn to know her. She looks as though she's on the point of walking out across the grass and away up the hillside. She seems to lean forward slightly, off her heels and on to the balls of her feet, and when she turns back she is smiling to herself – but a broad smile for anyone to see. He looks away. He feels a sudden dart of jealousy for whoever was caught up in the wide net of that smile. He would like it for himself, and shocks himself to feel such a thing, looking back down at his paper, half wishing he could leave. Soon, he thinks, just not quite yet.

She is wearing a light grey suit, neatly tailored out of some stiff-looking fabric. Serge? he wonders, then asks himself if he can be right about her. An actress? With that silk blouse buttoned high up against her throat, there's something almost schoolmistressy about her clothes. But in the way of women he has noticed in London, stepping briskly into taxis, tiny beribboned boxes dangling from their wrists. Her hat is the most flamboyant thing about her – a small black felt hat pinned almost like a military cap on the right side of her head, its pheasant-feather twitching with each movement. Vermilion lips beneath a wave of silvery blonde hair. Very pale skin. Yes, she's definitely an actress or some such, he thinks, looking across the tracks where the taxis and private cars wait for passengers. Perhaps that is where someone is waiting for her, and she has not noticed. But there is only one car there now, and it is empty.

He thinks about her clothes, the way that, like her gestures, they loop attention right back round to her: the stiffness of that suit only emphasises the softness of her body beneath, and all its slender loveliness is made more noticeable by the hard shell she's set about it like an oyster building up its layers of protection. She looks as though she'd face the wall to undress, even when she's alone, he thinks, and blushes, wondering when someone will come to take her away.

There are only a few other people left on the platform now – two young boys smoking, sucking in their cheeks, their eyes narrowed; a businessman he does not recognise scanning the timetable; the station cleaner hovering about a bin, whistling lightly through his teeth. There are no cars approaching, and the air is still. Birdsong is in the nearby poplars and sparrows have descended to the silent tracks.

He hopes that the cleaner does not approach any further because he knows that the man will recognise him and make some sign, and suddenly he wants to be as free from ties to this place as she is. How else might they meet? He tells himself that this is the only reason why he hopes the cleaner will not speak to him, though secretly he knows it is not true. To be linked so clearly with his life will make him impossible to her – and here he stops, disgusted with himself. The man is already beside him, respectfully mentioning his father, touching his hat as he passes by. Jack can tell that she is watching the exchange and he feels indignant at his own shallowness. She has caught him out. He sets his back to her.

The sunlight has shifted in the few minutes of his being here, so that the platform is cut in two by light and shade. All the other people in the station have gone, leaving them alone together on the empty station. He feels foolish. He walks over to her.

'I'll take you, if you like,' he offers. 'You're staying at the Grand?'

'But my bags.' She does not meet his eye and looks down at her luggage. Only a suitcase and a leather grip. He hesitates, waiting for her to show a sign of consent. But the abruptness of their exchange seems to have caught them both off guard, as though they were picking up an interrupted conversation. To continue speaking is to admit all this. Both fall silent and she looks up at him as though in recognition. Her mouth twitches slightly in the right-hand corner.

Later, he will recognise this as a sign of nerves or worry, not indecision, although he cannot imagine that she might be afraid of him. He does not see himself as a stranger to her when already, without even being aware that this has happened, he has run her across his life like magic ointment, so that it glistens with possibility. He has a sudden vision of it being perfectly natural for them to link arms, throw back their heads in laughter at not having met sooner, and simply dash off into the fading day – leaving her luggage sitting there as evidence only of a fast-forgotten life.

He looks down at his shoes in embarrassment, as though he has just spoken this thought aloud. His desire to tell her what he feels is overwhelming, and to stop himself mentioning it, he fills the space between them with chatter, saying that it isn't far to the hotel, that he's little else to do and would be happy to help, that it'll be quicker anyway than ordering a car – this last thing he's uncertain about, suspects it is a lie and hurries past it by lifting up her bags, saying simply, 'Look,' as though that were proof enough of the rightness of his suggestion.

'Please,' he adds, alarmed at the sound almost of invocation in his voice. The dusk expands the day and the hillside seems suddenly closer, the trees rustling as a light wind starts. She looks up at the sky and back at him. She smiles. 'It'd be no trouble at all,' he tells her.

She glances beyond him down the platform to where the cleaner has re-emerged, and is rattling his pail and brush. This is what decides her: she trusts him because a few moments earlier she had seen him talking to the station cleaner. She can tell that he belongs here, he can sense this plainly enough, and his thoughts are torn between gratitude and sadness. The very thing that is making her trust him has set him at a distance from her, and secretly he is cursing that this might be so, cursing still more his own lack of independence, and his age. Close up, he can see that she is perhaps a few years older than him, which only makes him want to possess her with a strength of feeling he has never known. He wants to run himself right through her with his youth and that way bring her into balance with himself – a kind of gift, all he has, he thinks with scorn, deciding to take her bags to the hotel and then be sure he doesn't see her again – leave town if necessary.

He's conscious of her looking at him, her gaze steady, her eyes widening as though she's been darting with him along the wild tracks of his thoughts, and been exhausted by them, and surprised – but not horrified, he thinks, and starts to hope, forgetting his plan of two seconds earlier to leave as soon as possible. 'No,' he says aloud. She smiles, as though understanding perfectly what he means. 'I'll take you to the hotel. It's not far.' He has already started to go and looks back at her to see that she will follow.

That way, with him leading, they walk together for the first time through the soft descending day. Birds scatter from the hedgerows as they pass.

It was early morning when David set out towards the dig. No one else stirred as he left the hotel, and he was relieved to find the front door already unlocked: he had dreaded having to disturb the girl who kept guard over the front desk. When he looked back from a high point along the road, the hotel buildings were almost entirely obscured by trees. Only the first two letters, the 'Gr', of its name were visible. Distance edified the place, he noticed, remembering how last week he had seen a builder patching up the guttering; great rusted handfuls falling as he went inside. 'Sorry, mate, didn't see you.' But from so far away even the mildew and damp-furred walls attained a kind of glamour, deepening the richness of the stone. The slate rooftops showed platinum in the early light.

He struck out across open countryside. The meadowgrass, thigh-deep in some places, was heady with the scent of cow-parsley and the popping heads of ryegrass. He snapped off a young switch of birch, and slashed a metronome of guidance before him where he aimed to walk. He whistled to himself, and was very happy.

In fact, it was because he had been so lost in thought and pleasure at the day that, looking back from the brow of the hill, he could see how poorly he had navigated; now he was way off course. He sat down to rest for a short while at the top, perching on a collapsed part of the old stone wall where he could see down both sides of the incline.

On one side the meadow, about half a mile long, reached out towards the town. He could just make out the two tall chimney stacks of the hotel. At the base of the slew of green, viridian with rainfall, a huddle of trees separated the land from the first buildings; one of these was the old station house, now obsolete - at least, it had been converted to a private residence. The tracks were dismantled twenty or more years ago, or so he'd been told, and had been borne away, leaving only the ghost of themselves like the faint veins of an autumned leaf; the cuttings still remained. From here, the path they followed around the limits of the town, over the iron bridge that crossed the gorge, and then away along the baseline of the valley – all this could plainly be seen.

Even the lines of trees – willows and breezy poplars, aspens, elders, beeches and massive sycamores – all observed the old route. He half-expected to hear a train's bustling cut across the landscape, see it plunge and emerge from the tunnel of trees, their branch-tips whipped back by the rush of metal.

On the other side of the hill, moors rolled away towards the hidden sea. This landscape was the reason for his being here – the rare formation with its long-secreted hoard: fragments of a Viking longship. A jewel-bed, David smiled, the land like velvet over Jurassic bones of oolitic limestone to the east, the svelte imprecations of blue Lias clays and shales to the west, so that now he was walking a line between two ages that pressed one against the other and folded up into the backbone of a body, flesh – sunk now but discernible by the skeletal relic stretching northwards.

The boat was discovered not entirely by accident. In the chalky downs, thirty years before, excavation of a Bronze Age settlement revealed a Neolithic burial pit, thought to date from 4500 BC. Picking over the spoil-heap, Viking flints and arrowheads widened the search and brought it surfacewards again. Traces of the ship were found, barely a mile away, in the red clay crust of the earth, so near to the uppermost skin it seemed that had they waited longer it might have revealed itself to them – or to some future generation – cresting the surface after a heavy storm had worn away the limits of the land.

'A child digging for Australia might almost have found it.' David's father put it to him this way when he saw the photographs, sent down the line to him in Alexandria. 'Better get back to my books.' He had sounded bored. By 'books' he meant stone fragments from the third century BC.

But the land had given up its riches, and in that way it had defeated time: Armorican mountain ranges were worn down by sixty million years to create the perfect space beneath their folds to hold the longship steady.

David's part in the dig was minimal – that of an apprentice. At twenty-four, he was only 'starting out', as he preferred to think of it, as though the decision had not already been taken for him about what he ought to do. He imagined himself standing at the edge of his life's decisions, watching them gather weight and impetus. He had no wish to jump in anywhere. He wasn't sure what that might mean. He felt that to jump into the life expected of him, to become an archaeologist like his father, would be to leap backwards, not forwards, as though he was expected to travel back in time and reset the tenor of his father's life that had brought so much unhappiness with it: his mother died when David was eleven.

But he knew that it would make no difference. He could sacrifice himself and it would change nothing. The grief would remain, and they would merely rediscover it in a different layer of time, or in another place – just the way that an ammonite might be found in silent marble or on an empty beach beneath a strand of sea wrack shifting in Saharan wind.

Pausing for a moment on the high point of the landscape's

folding, David felt caught in the crossfire of two ages so remote it was incredible to him that it should also make such perfect sense. It was as though the land itself was thick with signs: a map of constellations flattened into geography and set alight by time. The miracle was that the signs were readable. They worked on the dig and, like a puzzle, it showed itself as liable to be solved. The remains had for the most part been removed. The wound left in the land would soon be healed. And the scar was incised for a purpose; their knowledge of this place had been transformed.

David had played his part, and he was proud. He felt the melancholy of departure – the work was virtually finished. But this also was a reason for pleasure: the site had yielded everything. Walking up there that morning, he felt the inadmissible yearning at the fact that there was no further mystery to be unveiled.

Uninterrupted, the darkness of heather, like blackened pumice, spread out beneath his feet. Looking out this way, David could see its logic. The moor was the tufted hair, the very limits of a massive depth of limestone. This point, his perch, was the fragile coccyx of a spine that built into the Alps and right on up to Everest. 'The backbone of the old world.' David felt the shape of it beneath him.

So he sat there in the morning, atop the riptide, momentarily subdued, of two opposing flows of time. He was very quiet, retreating into his thoughts. There was a freshening breeze running low to the earth, reaching him from a south-westerly direction. It carried the scents of moorland with it – the richness of peat, and when he breathed more deeply: saltwater, too.

Approaching the end of June, long weeks of heat had been barely touched by rainfall. Only the last two days had threatened thunder, and when he woke that morning he could see that there had been a downpour in the night, so quick and silent that it did not wake him. Now, the meadow's monotony of green was swollen, the grass seeming to grow at double speed. There were rare wildflowers, too. Orchids and wild lilies flourishing in the humid atmosphere, as though the rainwater had penetrated an ancient season, waking to new life the hidden species that lay dormant there.

Even in the early morning, not long past dawn, the heat warmed his limbs. It sat pleasant about him so that his few minutes' rest at the top of the hill felt like an extension of waking up. He was happy to be caught between sleep and waking: shutting his eyes, he felt the nearness of dreams; opening them, he could see a landscape still misted with the last clouds of nocturnal dampness, the quickly risen sun turning the mist almost phosphorescent. He felt clear-headed, and his clarity gave him purpose. But it was the clarity of preoccupation, and when he set off again from the hilltop, striding out towards the start of the moorland, again his course was way off mark.

He could see the orange tape, falling in and out of view beneath the atolls and swells of heather and boggy turf. But the mist clung low to the ground, and the colour was muted as sunset behind thick cloud. He aimed for the flashes of orange, working crabwise across the mounds of heather, following the sheep-tracks and the wizened paths of dried-up streams with the pebbles crunching underfoot. Sometimes, he leapt forward on to what looked like a firm nub of turf, only to find that he was jumping on to a shifting sponge of marshgrass that gave way the moment he put his weight upon it. Had he taken the more direct and well-trodden path down from the hilltop, he would have been there by now, and he cursed lightly to think of this, although he was in no real hurry.

The path had been worn by over a month of use. Around fifty people, in a sparse rotation, had worked the dig. A few of them were left in the town. But now that their finds had been taken away, there was no reason for them to stay. His own work almost over, he was due to leave the next day. There wasn't much left to see. The site had been picked over, photographed, all its secrets divulged and recorded. The major pieces would eventually go on show at the British Museum.

David was glad to be left alone there now. He felt as though he had been holding his breath until the work was declared finished. It wasn't so much a feeling of trespass that bothered him: discovery was excitement, a slim hitch forward in drafting a map of the past. It was more an instinct of worry. As though by removing that layer of history they were opening up a space that was only nominally empty for, logically, something must be there.

'No such thing as a dead end, only insufficient evidence,' his father had once told him. And this was the thought that made him pause that morning, his brow wrinkling, nerves unbending, wrestling in his stomach, making him feel shrunken and myopic. He wondered at the worth of something, once it was taken from the rich soil that supported it: how could its value be assessed aside from the alluvial fabric of its setting? Taken from its context, even truth could turn to lies. And yet with no dead ends, the path must lead somewhere, even if they could no longer find the way. He worried at what might be revealed in tandem with their discovery.

Balance – he was once told – everything reaches its balance. Dislodge one pebble and the upset might change history. He couldn't remember who had told him this. Not his father, certainly. Perhaps he had heard it on the radio, or maybe read it somewhere. He couldn't remember. But he had had the thought, and it had worked its way through his understanding of things.

He imagined the carbonised beams of the boat, the skeleton of the hull emerging by inches from the earth, the faces pale with ecstasy crowding round – the closest they'd ever come to spying on the truth of the past. The scent was ancient. He was there then and he saw the quiver of the palette knives, the tentative flash of badger-hair brushes revealing the quarry, grain by grain the veil of sand and clay pulled back.

But there were questions none of them dared ask. The answers reflected too keenly on themselves, exposing their uncertainty. It was more than an anxiety of superstition. It was a very definite kind of haunting. As he approached the empty site, miles from the sea, even the land itself appeared to reveal the lack, seeming to him to be more than ever the shape of a shallow sea bed, or the cup of an estuary, a vast natural harbour curving round and up to the hilltop where earlier he had paused to rest.

In fact, had he been there even just two thousand years before, he would have been sitting beside an inlet of the sea, looking out upon the water from a natural promenade. Approaching the site, he would have walked fifty times his height beneath the waves. The thought made his spine twitch, stiffen with imagination of that fact.

The sound of wind through the heather was almost indistinguishable from the sound of a sea breeze whipping up the surface of water to a fizz of whitecaps. Gulls, some way distant, wheeled by in silence, their wings angled to scythe the deep green with the ravenousness of pterodactyls, beaks gaping, soundless with faint menace.

Although he could not see the coastline from down inside the soft hollow that marked where the riverbed once twined along the inverse backbone of the hillside, he could tell where it must be by the sight of gathered clouds, almost violet in the misted early morning. There will be rain later, he noted, and plenty of it.

He paused for a moment while he decided which way to leap. He could not think what made him take this cock-eyed route towards the site. He had approached it like a boat beating head-on to the wind, tacking back and forth with massive waste and necessity of effort. His legs felt giddy, drunk-ish, and he cursed in earnest, seeing that he was surrounded on all sides by marshgrass and deep cuts of peaty water.

Just downhill of where he stood, he could see the water moving slightly, flowing downhill with some force – and he guessed this must be the source of the spring he had heard mentioned. Last night's rainfall would have filled it up to overflowing, the water table rising after months of wet. Above the spring, the grass appeared firm, and he leant forward to grasp a handful of it to haul himself clear of the brackish pool gathering about his feet. He could feel it coming loose, but it gave him the leverage he needed to leap across to firmer ground, glad to find his foothold among packed sand and flints. Minutes later, and he was ducking beneath the orange tape that cordoned off the circumference of the dig.

He worked there through the day, watching the rainclouds move towards him from the sea. He could feel the dampness approaching in the wind, the air itself growing incrementally limpid. He expected thunder. There was purple low in the sky and in some places a depth of blue that on a fine day would have meant the deep azure of heat and sunlight, but today meant only rain. Yet the weather seemed to hang in the balance, and he thought that he would not have set out at all had he known that it would turn so quickly. This made him frown, bending closer over the earth in the shuttering light, resentful and impatient.

He heard the earth shift before he saw it. There was the sound of tearing, as though someone with far stronger hands than he had taken hold of a hunk of grass and was ripping it somewhere out of sight. He looked up, could not understand what the noise might be until he saw the platform of turf that earlier he had used to hoist himself clear of the spring start to slide free of the bank that had held it, pushed aside by the weight of water bursting out from deep beneath as though someone had carelessly unplugged a geyser, that now, with a champagne cork's power of explosion, was shifted aside to let the spring flow back along its ancient course.

David set aside the soil samples he had collected, trying to be careful although his hands were shaking as he watched the spring's path, wondering which way it would fall. He feared for the hollow of the dig. Perhaps something had been missed. But how long had the spring been covered by that plug of turf, he wondered. And by that accident of his having to cross it earlier, it was now released.

Everything reaches its balance – he could almost hear the echo of his earlier thought – and here's the proof. As though by his being here at all, by delving into a layer of time revealed in sediment and quiet silt and rock, he could not help but wake up what lay dormant there, and not merely what he had sought, or in any way expected.

Nothing is so definite that by looking at it, or even just searching for it, we don't also change it, give it life to a degree – he had always argued this, against his father. 'No, we record what's there, that's all.' David could see the way the blood drained from his father's face as he insisted, 'When something's dead it's gone.' His voice was cracked with anger. 'It's not our job to bugger about with fantasies about what might have been. Everything settles down into its right order. You have no hand in what happened before you came along.'

His father finished his drink then and left the room. Neither mentioned his mother. Yet she had been the unspoken subject of their argument.

But there are degrees of existence just as there are degrees of heat and cold, David had wanted to say to him. And just as colour doesn't exist without the prismatic effect of the light that shines upon it, we contribute to the making of the things we see, so that they're part of us, and losing them, we lose that aspect of ourselves. (He could hear his father slamming drawers of his filing cabinet in his study upstairs.) So to have lost my mother, your wife, is not the same as to have lost some scrap of manuscript or to wonder at the death of Sheba.

And yet earlier that day David had seen his father smash a glass in rage at just such a loss of a bit of paper. He had not seen such violence of emotion when his mother died.

'It's done, and so it's over,' his father had tried to console him years before. 'She has left us absolutely, and so there's no point in being upset. It'll do no good. It won't bring her back. You must try to forget.' David knew that his father was wrong, and that night, in teenage silence, he cooked: salt cod with tomatoes, thyme and bay, black olives, capers and red wine. They had eaten the same dish in a restaurant in the hills above

Nice. David had been too young to remember. For him, the evening was composed of eucalyptus and aniseed, with the hillsides shadowing to blue instead of night. But his mother had cooked the dish while they lived in England. It had been her speciality, or so she called it, smiling at her husband as she said this.

When David cooked it, his father cried as he ate. David hated himself for doing it, but he hated his father more for saying that it was not true. 'See?' the food told them both. 'Here I am still, and you remember everything perfectly, don't you? Of course I have not left you.'

Certainly there are degrees of existence, and nothing ever truly dies, he thought, watching the underground spring flow free. Things just sink back weary for a while until someone riffles through the layers of time that have blanketed over them, and gives them life by that exposure.

But he could almost feel his father's breath upon his neck, as though he stood right behind him. This is how he most often thinks of him: standing one pace behind him, hidden from view, describing something that, as a small boy, he could not see, as though pointing to a future he has already mapped out, diminishing the child's freedom with a flick of his hand. 'She has left us absolutely. Look – the future does not contain her.'

'No,' David wanted to shout. 'She's still with us, and right here now. Can't you see?'

He looked at the gathered stormclouds, could see only the magnitude of his sudden fear. He felt as though he had summoned up a ghost. He shook his head, rubbed his knuckles between his eyes as though to press away its source. But it was no use. He felt the fact of his haunting more nearly than the fact of turf beneath his feet.

The stream flowed fast now, coursing through the empty veins that ran along between the heather. He followed the flow of water back up to the source. It rose knee-high as he waded upstream. The water bore the rich red mud of long-hidden silt and peat along with it. When he looked down at his legs it appeared that he had been wading through a stream of blood.

From a few miles distant, the place is almost exactly as Anna imagined it would be. The road follows and then diverges from the train tracks, which no longer run as far as the town but stop at the nearest city, yellowing the horizon at dusk. The single-lane road appears to be the only route into the town.

In her mind's eye, she had imagined a stream of brisk summer traffic, but the road is deserted, and with the engine off as she stands looking over towards the town, the air is close to silence, filled only with the softness of pollen-heavy bees. She can see them gliding low among the heather. The day's last sunlight flashes on their wings, catching, too, at the clittering wings of cobalt-bodied dragonflies and the rare, pale gilt of moths.

She stands there for a few minutes, the earth seeming to reveal itself slow about her. Last night there'd been a rainstorm that the day's sun has done little to conceal. Along with beesong, she can hear the gush and chuckle of a stream running downhill in tandem with the road. And in this last part of the day, the moisture is risen from the peaty soil so that the land glistens - as I knew it would, as I imagined it would, she thinks, smiling.

She has in mind a scene just like this one. Midsummer, late in the day, the town seen from a few miles distant. They have walked up through the meadows to a place where the long grass gives way to moorland. It is a point the author had made much of, for reasons more important than the fact that it is startling. To Anna, it looks as though an argument in the land has gone unreconciled.

On one side, the meadow is bright green, the earth raw ochre, almost bloody beneath, visible only at its limits as though for emphasis of contrast. On the other side, the moor has sparks of hunked granite and flat slews of shale within it, and with the sun sinking into mist behind it, it seems to be fading into violet, the colour evaporating, the line of horizon dissolving into cloud.

She watches the shadows settle with the weight of evening on the land. The scene ahead of her matches almost perfectly the vision she has carried with her now for months. This was her earliest chance to come here. She took it. It will be her summer holiday.

But she has other reasons. Insubstantial, but real enough for her. She can feel them lagging slightly behind her, as though at any moment she might turn to find someone waiting for her, a few feet behind and undeniable. She does not want to turn round and see that it is not true. So she keeps her eyes fixed forward and feels the pleasure of almost absolute recognition. 'Almost' absolute, because she is seeing the town alone.

Still, the image of the town ahead of her sits very lightly across the imagined town in her mind, as though to take a pace towards it might not be to walk out on to the springy turf and moor, but to step straight into the story.

A wind is gathering. It is warm against her face. It is pleasant as it touches her skin. It makes her smile. But lingering there, she feels the space beside her as vividly as though someone has just stepped out of it to leave it empty. She misses this life she has never possessed, and feels a pang of yearning for a love she has only known in the body of a story and in no other place – in no other person but herself, reading. She wants to lift herself from the picture to find the story's gemstone shining there. But she is afraid that were she to do this, she would be left with nothing – just the empty landscape closing tight around its secrets.

In the novel, the lovers stood on a spot very like this one - perhaps this exact place - and looked down towards the town, deciding to stay there, to escape there. He turned to her at this moment, saying her name very softly, so soft that it is dissolved in the sound of wind through heather, the bees similarly loud. He says her name, and calls her his love, tells her he'll love her always, and that she never has to fear she'll be alone because she has him, and he'll never leave her.

That day, they had gone down to the sea and swum naked in the cool water of a hidden cove. And when they kissed, just then, they tasted the salt that had been carried with them on their skin like pollen, their kisses scattering it to the air in this high place, miles distant from the shore.

Dusk has given way to evening by the time they reach the hotel. And by then Jack has already lied about two things: that it is on his way (to where, exactly?); and that it isn't far. In fact, it is around half a mile from the station where he had found her. But the idea of letting her out of his sight made him go cold with panic.

They are small lies, he tells himself, and can do no harm. Although looking back to the start of things between them, he hates to see the significance in that premise of untruth, as though some form of deception would shadow them ever after.

He remembers that when she remarked on the distance, she smiled, looking at him sideways. And when he changed the subject, commenting on the scent of white jasmine, just in bloom, she merely laughed, and he knew that she could see what he was thinking.

They stand together outside the main door of the hotel. He has had no reason ever to go there before. She mistakes his reticence for manners, and mutters something about 'you English', entering the hotel ahead of him. He hadn't noticed her accent until then – the accent beneath her American voice – the Germanic flattening of the first vowel, and is on the point of asking her her name when one of the staff approaches her, addressing her directly, his voice lifting with relief. He explains that they had been expecting her on the six eighteen, but that he had just discovered no car had been sent, and they were worried – at which point he falters, noticing for the first time that she is not alone. A young man is carrying her bags.

The words 'message . . . husband . . .' fade, are restored through the habit of deference and faint indignation, as the concierge hands her a folded slip of paper with the words 'Mrs Greenwood' written there, distinct in unambiguous copperplate.

She takes off her gloves. He notices her wedding ring.

He sets down her bags, turns from her, attempting to smile but feeling the grimace there, hoping that she won't look at him just yet because then she'll be in no doubt about what he's thinking, and his thoughts horrify him. She is married, of course. He has no business here.

But she is holding out her hand to him, still that smile, which now he assumes means no more than an exhibition of her natural gracefulness and charm. And it is true, she has the same expression for the concierge when she presses a coin into his palm as she takes the note from him. The man hovers. She dismisses him with a slant of her shoulders.

She is still holding out her hand to him, saying her name. 'Elena', no 'Mrs' and no 'Greenwood' this time, just 'Elena'. 'Jack,' he replies, the small admission making him feel bereft. He half wishes he had thought to give her a false name, and he hesitates before taking her hand, wondering if she'd think it absurd if he does not take it, because how can he, now that he knows just how out of reach she is? But he takes it anyway, the skin warm and smooth against his own, his fingertips brushing the fragile blue inside her wrist where the blood seems to jump up towards him inside her skin. He prays that she does not notice that he is shaking.

He tells her 'goodbye', his voice too quiet to be entirely polite, as though whispering intimacies he did not wish to be overheard. She has to lean towards him slightly to catch what he says. Hearing that it is merely 'goodbye' she draws back and shakes her head at him in laughing disagreement.

'You see, they'd forgotten all about me,' she tells him. 'You found me.' She smiles, her eyes seeming to mock him. Or is she offering him some kind of challenge? She confuses him. He raises his hand in farewell, backing away from her, conscious that to turn from her is an effort hard as fighting through an opposing crowd, invisible, massed about him. To leave her at this moment is to force his way backwards through the minutes since he first set eyes on her, as though they had not happened. It is a kind of lie. He is aware that his mouth has parted as though he had just spoken these thoughts aloud, and she glances up at him as though she heard.

He cannot bear it; he turns away, and she turns from him at exactly the same moment, as though, unconsciously, they are mirroring one another. So if I turn back now and just take her in my arms and kiss her? He stands very still. He is aware of her, no more than a few feet from him, similarly unmoving. He holds his breath.

So vivid to him is the image of their embrace that the noise of her footsteps on marble is strange as muffled gunshots, waking him from sleep.

3

Overhead, late blossoms tremble in the dusky breeze. They shed petals on Jack's head as he passes by beneath. He can see her still in the hotel doorway, her blonde hair blazing in the lamplight's gilt.

By the time he turns back to her, she has already started to walk away. He can see nothing but her silhouette, poised before motion at the foot of the wide staircase.

He is angry with himself for looking. He feels found out, as though he'd just blurted his worst secrets to a laughing mob. But even he knows that his anger is at best superfluous: the fact of her marriage has nothing to do with him; *she* has nothing to do with him. She is from an entirely different world. But his hand still burns with her touch. It ought to have been impossible for me even to catch hold of her, he tells himself, reassured that it was not. But it is a faint-hearted reassurance. He feels little better than an interloper, a spy peering in at the window of her life.

So he watches her standing there, with the blossom dropping steady and snowlike about him, and he feels the dislocation of the scene like a mismatch of time frames or climates. She is bathed in sunlight. He is stuck out here in the cold.

He tries to tell himself that she has ruined everything, even the richness of the season. He tells himself that for him, now, the rest of the summer will be joyless. He tries to think of her presence here as, in an obscure way, corrupting – an apple-munching temptress in Eden. But the visions of blame only make him see his own foolishness. She has done nothing. It is all him.

As he watches her poised to move away, she seems almost to hover, her figure luminous, remote, and he tries to tell himself that the only reason he even noticed her was because she is the manifestation of everything he does not himself possess, everything he has no part in. She is the negative against his positive, a kind of cancelling-out of his stake in life. It is as though, with a wave of her hand, she could make negligible generations of his family's effort. Not only does she seem to be remote from him, but haloed somehow at one remove from life.

That is freedom – he watches her as she starts to walk away into the bright interior of the hotel – to be able to skate with such detachment across the surface of things, not giving a damn, feeling nothing deeply, letting life slide effortlessly by as though nothing can touch her, because nothing maybe can touch her very deeply. How could anything imprint itself upon a woman like her? he asks himself. A woman who doesn't even carry her own luggage, who has no burden of life to bear around either on her back or in her heart. Whose every effort is aimed at giving the appearance of having no history she'd ever want to speak of.

Jack pretends that this thought amounts to a dismissal, although still he cannot quite make himself walk away. What, and lose sight of her?

His fascination unnerves him. He tells himself that his feeling has something to do with jealousy. And he thinks of his father's sacrifices on his behalf, the sweat it has taken to see him through his college education, when he himself had had no such chance in life.

But he knows that it is not that, that he does not feel any kind of resentment towards her. In fact, he feels sadness, and yearning, and all his anger is towards a world that has slipped itself between him and the object of his longing, setting up a barrage of objections that he'd like to see brushed aside by that elegant little hand of hers.

Yes, he thinks, she could swat into oblivion everything about me and her and these shadowed times we're both caught up in, just like that, all queenish for just one second, that's all it would take, and nothing else would matter. We'd neither of us have any history to scupper us then. She'd no longer have any husband. I'd be parentless. And that flunkey who even now is rushing up to her to take her coat – Jack watches still from beyond the doorway, seeing her move towards the wide curve of stairs, her shoes snapping delicate and resolute on the Purbeck marble – yes, even he would tremble and disappear, just at the sight of us standing steady there together.

Jack smiles to himself. He can still see her as she takes the stairs. She does not look back at him. And when she disappears from view, he realises that this was what he was waiting for – some kind of sign. To have been denied it amounts to a rejection, he tells himself, although he knows that it is even less than that: he does not exist for her. Why should she turn round? But he feels her disappearance like a sickness, suddenly explained to him, as though he has been labouring his whole life under the illusion of good health.

The sound of laughter from inside the hotel mingles with the sound of a band tuning up for the cocktail hour. The evening is still gleaming with June sunlight, and behind the hotel the poplars are dancing in a freshening breeze. The day is pretty with motion. Even the insects seem lit with joy and life, eager in their commotion beneath the dappling shade of Chinese cherry and the fragile green of limes.

With an unseen hand, someone moves about the drawing room on the ground floor of the hotel, lowering to half-mast the muslin blinds. Jack watches as this clockwork task is performed, fixed tight to the minute of seven o'clock. It startles him, makes him step back a pace, as though someone had shouted at him to clear out, or as though, in secret, somewhere far inside himself, he'd imagined that by meeting her, time had been unhooked from its usual ratchet and rolled into a kind of nakedness, all surface fuss slipped easy to the silken floor with a thumb-forefinger act of stealth.

He can see exactly how this gesture would be performed. And yet here's this person, unseen, setting down the blinds across the windows, excluding him.

Jack watches the hotel, knowing the absurdity of his doing so, imagining her expression if she chanced to look out of her window to see him standing there – although this is nothing like enough to make him leave just yet. I am already far beyond any shame at such a thought, he tells himself, suddenly relieved at the certainty of what has happened to him, as though the effort of his heart's remaking occurred while he slept, and he merely woke to find the feat accomplished. There was nothing he could do about it.

Only when at last he turns away does he contemplate the error of his first opinion about her, realising that in truth there are in fact many different ways to be removed from life. Her, by the remote power of her glamour, making her so untouchable. Him, by the narrow impotence of his youth, for he has nothing that conceivably she might want. And he is trembling as he turns away from the hotel, as though stepping clean out of armour he's worn all his life.

He kicks the gravel, wanting to kick out at his former self for being so stupid in his confidence. Because it is as though the mere fact of her has stripped him, leaving him defenceless not so much against her – for this is a vulnerability that he craves – but defenceless against the world, which even as he walks away from the hotel seems to have grown, become brighter, encroaching on him with such sweet threat – a kind of unimpeachable lure – that it makes him astonished he's not noticed it before.

I must've been blind, thinking I was separate from all this, as though I thought the world could change and I would not change with it. The revelation sneaks like bindweed round his thoughts, stifling them from the roots upwards with a look of beauty that is anything but harmless. Because already she has changed everything for him. And as he walks away he hums to himself — a child trying to stave off bogeyman fears.

The hotel lobby has a faint smell of salt, as though the sea were nearby, and as Anna looks through the main door into the evening, the pines rustle like low tide. Electric light catches their branches, transforms them into ocean swell. Anna sits down beside her bags in one of the armchairs, the loose chintz covers shiny with wear. The hotel is silent. But there is no sense of hidden industry, only abandonment, and she wonders if something is going on elsewhere in the town that has drawn away the guests.

There is a spring loose inside the armchair. It digs into the small of her back. There are potted palms, too green to be real, Anna thinks, although the pots they stand in seem rather better than standard hotel issue. A narrow strip of red carpet runs the length of the hallway, leading to the front desk. Either side of it, the floor is dark marble, speckled with ochre whorls. On the far wall, above the empty sandstone fireplace, a large gilt ormolu mirror is age-spotted to the colour of lead. The lobby is decorated with black and white photographs, portraits mainly, some of them signed, and a collection of movie stills. Most are unrecognisable on first glance, although one or two stand out as being familiar.

But the place is cold. Anna doubts that it is heated. She thinks of the thin summer clothes she has brought with her, curses herself for not bringing anything warmer. She takes a newspaper off the table beside her. It is a local paper, one week old, still neatly folded, unread. She hears some movement in another part of the hotel – not entirely abandoned, then. It has no air of dereliction, certainly. But there's the sense of it being like a large, once-grand ship forced to run on a skeleton crew who have pretty much lost interest in its course. It is still beautiful, she thinks, and picturing it by daylight she can see its charm. When she arrived, it had frightened her. The blank windows, unlit, gave it the appearance of a sanitarium, the inmates forced into early beds.

She waits for five minutes before anyone comes.

'Bell don't work,' the girl tells her disgustedly, when at last she appears. She brings the thin heel of her hand down on to a front-door bell Sellotaped to the reception desk. 'Nothing, see?'

Anna smiles. The girl wipes her hands on the front of her skirt. Her movements are quick and pointless, giving the impression of impatience at innumerable tasks to be performed, though elsewhere, and this one certainly the least of her concern.

'For a week?' the girl asks, when Anna mentions her name. She looks at her with incredulity, almost scorn, as she hands over the room key, leaning across the counter to peer at her bags as though for clues.

The girl does not offer to help, but then remarks, as if remembering herself, 'He's off-duty now, or he'd help you with those bags. They look heavy.' This last comment is said with a sudden hungry expression, and Anna can see that the girl wants to know what she has brought with her. She says nothing. She imagines the girl's disillusioned 'Books!' if she told her, so she merely smiles and follows the instructions. First floor, second from the end on the right as you go up.

Anna hesitates: she had wanted a room on the top floor, with a view of the countryside. She asks the girl if this is possible, but she frowns as though Anna were mad. 'All locked up,' she tells her, as though she ought to have known this already. 'Just storerooms now. No one stays up there.

'Watch the carpet,' the girl tells her, appearing to cheer up suddenly. 'It's loose on the landing.' She leans on the desk, watching Anna pick up her bags. 'There's a minibar in your room,' she adds, with a flick of her head, and Anna can detect a sly emphasis on 'your', as though she has been singled out for special privileges.

The girl picks up the phone when Anna is almost out of earshot. She hears her stifle a giggle, whisper, 'Tell you in a minute, hang on!'

Upstairs, the corridor is lit by fake candles, wall-bracketed with tarnished gilt sconces. They have a red gleam at their tip in masquerade of flames, and give off even less light. The one beside her room is out.

She feels duped. She remembers the brochure, the elegant line-drawing on the cover that she supposes now should have been a warning: surely they would have used a photograph if they'd wanted to tell the truth? The drawing showed people in intimate clusters on the terrace, sitting beneath parasols, taking drinks at dusk – or so it appeared. She knows that no one has taken her in, or given her any reason to imagine that the place would be any different from how she now finds it. But she has brought the novel with her, too, and it sits in her bag like a reprimand, or like a warning against too-keen belief. She tells herself that it is too soon to be disappointed. But what was she expecting?

The key is awkward in the lock, as though the room is seldom used. The door sticks in the frame, the fireproof board that has been put over the original panelling making it too large for the space. At least they haven't torn the doors out, Anna thinks, feeling the weight of it as she pushes it open, the brass doorknob cool to the touch, as though unheated by anyone's hands for years.

The room is in darkness when she enters, the only light coming from where the curtain, ill-fitting, allows in the last faint gleam of evening around the edges. It frames the tall sash window like a bastardised eclipse, not circular, but emphatic none the less.

The birds are growing loud now in the quickening breeze. Looking upwards from beneath the greenhouse glass, Jack can see them circling, starting to descend before the evening and the storm. Gulls are often blown here, fifteen miles inland. They gather along the join in the land, the point where the moor meets the chalky upland, as though their compasses are millions of years out of date, remembering an ancient strand that's long since lost its sea.

Even now, it is the gulls that are most boisterous, Jack notices, watching the way they seem to swarm like fishes caught in an invisible net, mingling, escaping. And as the sky grows darker, they seem to break the surface of it like cresting waves, their white wings flashing against the blue. Rooks are risen from the coppice, noiseless by their distance.

David has been inside the house for barely a few minutes. But in the second that he reappears, Jack wonders who he is. He is caught momentarily in the shadow of the doorway and seems to falter, in that attitude of indecision startling Jack, as though he isn't watching someone else emerging from his house, but is being shown an image of his younger self. David pauses, sees Jack, waves, 'Thanks for the phone!' then starts off in the direction he came from, back up the hillside, following the line of crushed grass towards the top.

Jack wonders if he knows that soon the rain will come, delivering nightfall many hours too early for the time of year. And does he know what it's like up there beyond the lip of the hillside where, lightless, the moor rolls on without either landmark or any sign of beginning or end, the very second you've gone beyond that topmost limit of the hill? Jack's knuckles feel cramped inside the tray of soil, the damp of earth and approaching rain making his joints ache, the cartilage along the ridge of his spine cracking as he stretches.

The air beyond the glass is alive with the flight of insects. And beneath the wilder sound of wind and birds in harried flight is the soft throb of wood-pigeons echoing inside the chimney stacks and beneath the eaves.

He holds his breath. He can still hear the gunshot ricochet around the slate rooftops and stone-flagged streets – the sound of wood-pigeons being brought down in the pines around the hotel. They'd annoyed the guests, apparently, who had found their lullaby too demanding, keeping them from sleep.

It was the day after she arrived, and he had imagined her in a sudden blink of wonder, commanding the destruction of birds he'd always loved to hear around the vanishing mist of twilight. He thought of her doing this and frowned, as though she had deliberately set out to hurt him.

But it was one of the first things she said to him the next time they met. He had simply gone up to the hotel in pretence of visiting a friend, and there she was, stepping out of the hotel doorway as though straight from the moment he last saw her: they stood together on the driveway, without even saying hello, continuing their conversation from two days before. 'But can you believe people shoot at wood-pigeons?' She'd been pale with anger as she told him how she'd heard the sound of gunfire and it had frightened her, and so she'd gone downstairs to see what it was all about and, discovering what it was, had caused some kind of rumpus with demands to see the manager – 'the full works', he smiled in admiration – and had it stopped.

'Can you imagine why they'd do it?' Her hands pressed the air in the particular gesture she would make when she was enraged, her hands seeming to reach down to protect a child, invisible, standing beside her around thigh height. And her eyes lowered as though to slow down an impress of approaching images – all the things that he could only guess at.

Even now, he can recall his anguish at that moment, hating himself for being so easily duped into thinking that he knew anything of consequence about her; hating still more that he couldn't nestle down there alongside her in her anger, and see its first thoughts, discover where it came from. He wanted to tell her this, even then, and could see the madness in that wish: to travel back in time to see her grow, discover just what had made her.

The light failed fast as he left the hotel that first time. Or was it, he wonders now, that I stood there like an idiot, over-long, watching the hotel, the ebb and flow of life within it hidden from view. Hidden, apart from the shadows that it made on the drawn blinds and curtains, a kind of puppet-show in faint relief.

Certainly, by the time he retraces his steps along the narrow path he'd taken her – the secret route, he told her, meaning only that it wasn't the kind of pathway she'd have been expected to use – the way beneath the trees was full of shadows.

The scent of warm grass and the heated threads of pine-sap gleaming in the last gold of sunlight – all this is again vivid to him. Then, it was as though by retracing his steps he was being given the chance to drink in everything he had missed when he walked that way before. He had missed it for a reason: she filled his sight, ran through all his senses, as though he'd not been walking quiet and polite alongside her, but had been pressed skin to skin, finding his way all around her secret dimensions by touch and scent, so that to draw away from her was to carry away with him a perfect impression of his desire.

It was always this way with him. The minute she was gone, all the things he'd meant to say and do with her leapt devilish to the front of his imagination, so that he could see them far more vividly than if they'd happened.

Now he can almost feel her breath against his neck, and his chest feels warm as though she'd reached her hand round to cover over his heart with her outstretched palm, the way she'd often do. He lifts his own hand up as though to meet hers there, pressing it instead against his ribcage where he can feel the thump and pulse of troubled blood.

He shuts his eyes, and tilts his head like a conch shell, slightly sideways, as though to catch the song of wind inside his thoughts and that way dilute them. They are too fierce. He wonders that he's able to contain them. Wonders that he doesn't just keel over at moments like these. He can feel his mouth twist with a depth of sadness that bears down upon him now with the weight of tides. Why is it that this moment doesn't fell me, simply knock me down?

When he opens his eyes he looks through glass to where the day is darkening. The first grey thunder approaches, though slowly, very quiet, and still from some way distant. The greenhouse roof is opaque silver.

As a boy with a knack for story-telling, his father looking at him with pride, 'You have books in you!' And he'd thought then how pleasant it might be to get them out, like unlocking a forgotten library.

The phrase returned to him when he met her. Meeting her was like setting light to a library and never once rushing for the water-pail to douse the flames. Even had he wanted to, there would have been no way of explaining what had happened to him. His love was not translatable. She burned through everything, and left him speechless.

He feels the giddiness of memory almost tip him forward with the force of years. He steadies himself with a hand against the arm of his chair. It is cold to the touch, his body giving off so little heat. It is the loneliness he cannot stand. He felt it from the start. He feels it now. To say what happened between them is to ask to live lost time.

He stops here, seeing with such clarity the gold nub of all his sorrows then revealed, as though dug up from miles beneath the surface of his life.

There's a growing noise of weather outside the greenhouse. It makes the glass tremble where the breeze touches it, the breeze no longer soft but gnarly where the birds have broken it – Jack watches them falling into the outstretched arms of trees.

He looks at his hands, still embroiled in mud, the fingertips reddish with the peatiness of soil. Troublesome hands, he thinks, peering outside into the darkening day. Is it still possible to see the boy? He is almost at the hilltop. Years have run through him while that boy has travelled only yards.

He listens to the rush of wind keel round the back of the house, run through the garden, whipping up the ancient horsetail ferns, almost unchanged in many million years and still so potent in their beauty.

When Jack looks back up at the hillside, David has vanished beyond the line of near horizon.

He reaches out, fumbles for a cloth to wipe his hands free of the black soil. Certainly, he tells himself, she was with me in that loneliness of love. We held each other there, however briefly. But that it was only ever her who witnessed what lay between them now makes his breath grow ragged with that weight of secrecy – a secrecy he was sworn to for good reason.

Elena is wrestling with the window lock. It is the first thing she does whenever she enters a new hotel room: opens the windows. Day or night, it is her ritual, her way of feeling as though she has a right to be in the new place, breathing in its air.

If she is with her husband when she does this, he laughs, calls out her name in joking reprimand as though he has no idea why she might wish to do such a thing. She is careful not to look at him then, because despite his laughter his chin is always lowered like a bull and she can tell that he is annoyed. He thinks that it is childish of her to stand this way, her nose sticking so indecorous out of hotel room windows. Once, without laughter, he commented, 'People will think you're a bloodhound, Elena.' And she could hear the dislike in the word 'bloodhound', and her name sounded like an oil-slick – dirty, liable to flames.

But now she is alone. Seeing the view, she almost runs to open the window. The bellboy follows after, with her bags. He, too, laughs at her, although he pretends it is a cough, and turning, she can see that he is smiling as he trots off without a tip: in England, young men seldom take money from ladies. Idiot, she would have done so in his position, she thinks, reminding herself to give him a gift of some kind when she leaves.

But she had another reason for dashing to that window, and she is glad that the bellboy has gone. She wants to find out if she can still see Jack.

At last she works the catch loose and raises the tall sash window until it stands wide open. The light is soft at the end of the day and she can hear the wood-pigeons' ululations echoing in the chimney stacks. From down inside the town there is the sound of laughter and two rival dogs *raffing* the warm evening in syncopation. Sounds of her girlhood in Bad Homburg. Slate rooftops reflect the last of the light.

A bell chimes seven o'clock inside the hotel corridor. She had passed it on her way upstairs: a grandfather clock so similar to the one her mother inherited, had recently been obliged to abandon, that Elena had stopped beside it to take a closer look. Now all they have of that clock is the engraved key that was used to wind it. Elena carries it with her always. She has it with her now, tied with a grey silk ribbon inside her handbag. Of course that clock was not her mother's. But the similarity was astonishing. Perhaps it had come from the same watchmaker's in Düsseldorf, in Kasernenstrasse?

Perhaps. Elena had walked past it to her room, telling herself to give it no thought; and then it chimed. She thinks of the Krannenbergs. They carried on the business after three generations at the same address. She wonders if they decided to stay. She can see her mother's head-wag of anxiety, her eyes sliding from her daughter to her daughter's husband, the man who insisted that they leave that spring for America. Secretly, her mother worries about the entanglements of their situation. Her daughter's businesslike marriage; the husband's endeavours to secure their US residency. She is not comfortable with the nature of their indebtedness. Now they are staying in an airy modern bungalow in the hills above Los Angeles. It has terracotta-tiled floors and a landscaped garden sprouting palms. 'It's new but it's not home.' Her mother's sadness is also gratitude: she watches the newsreels, reads the papers, has stopped hearing from certain friends. But it is shame, too, and she brightens only when Elena tells her how happy she is to have them near her, as though this alone were the reason for their being there.

The light is changing each second, and she cannot see Jack. She supposes that he must already have left. Why would he stay? But the speed of the light's failure makes her hesitate. She has the sensation of having been running since the moment she first saw him at the station. Now she feels breathless, and physically taxed. Her body seems to have paid a great price for something without her having been conscious of any expense or barter. She feels frightened, as though she obeyed a gunshot to race, instinctively, without her consent. And now she cannot see him and is so surprised by this that she puts her hand across her mouth for fear she might make a sound. She does not wish to know what it might be and so she does not permit it.

When she suddenly catches sight of him she steps behind the curtain so that he cannot see her – and he does look up. His eyes seem to come straight to her window on the first floor, although she has not mentioned which room she will be staying in.

She stands there for a long time. Long enough for the room to grow dark around her. She does not put on the light: he is still there.

He is no longer looking up at the hotel, but is standing at the edge of the hotel gardens looking out across the lawn. The yew hedges are cut in the shape of monsters, she thinks – at least, this is how they seem from her window; fantastical beasts, contorted. The scent from the rose-garden is vivid as she stands beside the open window. She imagines its pungency in his nostrils and wonders fleetingly what he makes of it. Is it the reason that he lingers?

Someone has watered the gardens that surround the hotel and perfume reaches her in layers. The roses come first; then herbs – thyme, rosemary, mint, and a thick swathe of lavender suddenly, as though someone has just rushed their hands through it. A young wisteria is pinned to the south-facing wall of the garden directly beneath her window. There is honeysuckle, still hidden in bud, and jasmine too, so that the deepest part of dusk makes her think of the coast of North Africa. She has a sudden vision of Jack plucking a white jasmine flower and planting it behind his ear. She can almost see him sway off into the town to the call of the muezzin.

And yet it is not his foreignness but his nearness she is transfixed by – as though she has not met him for the first time, but found him, after years of disbelief and searching, already waiting far inside her. She is conscious of him as an exile yearns for a homeland reluctantly relinquished, and so long ago that their memory of the place is not a definite series of events, impressions, people, scents – but a rich stratum of astonishment at being so removed.

Her distance from him seems incomprehensible. She cannot understand it. She tries to explain the feeling to herself, but can only think that she misses him as the dead might long again for life – with great tenderness and sorrow. For her, he is shining. When she first saw him, she was sure that she recognised him from childhood. She had the impression that she had seen him at another station, perhaps her home town. But many years ago. To feel that she remembered him as a girl was to transform her to a girl once more, and she had turned away, thinking this, walking to the furthest end of the platform so that he could not see her blushing. She had wanted to run to him like a child, in perfect freedom at the sight of a familiar friend.

Now she can almost hear him, although he makes little noise outside – he lights a cigarette, kicks gravel with the toe of his shoe, stands square on the grass for a while so that she thinks of him there, barefooted to claim his patch of land. She touches her hair and it is static, floating about her head like an experiment in electricity, or like the threads of a jellyfish buoyant in nocturnal seas.

Beneath the perfume of the garden run the deeper textures of the land. Not scents at this time of day so much as aspects of the dusk itself – the impression of riot where weeds begin after the ordered quiet of the formal gardens; the nest of pine forest; grass cuttings given a crust of hay after just one day's heat – a hive where things can burrow; the tilting meadow run to fallow, thick with ryegrass, and the dandelion suns showing through on milk-sap stalks. Beyond the hilltop, the moorland is a surrogate sea. Its silence is immense, obvious. The horizon, vanishing in the gloom, looks to Elena like a strip of black velvet.

Below her, at the edge of the garden, she hears Jack make some kind of noise in his throat, and she thinks that he is addressing someone and for a second she fears that it is her – that all this time he has been watching her, as though they have been twinned in a parallel intimacy, enjoying the evening. She stands further back behind the curtain. She can hear him still, and she realises that he is humming to himself, half singing between kisses to his cigarette.

She wishes that at this moment, without his noticing, she could reach out to where he stands and lay her hand upon the dark smoothness of his head, to stroke him like a cat. Stroke a cat, she thinks, and the cat becomes more feline, conscious of itself. This is what he sounds like now with his private song: like a cat purring. She wishes that she were the cause of his consciousness of these moments in his life. She would like to set her hand upon his silk-cropped head and feel his life's unrepeatable warmth, listen through her fingertips to his boyhood, singing.

He seems so near to her at this moment that she half imagines she could do it – that just by reaching out her hand she might run him through her fingertips, snag there, delaying, if she liked.

Of course she cannot do this. He is much too far out of reach. So instead she wraps her right hand very tightly about her waist and listens to the shifting timbre of his voice upon the cooling air. The noise grows fainter. She had not heard him move to leave. She does not dare to look out for fear that he might glance up at her window and realise how long she has been standing here. His voice fades and finishes, and she imagines his footsteps vanished on the grass.

4

Evening has come early with the sky so full of clouds - rain-bearing, David can tell, and he's anxious as he peers at his watch-face in the diminished light.

The way ahead is indistinct. He'd hoped it would be easier. Every inch of the way is, or at least he thought it was, imprinted on his mind. He wonders if this is all that's meant by people when they talk about time slowing down at moments of great crisis. He imagines it as his brain shifting down a gear to manage the greater speed of experience, as though it's giving him the chance to grasp and store away each otherwise unmanageable moment. The meadowgrass catches at his legs. His chest is tight with running.

But he is glad that he's alone. He strides on uphill, and feels his life gathering in every stride - no more the shadow lagging a few paces behind, no longer his father's flattening predictions, damping down all his excitement, all his innocence of discovery. His life feels rolled up tight inside his flesh. His bones ache with it, and he can't wait to get back to her - can't wait, those words making him grin now in the secret darkness.

Briefly, at the hilltop, he turns back. There are no lights following after him, as he'd imagined there might be by now.

He telephoned almost thirty minutes ago. The only light is the yellowish dish of the town, and the solitary gleam from the station house on the periphery, a satellite set in darkness. He hesitates before stepping downhill on to the moor, again that sensation of stepping into and beneath water. The way ahead is entirely lightless. There are no more points to navigate by, and the wind is growing twitchy as the night descends.

He has only a small Maglite but its beam is strong. He worries momentarily about the batteries, but is sure that by the time they start to wane the others will have long since arrived. He can almost see their miners' beams as they searchlight their way across the ocean waves of moor to find him.

There's still some light left in the sky, and he knows that were the gathering storm to shift its course, even by one mile, to lift off this stretch of land, then the sky beneath the clouds would still be bright with the last of day - for perhaps two hours yet. Darkness does not come until ten o'clock at this time of year, and sometimes, especially around the crescent moon, as now, the light seems to linger for a greater length of time, the stars emerging wet with glitter.

He looks up, can see nothing of either moon or stars but instead a kind of watery mottling of early night that seems more like the surface of the sea than sky. The sky remembers the shape of things beneath. He shivers. The air is cooler on the open heath.

He moves forward along a path that he suspects is erratic - following a trajectory that he doubts is the same as the way he came before. But he walks fast. He has the sense of the fixed point in his mind, and he tells himself that that is enough. He expects the others at any second, though there is still no light for evidence.

Although his route is steadily downhill, there are certain sudden gradients, and some of these he recognises, seeing the way back to the place as a rough angle cut out of the landscape, leading him inevitably there. But this thought, too, worries him. And in a sudden stab of doubt, he imagines the land leading him along a false path, keeping him away from his discovery, making him rush off to the middle of the moor like a sailor in vain search of the greatest fish - mythical, uncatchable.

He slows down. He feels foolish in his eagerness. He tries to steady his breath, peering ahead of him like a blind man able to see nothing but a muss of cloudiness and dark - all landmarks illusions, all his confidence liable to deceptions.

He glances over his shoulder, worrying that there is no following light. He tells himself that his anxiety is little more than impatience at their inefficiency. How can they not have followed straight after him, the second he called? But he knows that his unease is not because of that: the darkness does not feel empty.

He tries to stretch his torchlight's beam, scatter it more widely on the heather, but it is too narrow to reveal much beyond the nearest shapes of turf and purplish soil directly beneath his feet. Sphagnum peat, he names it to himself, imagining the forest once here at the shoreline, the birch trees, alders, hazels, oak and pine. The wind twitching through the heather now makes a sound that could almost - he tilts his head, pausing to listen - yes it could almost be the whisper of that lost wind's tongue inside the forest now reduced to peat.

Of course, he thinks, there will be things living on the heath. Sheep and rabbits, nothing of consequence. But it isn't this that bothers him. He walks more slowly, minding every footfall, trying to remember his way in the gloom of abbreviated light. He picks out certain outcrops and undulations of ground, the smooth face of flints embedded in the earth – things he seems to recognise. But the second he thinks they seem familiar to him, with the next inch of movement forward they are transformed, and he realises that he has never set eyes on them before, that already he might be way off mark.

Where only minutes ago, brinking the brow of the hill, he'd felt the power of discovery, now he feels only impotence, the massed black weight of darkness tight about his sight, blindfolding him in unknowing. It is as though the reverse of what he'd imagined has happened. He has discovered nothing; rather, something has discovered him, and he has been found out. Time has found him out, and caught him snooping in its velvet layers. He slips, steadies himself, cursing the stupidity of his earlier confidence.

The heather is crackling now in the wind. He imagines devilish fingers pinching the brittle stems to break them off and cast them to the wind, which seems to come from all directions, its motion inconstant, circular. One moment he leans into it, his shoulders braced against the pressure; the next, he's leaning into nothing, and staggers forward.

Strange scents are delivered to him that he does not recognise. Among the familiar salty samphire tang of distance, and the brown mulch-scent of peat, there's something sharper – like the smell of alcohol or vinegary wine; and then beneath that comes the wet-pollen sweetness of summer flowers, making him think he's closer to the meadowlands than he'd thought. He feels like a lost dog, tormented by false trails back home. And yet it is not home that he is seeking, but something that once he finds he'll have to wait beside until the others come. He falters at this thought. That's the extent of my cleverness, and my courage, he tells himself. To sit beside my discovery like a whimpering dog grown fractious in the unfed night.

He steadies his pace, feels the land start to tilt sharply downhill beneath his slipping toes; with every step the darkness seeming more substantial, as though to reach out into it would be to touch warm velvet, or an animal's wrinkling back bunched up in mysteries of pleasure.

The air is damp now against his face. He guesses that his downhill route will lead towards the one-time riverbed, and from there he'll find his goal. It won't matter if I approach it from a different angle, he tries to reassure himself. Just so long as I get down to the bottom I can work my way along until I'm back at the dig, and then I can find it from there. The wind lessens as he descends. The air against his face grows warmer, almost humid, and he imagines the steam rising from the waterlogged earth, tries to imagine what steam might look like in the darkness. Still the noises of snapping heather, as though the land around him must be crawling with beady-eyed creatures with strong-muscled hands, gripping, unclenching.

His neck is straining with the effort of looking only ahead of him, and of not swinging round with every noise and undiscoverable flutter. He walks on, the beam of his torchlight seeming pathetic to him in the face of so great a darkness. He wonders if he wouldn't be better off trying to find his way without it. But he knows the real reason why he'd rather go forward without a torch, hidden that way inside the glove of night. Why? So no one can see him.

And by no one, he asks himself, what do I mean? He cannot answer. But he feels that with every pace his feet are nudging something awake, disturbing a great animal that he'll never be able to coax back to sleep. If he were hidden by the darkness then perhaps it would be different, perhaps then he could slip by unnoticed. Because at any second, he feels sure, his torchlight's beam will pick out the reflective dazzle and wetness of a watching eye, and what will he do then, knowing that he has been spied on the whole time he came down here in the darkness, rushing out here like a fool to claim his prize?

One second the ground is soft with the springiness of underwater caverns running on in secret; and the next, there's only rock, impermeable hardness, misleading grit. The vacillation between hope and despair at ever finding the place again is more exhausting than any delivered fact of impossibility might have been. He feels as though he's being played with. Watched and played with. His throat is tight with tears he won't let fall but keeps suspended there so that at least he can navigate by that one point of pain.

He hates the look of the Maglite's faltering beam upon the earth. He hates the meagre points of reddish soil that it illuminates, the heather's battered purple, the occasional wet gleam of flint – it tells him nothing. It horrifies him for being so unrevealing. He had imagined that, by now, he'd be at the centre of a circle of watchful and admiring faces, peering at his discovery, their arms around him, the day returned in an instant by their floodlights' solid beams.

Instead, this: no sign of life beyond his own, and that sign diminishing to a point of deepening illusion, where with every step downhill the way grows more unclear. His torch-beam flickers, fades in and out of blackness. He turns it off, cursing, stands still for a moment in the flat black night, setting his feet square on the ground to get his balance.

The moorland rumbles and seems to shift in layers of darkness about him. He feels the first large drops of rain fall on his face.

Elena wakes just before dawn to the sound of shooting. The gunshot echoes beat back up into the air off the black slate rooftops, and where the rooks rise, it looks as though shattered slates are being thrown up against the pale dawn sky.

These are not her first thoughts. Before she runs across to the window, she lies very still in bed and thinks of him, has a sudden prayer that he is safe. Jack. She does not even know his surname. She must find it out. She must also tell him hers, that buried underneath her married 'Greenwood' she is really 'Leeman'. She must tell him everything about herself, and about this moment of realisation: that the time between seeing him yesterday at the station and now – the hours of sleep – has formed a kind of unbreakable thread that has bound her to him. Can he even guess at its strength? she wonders. It has changed everything. It has returned her to herself, and now her one thought is to give herself to him.

There's the sound of birds descending. The air enters the room through the open window and she can feel it dancing cool about her naked skin. She stretches, listens to the soft flutter of wood-pigeons returning to the eaves. Just this way, she would lie half sleeping in the cool night air at home.

The first sound of daylight would be her father lighting the boiler in the cellar. His movements would reach her as a faint hiss and ping from deep down inside the belly of the house. If he hit the pipes hard enough to release a bubble of trapped air, she could feel the vibration against the palm of her hand pressed against the copper. It was a comfort. She slept in the certainty of her parents' having so much of the day inside them already, before she woke. Still faint with sleep, their morning liveliness would affect her like a gift, and she would be able to face the day with strength, because of them.

She starts to fall asleep again. Perhaps those gunshots were a dream. Her eyes are heavy. She slips back to her dream of him and home, so naturally entwined. But the gunfire comes again. She runs to the window. Someone is shooting at the birds. She puts on her dressing-gown. He seems to walk beside her as she goes downstairs.

Jack is transfigured in the first wild crack of lightning. He snaps his head back to look up through the glass ceiling of the greenhouse where the clouds seem full of iron, too heavy to hang without falling.

The meadow is violet beneath an electric sky. Loud raindrops start to fall, spaced so far apart that it looks as though you could dodge between them, and he has an agile vision of his younger self reaching the side door of his house before the worst of it comes. Instead he settles back in his chair, as at a performance, and watches what will happen.

The sky is slow to give up its rain and the air seems empty of everything but the noises of worry – late birds finding shelter; over-brave dogs petulant in kennelled safety. Each sound reaches him neatly squared-off so that he feels as though he can pop them one by one into his mouth to taste.

He can hear the way the town looks. He can see the sash windows slipped shut, feral cats making nests out of needles beneath the covering pine. He can see the tandem faces peering upwards into the gloom before turning to one another, and smiling not to be out there. But still the rain comes slow, in wide-spaced drops, and Jack thinks that he can almost hear each one in isolation as it falls.

Inside the breast pocket of his old tweed jacket, he carries the only photograph of her he ever possessed. It is slipped deep inside the guts of his wallet, hidden inside a fold of paper – a piece of paper torn off one of the hotel notepads, upon it a hasty word of love she'd pressed into his palm in a moment of indiscretion: she could so easily have been seen.

He remembers the moment she handed it to him. Since

he first saw her, a week before, they had met almost every day, in secret. He was sitting in the hotel lobby as though waiting for someone else, as they had agreed he should. She'd passed him, hesitated slightly beside him, looking in her bag in pretence of searching for something, and then moved on – though not before addressing him, 'Would you mind?' indicating a copy of *The Times* that lay on the table in front of him. He handed it to her, and she had slid the note into his palm.

She did not look at him. The lobby was busy. No one appeared to notice. She walked away swiftly, heading upstairs to her room on the first floor. But as she reached the far side of the hallway, he noticed that she paused beside one of the large potted palms that stood either side of the sweep of stairs, and seemed to wrestle briefly with something. Her handbag strap had hitched itself on to a frond of palm and she had to unhook it. Their eyes met then in laughter at the silliness of what had happened. She disappeared from sight.

He waited a few moments before folding up the newspaper that lay in his lap. Then he tucked the note into his jacket pocket to read later – the second he was outside. It named the time and place they were to meet that afternoon. He half turned, wanting to call after her to mention his uncertainty about the weather. Hadn't she noticed that it might rain later? And, if so, would she still come to meet him? He wondered if she wasn't perhaps giving herself an excuse to avoid him, and worried briefly at this thought as he looked back at the hotel, glancing up at her window, which the previous day she had described to him: second from the right on the first floor.

She was standing just inside the casement of the tall sash window, hidden partially by the velvet drape of curtain so that he could see only the line of her face and shoulder. But he could see that her right hand was raised towards him, moving once briefly from her lips to the window as though impressing him with a kiss, and he knew that he was wrong to doubt her.

He smiled back at her, touched his breast pocket to show her that he had her note, and that it was already dear to him and near his heart. He didn't risk waving. But he knew that she would understand and he thought that he could see her smiling.

He turned for home and for waiting – three hours before he would see her. He remembers now how he had a sudden vision of himself placed for ever in that posture of passivity, waiting for her. He did not mind. He relished the freedom that it gave him. Freedom meaning that he was at liberty to do nothing but love her; and he could think of nothing else. Three hours would be easy, he told himself, in his mind's eye already the warmth of her beneath his hands. But he knew that that was a lie: three hours would be a kind of void with nothing in it but the strangeness of their separation.

The rain is thickening against the gravel pathway and the greenhouse glass, flowing across it freely now so that he can no longer see the sky, only a river overhead, the crystal room beneath it pungent with the scent of hothouse growth – tomatoes and ripe strawberries, the acid sweetness of the vine.

And if I'd known that waiting would be this long? He reaches his hand inside his breast pocket, the gesture little different, though perhaps stiff now with age, from the gesture at that moment of departing from her. He had waited until he was out of sight of the hotel before he'd dared to read the note again. 'Meet me at five in the coppice, darling? Say yes. I have important news. I love you. E.'

The first time he read it, he remembers how he'd misread the punctuation, seeing in her quick scribble a colon between 'news' and 'I' – so then taking the news to be that she loved him. Only on that second reading did he see his error, and it troubled him, until he remembered her waving at him from the window. And the tenderness in her posture made it seem impossible to him that she should have anything but pleasure for him. Perhaps the news was good. 'Good' meaning, of course, good for them.

He takes out the note now, remembering perfectly what she had meant by it, and all that her news had entailed. He presses the paper to his nose and breathes it in. Of course the scent is no longer of her. Perhaps it never was. But it is still of the moment of her handing the piece of paper to him, and this is enough.

He has her close beside him for the seconds of his remembering. He can feel the slight brush of her fingertips against his hand as she pressed the note upon him. I should have taken hold of her right then and stopped everything in its tracks, he thinks now. I shouldn't have let us go another inch along the pathway we were caught on, but announced then to the world that we were going to be together and that alone would have shifted everything on to a different course. Perhaps then she'd even be beside me now.

He holds the paper there, breathing it in. He cannot bring himself to look at the photograph beneath it. Not just yet, he tells himself, as though storing up a pleasure. But he knows that it is not pleasure he is postponing, but the sureness of pain: he has looked at her photograph more often than he has looked at her.

He glances up at the sky, darkening every second, the boom of thunder distant but strong, as though echoing in a deep cavern or well of his remembering.

That is it precisely, he thinks, feeling as though he can almost see the sound of thunder because it is so multiplied by the depth of his memories stacked one upon the other, overwritten, incrementally more loud. I haven't lost her by this secrecy, but allowed her memory to multiply. So that soon – he shuts his eyes and hears the rain on the glass roof above him – soon the layers of time and thinking of her will be lit up. Each emotion will be readable, exposed, the secret unearthed, gloated over by the world.

He rubs his forehead with his right hand, and with his left presses the paper back inside the pocket, where, give or take a succession of different jackets, depending on the temperature of the season, and on their general wear and usefulness, he has borne that slip of hotel-embossed paper, and that photograph, around with him for almost a lifetime, hidden close against his heart.

She must have fallen asleep unintentionally, because for a second Anna's thoughts appear to be composed of two distinct layers - what she can see, and what she knows - and the layers conflict. She rubs her eyes, stands up abruptly so that the book falls to the floor and she knocks over her now empty teacup.

The rim of light around the curtain edges has vanished and the room is in darkness. She can just make out the shape of the lamp on the small table beside her, but she does not know where the light switch is and hesitates before trying to find it, not liking to name the reason why, although the image of herself being caught at a disadvantage, bent over and fumbling with a switch, makes her stand there, her breath held, listening, and trying to see in the dark.

The room is silent. Yet she was disturbed so suddenly from sleep that the noise of running on gravel, now faint, seems loud with menace, even as it is swallowed up by the rush of wind. But there is something else, a much lighter sound, like someone passing tentative hands through thick velvet pile or short grass, a kind of slippery whispering. There is someone outside her room.

She can almost see them hesitant there, perhaps with an ear pressed against the wood to see if she is awake and moving about.

She reaches out fast and finds the switch. With the room lit, fear becomes anger, and she goes across to the door, meaning to throw it open and confront whoever is there. But she cannot do it. She checks that the door is locked and leans towards it, straining to hear. A sharp draught blows beneath the door on to her naked toes. She has the impression of windows being propped wide open at either end of the corridor to let the night breeze flow through the empty building. She thinks she can hear the whispering sound still, though grown further away. She flicks on the main light, and knows that she will not sleep.

From outside her window, the sound of running is now completely lost beneath the noise of gathering wind. She can hear a loose shutter rattling against one of the upstairs windows, and the lisping hush of the pines pressing close against the west side of the building. Again the sensation of being in a ship at sea.

She goes across to the window, peeks out at the night from the side of the curtain. At first she can see nothing, then she can make out the shape of the sky – not black but inky with a roll of clouds moving swift before a storm. It is not raining yet, but she can see that soon enough it will be. She supposes that that is the reason for the sound of running footsteps and peers to see if anyone is visible.

Over to the left where the open countryside starts, just a few yards beyond the red-walled garden of the hotel, the land is faintly visible – radiant where the town casts light across the grass. There are no stars or moonlight. Both are hidden by the bank of clouds. But on this stretch of land, Anna thinks she can see a small light falling in and out of view, as though disappearing beneath waves: the runner? Then it disappears entirely, and she wonders if she was mistaken.

The ancient wisteria on the garden wall rustles sere-purple, the colour deepened by the pitch of night. Where the hotel lights catch it, it appears to smoulder, as though a secret fire has been lit along its trellis that, any moment, will burst into flames. Anna closes the curtains against the sight of it. She tries to steady her breath. She thinks of how she will merely go down there tomorrow morning and admire its pendulous bunches of flowers and it will be harmless, a beautiful plant again – and not as it seems now. She curses herself for being afraid. She fixes her mind's eye on the thought of daylight.

Apart from the main door to her room, and the one leading to the bathroom, there is another, with an armchair set halfway across it. The panels of this door are also boarded over, and fire instructions are pinned to it on a laminated card. She tries the handle. It turns but does not open, and she notices that a key is hanging on a hook pinned to the wooden frame. She leans towards it. Is someone next door? But it is noiseless.

Perhaps at one time this was a suite, and the door led through to another room. She wonders if on the other side there is also a key, so that someone would only have to use it to come in here while she slept. She notices a small bolt at the top. It wouldn't be enough to stop someone breaking the door down, but at least she would hear them. Perhaps that is the reason for the chair. She notices the arc of flattened carpet: the door would open into her room. She shifts the chair closer up against the door and frowns.

Standing very still, she is sure that she can still hear a faint noise coming from somewhere close inside the building. Perhaps it is nothing. Just one of the other guests. But she has seen no one else yet, and cannot imagine what kind of people might be staying here. She thinks about the empty attic rooms overhead. Perhaps at one time they were the servants' quarters. What had that girl said? They were now just used for storage. But what was kept there? She imagines the stacked mattresses and the abandoned hotel linen, all the dreams remembered only as dust inside the fabric. She thinks of the layer of lost life above her and is saddened by its weight. How can those rooms be empty?

She holds her breath, straining to listen. The bedroom feels as though someone just left, leaving it entirely empty, even of her own presence. The overhead light lists in and out of brightness: the storm must be interfering with the electricity supply, and she thinks of herself being left alone in the hotel – she imagines that downstairs girl living with her family, not here, and even now snug before a front room TV once her shift is done. Who else will there be? She thinks of the laughter she'd hear if she risked the idea of telephoning for room service. But she supposes someone must stay overnight, perhaps the daytime-only bag-carrier – the 'he' to whom the girl referred earlier?

She walks across the carpet to the door, unlocks it, and looks out into the corridor, where the wall-lights have been turned off. Only at the far end, at the head of the stairs, is there any light. She catches her breath as she looks there, shuts the door fast, runs the safety-chain across, tells herself that there is nothing to be alarmed by, although the sight has made her tremble, the back of her neck grown cold.

At the head of the stairs, the figure of a man dressed in some kind of uniform was holding what looked like a short knife, or dagger. The blade flashed where the light caught it. He did not appear to see her. He was turned to the wall, leaning in towards the grandfather clock. He seemed to be wiping the knife on a cloth, and she realises that this must have been the noise she heard earlier, as he passed her room. Or was it that he was sharpening the blade?

She wants to open the door again and see that it is not true. But she cannot do it, and what if this time he has come closer? Her breath is high and shallow in her chest and the sound of rain fingering now at the window does nothing to rub out the image, indecipherable, that is fixed across her thoughts. She hesitates in the middle of the room, waiting for the right moment to cross over to the bed and try to sleep. But the thought of stretching out there in the darkness makes her shudder, and she knows that when she lies there, no sleep will come.·

The rain, louder now against the window, sounds like earth drumming on a hollow wooden box.

When David stumbles into the opening cut of earth, no one hears his shouts. The others are still miles away, adjusting their coats, complaining about the bad weather, looking for more torches, sipping last mouthfuls of coffee. They take their time before setting out. They can't imagine that there is any kind of rush, or that a minute now might make any difference. 'It'll keep, it's kept long enough,' one of them jokes.

The landscape had grown familiar to him, and he had known where to find the body again – just by the blocked-up source of the spring. He had set a post nearby as a marker. But the wind had carried away the plastic tape, and the post was invisible in the failing light. Darkness made everything strange. When he fell it seemed as though he was falling into a trap: this time, she had found him, it wasn't the other way round at all.

It was so close to where they'd already been digging that they might easily have discovered it months ago. Ensconced in peat, its outline had emerged so plainly beneath his hands that at first he thought the body must be from the very recent past. He had covered his mouth and nose instinctively, steadying himself, trying to think clearly. He shifted away a piece of turf. It came loose easily in his hands, sodden by the unbound flow of springwater. But there was no smell beyond an organic tang, and he understood then what he had found. Widening the beam of his torch, he could see how aldehydes in the peat had preserved the skin through successive ages to the quality of a strong hide, a deep russet-colour with the strength and patina of weathered conkers.

Earlier that day, when he rushed back to the town to telephone from the station house, running fast across the moorland, he had had words with which to snare this body.

Celtic sacrifice. Neolithic ritual. He had seen bog bodies of this kind before, but only ever in museums. One, discovered in the eighties, was thought to be from the first century, and sometimes they were much older even than that. He had made a stab at what it might be, and perhaps he was right in one of his guesses. But those words seemed like the jabberings almost of another species now. They were vacant as a number that reveals nothing of the life it's meant to represent.

Now the earth fills his eyes and mouth, and he can feel the thickness of her skin beneath his hands, the way her body collapses in places where he presses against it, trying to wrest himself clear of her embrace. It feels almost as though she were breathing, stertorous and hot inside his grappling arms. She seems to want to pull him down and keep him there, not let him get back to the air above. He is crying so hard with fear that he feels as though strong hands are gripping him tight around his throat. The earth weighs heavy on his back, great hunks of it falling in about him, the springwater turning the peat quickly wet like an unwound pot dismantling on a wheel.

His dizziness makes him sick and his head feels full of blood, pounding where he cracked it as he fell. But even though he can see only darkness, he knows that he has been blind until this moment.

Overhead, the storm grows more wild each second. The earth seems to tremble beneath him. He can see the raised flint as it catches the moonlight. He can hear her cry, the warm body's tumble into cold. What was the crime, and who the judge, the executioner? He had had no idea what death felt like. But now he knows. He holds her in his arms.

II

In the right conditions the dead body of any organism, however frail, even delicate leaves, stems, fronds, might sink down to the sea bottom, or be held in swamps or the mud of rivers and there be petrified in the finest perfection of detail. When we come upon them again it seems as though time has revealed itself in a different dimension, as though the particles that smothered and preserved them were not grains of matter in space, but passing minutes; that these are infinitesimal lives 'fixed fast in time'.

Jacquetta Hawkes, *A Land*

5

He leaves the station house at a run. The express train is loud approaching, its engine smoke clapped like gunshot against the sky. A series of illusions: silver-lined nimbus in his mind's eye. He squints against the June sun. His feet spray gravel, reveal the mud beneath, and when he brushes past the poppies growing wild at the gate, the spores rise and he can smell their scent. His new-ironed shirt feels cool and dry against his skin.

He steadies up when he reaches the street, pulled between contrary impulses: to be unseen, pass by unnoticed; and to stop everyone to tell them of his happiness, which anyway, he thinks, must be shining out plain as day from every hair on his head. He feels as though he should have a leper's bell: not unclean but in love, for he feels similarly set apart. He casts his eyes down, tries to wear a serious expression, is sure that he must be failing from the way that – or is this just in his own mind? – people seem to dodge him, standing back to let him pass.

He imagines her as she must now be. He glances at his watch. He has four minutes before he sees her. He pictures her look of nonchalance as she strolls out of the hotel, the way she will feign indecision in the doorway, as though debating which way to go, although she knows perfectly which direction to walk in, and what is her goal: him, and she his. He thinks of the small town as a symmetrical picture, the two sides rough mirrors of each other, with him in one half, her in the other. They have only to fold over that picture to be together.

He smiles to think of her walking towards him, her hips smooth and strong beneath her dress, the fabric clinging to her legs as she walks downhill along the path beneath the trees – the same way he walked with her for the first time, only last week. He can see the last blossoms catching in her hair. He imagines the touch of them against her cheek.

The thought of her being alone there fills him with pleasure. She has transformed that fragrant tunnel for ever for him now. It means her. She has left her shapes there, and he thinks that at any time of day or night, while he's without her, he has only to go there and she will be beside him almost as vividly as when they were together. He speeds his pace. And yet there is no substitute for the fact of her, he knows, and feels his distance from her with a wave of anguish – how many hundred yards? He tries hard not to run.

She is there ahead of him and appears almost to be standing on tiptoe, as though the news she has for him is a fragile object and she is afraid that any heaviness might break it. Sunlight presses through the leaves of sycamore and birch to make the green seem luminous. The horse-chestnut candles have fallen; the brushwood coppice floor is littered with broken petals. She does not move towards him but lingers in the flickering light, as though to move might be to undo a spell or stray into a trap. His footsteps sound ludicrously loud to his ears and he is conscious of every tremulous motion around him – a bird's wing, the flight of a moth, shadows running into each other as he walks towards her.

When he reaches her he does not dare to kiss her. She stands in a green light and her face appears to mirror all the loveliness of the glade. He has never seen her look more beautiful and her eyes are bright with nerves and some kind of withheld eagerness, or questioning, that he has never encountered. He hesitates a couple of inches away from her, close enough to gauge her temperature. So close, still they do not touch, and he can feel his skin graze against his clothes as though each hair on his flesh is made of glass. To touch her might be to splinter. He can hear his breath and it sounds to him like the breath of a stranger. He almost has the desire to run from the sound; he has never heard it before and it frightens him. He can feel the blood drop fast from his face and he is conscious of the five-years distance between them. He feels stupid with youth, and wishes he were older than her.

When he takes hold of her it is to lead her deeper inside the covering of trees. Her hand is hot inside his, though dry, as though she has been holding it up to bathe it in sunlight. The vision of her doing this is almost intolerable to him: he would have liked to see her do it. He imagines reaching up to take her sunlit hand in his and haul it up against him so that it finds its heat from him, not from the sun.

He shuts his eyes as he stumbles through the coppice with her. He has no fear of crashing into a tree. It seems to him that he is so profoundly within his flesh that he is no longer an inelegant man with limbs and clothes blundering through the clumsy wood, but is in fact the blood itself, even now running free inside his veins. Yet it is more than this: the deeper inside himself he goes, the further he is from his life's heaviness, and already he is flying far beyond the treetops dazzling overhead. He has no thought of himself, and can only think of her.

Darkness shuts down across his lids, as though he has stepped inside a cave. They are in the furthest part of the coppice where it runs into a sudden density of pines, and later, the forest – too close-set to penetrate without coming away with scratches. They pause there for a moment, peering towards the dark green line of trees that looks almost like a drop in the land, or like an underwater shelf that seems incredible for being so deep, so abruptly. The air is cooler here and he draws her close towards him, her body appearing to diminish with the temperature's descent.

She is wearing a grey dress. Her hair appears moonlit in the watery light. She is hatless. The omission makes her seem half dressed, startling – as though she left the hotel in haste, barely conscious of what she was doing.

He holds her close, speaking her name. Her hair is against his lips. But she says nothing for a long moment, and he can tell by her silence that something is wrong, or very changed. When she tilts her head back so that he can see her face, she is smiling. But it is a smile of worry, and he is anxious at what it must mean. He is impatient with her, and wishes she would tell him what has happened. Tears suddenly turn her eyes glassy, almost false-seeming, and he draws back. But this only makes a tear fall and he can see that he was wrong to think her emotion anything but sincere.

He presses away her tears with his lips as though they were easily removed transfers, leaving no trace. But even tearless her face is changed so that he has to gather it up once more in his sight. Her grief has made her unknown to him. It shames him. It makes him conscious of how small a part of her he has acknowledged.

He holds her nervously and his throat feels tight. She buries her face against his chest, almost hurting him. With her face concealed, she tells him that she has received a message from her husband, asking her to return immediately to America. He himself is in Europe now, and is leaving for California in two days' time. She is careful not to suggest that she has spoken to him, as though to mention this might be to raise the spectre of the man in some way – to set him alongside her suddenly, right here in the forest. She does not lift her head.

They stand there like that, neither speaking, for several minutes.

He feels that to let her go will be to lose her, as though they have been sharing a dream and have simultaneously been roused by the sound of shattering gongs. So he clings to her and she to him, and he is conscious of the speed of change around him. Already his earlier vision of merely folding over the town in his mind's eye, and that way being with her, floats skywards like a scrap of finished ash, and he sees the distance still left to travel to her revealed even in their embrace.

It is then that she tells him that she is in love with him, but that there is a great deal he does not know, and when her voice lowers, the words falling into one another, her eyes are shining.

She takes a pace away from him and in that step seems like a child. Her arms rush up to take hold of herself, almost seize herself, as though claiming her independence from him, or as though intent on a strength that she cannot believe she might possess. He does not know what she will do if he tries to touch her. He almost thinks that she might strike him, or call out. Her shoulders are raised in an attitude of defiance. But she is so tiny that he thinks it only makes her look vulnerable. She seems almost courageous, and her longing for courage fills him with anguish: he is paralysed with the thought that he might have caused her shame.

'You are not responsible for what has happened.' Her voice is high and she speaks fast as though the words humiliate her to utter them. By speaking quickly, she appears to want to claim all possible denigration for herself, as though lighting it up with the largeness of her generosity will be to diminish it to nothing. 'It's all my fault. There are certain things—' She laughs, her chin tilted to one side almost with a look of contempt, directed only back at herself.

He cannot bear to see her behave this way. He imagines her barricading herself up so that he cannot draw any closer: she has immured herself against it; she will not allow it. He tells her, 'Stop, don't go,' although she had made no further move away from him.

He can hear his heartbeat onerous in his chest. He stares at her and she seems to falter, her eyes cast suddenly down, and he is conscious that he has never seen her acting until this moment, and he takes her in his arms again, telling her everything he feels.

They descend first to their knees and sway there momentarily, like two dignified ancients before an execution, holding hands.

Pine needles cushion their fall, the risen scent matching his first knowledge of her skin. Her lips taste of the forest floor and her hair seems like a hot cat's fur – alive with static to the touch as though even that dead part of her were liable to pleasure. He runs his hands over her hair repeatedly as though to earth the crackling static that might otherwise harm them. Her skull is beautifully shaped, he discovers, like a small child's. Her hair is very fine and he imagines her floating on the surface of water, the way her hair would spread out around her face. Then he holds her head between his palms, placing one either side of her face across her ears, and she shuts her eyes. He understands perfectly her need for that blind silence. He holds her there, upon that island, and she is smiling.

There is the scent of crushed leaves mulched to sweetness. The air is very still. When he tips his head back, the sky is mullioned through the leaves of a sycamore tree, the fruit helicoptering earthwards, scattering light like gold moths' wings.

Afterwards, a tendril of ivy curls around her forearm and he draws her closer to him, feeling her heat again, her bones seeming more fragile now as though stripped of the power that held them taut. She kicks away a fern that tickles the arch of her naked foot. When she stands, laughing, she is giddy as an infant and he jumps up alongside her to hold her steady.

There is a fine red scratch running laterally across her throat where a choker might be clasped and he kisses it, half wishing the mark were permanent so that she might bear that sign of his habitation of her body when they are apart – although the next time he sees her it is gone, possibly concealed beneath powder.

Yes, he thinks now, wondering at his hoard of memory, it was just like that. To hold her was to start to lose her. Everything I thought I knew simply vanished, or was concealed by a mist of unknowing. Being sure that we existed was like insisting on the presence of some kind of spirit: madness to make claims for. And every move towards greater intimacy brought an equal measure of loneliness and fear.

His mind's eye darts lizardish about each second of that afternoon as though he might taste it all again, just by looking. He raises his hands to his lips and smells the scent of peaty soil ingrained there. Her hair smelt just like that. Though soon enough, he remembers, it was scattered about with shiny needles of pine, and later, her head thrown back, she had to brush them out. They fell to the floor like raindrops, with a tiny crackling noise that made them both glance up. But the sky was still clear, although the day by then was nearly ended. Her handbag's clasp when she put away the hairbrush sounded like an impish gunshot, a small shock of metal: it was time to leave.

Dusk soon made the air seem smoke-filled beneath the lightless canopy of trees, and her smooth skin grew goosebumpy under his hands. They staggered where they stood, and clung speechless for a long time. Leaving her was never so hard as at that moment. He was afraid for her. He could not say why. Something had been resolved between them, he felt sure. But the second he let go of her, uncertainty covered him in doubt and he took hold of her again.

A soft peal of thunder arrived with the end of day. They walked together through the long meadowgrass, and when she faltered, he urged her on. He wanted to hurry her forward to the moment when they could, absolutely, be together. Her slowness made him jealous for all the time with her he had not had. He wanted rid of it the way a healthy person likes to shake off sickness – for his body to forget it. Knowing he had to let go of her made him feel the shock of vertigo. He couldn't bear to think of the times behind him when he was without her, or the moments ahead of him when she might still not be his, even after this – after confessing himself entirely to her. It made him hurry forward as though to bring the future into line with his desire, and not let it lag behind him with those times when she was not his; when she was not even known to him.

They parted beneath the disguise of a line of trees. He watched her leave a few moments ahead of him. Her walk appeared idle, vaguely curious, as though she had just been out for an afternoon's stroll. She was soon concealed by the long wall of the hotel grounds.

He imagined her hand on the wrought-iron gate that led into the last part of the garden. He could see it swing shut behind her as she made her way, unhurried, along the pathway between the tall yew hedges cut into the shapes of giant birds, and closer to the hotel, chess pieces. Their shadows would conceal her, her outline transmuted to the ambiguous quality of a ghost.

When she stepped into the gold light of the hotel, he could see how her hair would be shining like a patch of flaxen daylight, and maybe then she would blush, touching her hair, surprised at herself for coming out without a hat. Perhaps her breath stops then as she wonders if this is true. Or is her hat lying somewhere like a wild anemone beneath the trees, to be discovered by the following daylight?

Did she look back at that moment of remembering herself; see herself again on the forest floor, her pale hair tangling with the bindweed and ivy, her skin flushed with blood? And does she hesitate then, on the point of running back to him through the fallen evening?

He presses his palms against his face. He feels damned. Excluded. Perhaps that was the day I started to lose her. Perhaps it really was that soon – even before I had been able, properly, to hold her. The scent of her hair is in his hands and he cannot take them from his face. The fear of letting go of that minute remnant of her is a taunt: it was precisely this fear that destroyed everything, though not quite yet, and so in his mind's eye he lingers in that afternoon beneath the cover of the trees, listening to the sound she makes mingling with rainfall pounding on the greenhouse roof.

When he looks at his hands he cries. He hates his hands because they do not contain her. His tears fall on to his palms, gather in the hollow at their centre like glassy impressions of stigmata, which only makes him more enraged. He would gladly have suffered for love, had love meant her alongside him. He would happily have been her supplicant, her martyr. '*I would have died for her*' – he frames this thought aloud and it sounds horrible to his ears, like a lie: it was not possible.

His life seems to fall away behind him too heavy to be

bearable. Too long spent wishing and bawling out my secrets down a well. He swears to himself, looking at his hands with contempt for everything they have done without her.

She has seen nothing of the cause of their lines, he thinks, clenching and unclenching them. She knew none of the moments of their scarring and callousing, or of their fingernails' yellowing, or of their joints tightening so that they grow more difficult each year to bend and straighten out.

He has punished his hands for their lifetime of not holding on to her. He hates the sight of them. They are old. It seems implausible – some kind of dream – that they should ever even have touched her. It is an obscenity. He shoves them inside his pockets. His right hand finds a few rusted nails he'd been meaning to use to fix up a trellis that's come loose on the south wall of the station house. He presses his hand hard against the steel until he draws blood and this, at last, gives him a kind of pleasure, though it is full of malice and his heart feels sore with longing for her.

The rain has turned the heath into a sea, as though the land is swelling with memories of its forgotten self. David feels as though his blood is being replaced with water. His energy is failing him. His limbs are heavier than he has ever known. With every upward push he feels the earth seem to fold itself around him and then to heave him down again. His efforts seem useless and his senses are thrown off-course so that he half thinks he might be dreaming or gone mad with fear and isolation.

He has wrapped his hands around himself because to reach them out is to touch another's leathered flesh and bone and it terrifies him. It seems to choke him, or somehow have got inside his mouth, entered his lungs. His body seems thick with it. He can barely breathe. He does not know how long he has been down inside the crevice. Time is compacted by fear.

When he finds a foothold he pushes himself up with such force he sends a shower of earth and water skywards into the night. He feels the clods rain back down on his head like lava and he lets out a great roar that he barely recognises as his own voice. It terrifies him. He is shaking so violently now that he cannot trust himself to stand up when at last he works himself free of the pit, and he collapses on a rump of heather, crying with relief that this, at least, does not give way beneath him.

Then he sees the lights heading towards him across the moor. They are bobbing fast in his direction, and he realises that they must have been alerted to his position by the sound of his bellowing. It must be at least an hour since his torch gave out. He rubs the face of his watch free of dirt, peering at the luminous green dial. No, he has been underground for almost two hours, passed out for only some of that time after striking his head, so then awake, undreaming, for the rest, and this thought sits in his mind's eye like the worst danger he can conceive of, too close still for him not to run the risk of falling there once more.

He grips his upper arms to stop himself shaking. He curses loud and fast and wishes they would hurry. How much longer? Even sitting on the ground in the clear air, he feels as though he is falling, the moment of stumbling endlessly replayed. The night itself seems to slip from him. He can hold on to nothing. And yet he thought he knew what he had found, and had even felt the triumph of possession. 'I've discovered something'; he cringes now at the way he bleated out his foolishness down the telephone. And so when he fell, he fell as his father, seeing death as final, remote, abstracted into harmlessness. But he landed as himself, and the intimate nearness of death returned to him.

Yet we were both wrong. He touches his head, winces at the bruise, feeling the wet of broken skin. It is not so definite as the end, or just a matter of degrees. It is something else entirely. Something that can come to the living, too, so that they walk in its shadow, unlivened as ghosts, deaf even to their own loud cache of memory. But you only have to listen out for it, and you can catch its sound. He can hear the wind playing the heather like whitecaps, and still, though fainter now, the sound of the woman's cry, muffled by the earth.

He feels all this so close alongside him now, shadowing him, resting beneath everything – a dark, crowded place into which he might fall back at any moment. The crevice is partly hidden from sight by a lip of turf, and he dare not move for fear of slipping there again. He still cannot stop himself trembling. The earth seems to shift unquiet about him, and he thinks of it as a kind of cakewalk endlessly in motion. He feels as though he has waited for the right moment to jump on, squinting ahead at the future until his time arrived, and his delay has cost him dearly: he had not seen that the ground beneath his feet was also liable to just the chaos that he feared might lie ahead.

By waiting over-long, the past has written him. Time has looped right round and caught him hesitating, thinking his delay meant he stood still. But even standing still has proved a kind of sprint: time lassoed him, felled him, as fierce as though he'd rushed headlong towards disaster, his arms wide open, his throat exposed.

He should have broken the thread any number of times; should have stepped out of his father's shadow, not followed the shaded pathway where it pointed. But he did follow, and the sorrow of his mother's death rose up again in his future, seized him, and pulled him down; he embraced her and felt the pity of death inside the circle of his arms again. She seemed almost to breathe, and as he lay there her skin grew warm beneath his touch.

He has been cut down to the emotions of a child, and his brain feels shrunken with fear. He holds his head in his hands. He can see himself at the age of eleven, alone in the empty house soon after she died. The entire building is in darkness and he is too afraid to turn on the light. He tells himself that he is wise not to dare such a thing, and lies beneath the covers of his narrow bed chanting beneath his breath – verse, times-tables, lists, as though by this litany of familiarity he might drown out the louder sounds of his mother's absence, haul himself back to a place of light and calm.

It did not work. He could hear her still. He could hear her skirt rustling as he sat and read a book in the armchair in her study. He could hear her laughter when his father kissed her unexpectedly behind the ear, the softness of her voice when he embraced her, thinking their son was not spying on them and smiling at their joy through the concealment of his lashes. And even beneath his hopeless nocturnal chants, he could hear her entering his room, leaning down towards him, fitting the bedclothes more snugly about his messy limbs so that he did not catch a chill in the night, and, thinking that he was sleeping, even without hope of her being overheard, the way she would call him 'little angelchild' and kiss his sleep-damp forehead.

He could still hear all of this. So he persisted with his chanting. And his persistence, he soon found, was better than any alternative – either asking his father for help, or confronting the darkness where she was not.

And just so now, he finds himself running through loops of facts about the place around him until the torchlight grows near and he worries that they will hear him. He wipes his face with his sleeve and, as he does this, tastes the peat again and has to swallow hard to stop himself being sick. It is too close a reminder of the thing that lies just beneath the surface of the land, the thing that almost claimed him. He clears his throat, presses a hand against his chest to steady his breathing before calling out so that they will know where to find him.

They catch him in the beam of torchlight and he can hear their excitement. Some of them are even laughing. 'David!' someone shouts. 'You lucky bugger! Is it true?' The words startle him. It is as though – from the moment of discovery to his dash back to the town to telephone from the station house, to falling into the darkness, being forced to wait, right round until this moment – the whole episode was transfixed within a marble loop or whorl. Its circular fixity blinded him. Only now can he see what has happened.

He stands up, tells them, 'Over here,' although by now he is caught up in the torchlight. Someone slips, laughing. He warns them to be careful, explains that they should watch out for the sudden hollowing of the earth. 'Just above the spring,' he calls. 'The body's in there.'

There is only one light left burning in the station house and it gleams across the silent tracks like blame. The steel seems platinumed, wet as fine-ground knives.

Night has fallen by the time Jack arrives home: he could not bear to go straight there after being with her. He went right through the town to sit beside the river – at this time of year so low the banks show cracked where the water has long since dropped down to the depth of a stream. He could wade across it if he wished.

He sat there and watched the insect-boatmen stalk across the surface, their wings held aloof. Gnats and horseflies were still industrious about the mud, and when he walked through the reedy grass the moths rose spiralling upward. A lone firefly caught the first of the moonlight. A wasp crawled over his shoe and he did not bother to shake it off. It seemed sugar-drunk and slumberous. He didn't mind it.

Often, he goes to the river alone. His seat is a slab of sandstone, and that evening it was warm with the day's heat. He half imagined that it had started to smooth itself to fit his shape: he had been going there since he was a small boy. But he knew that that was foolish, that he could have left no impression there. It saddened him, and made him suspect his vanity. He has her shapes impressed upon his bones and in a flash he had a vision of his skeleton knocked by one degree out of kilter – the degree that they had tussled over. At this thought he felt the hair on his scalp lift as though caught by a breeze, yet there was no wind to speak of.

A willow tree screens his perch from the road that runs across the narrow sandstone bridge. There were no cars at that time of day, but three or four people passed by on foot, lingering at the centre, peering into the gloom. One person threw something into the water and Jack heard it break the surface, the sound as hollow as a frog's leap from a lily pad. He imagined it might be a good spot for fishing. At any other season, the water runs deep there, gathering in a natural pool where stones slump against the stanchions of the bridge. In late spring, the water is the colour of royal blue ink. With storms, it draws the ochre and shantung yellow of the clay banks within its depths and becomes muddy-as-the-Mississippi – or so, as a boy, he thought of it. Now it is meagre, the colour of string, and despite the recent rainfall it appears to have been scorched, or as though someone has beavered a dam upstream to staunch its flow. But its trickle is melodious, and Jack sat beside it and felt the sense of mute companionship once again. He wanted nothing to dislodge her from him – not ever, and certainly not just yet. He stayed away from home until the thin moon had risen high and he glanced up at it as though it were a reprimand.

Leaving the river that evening was like saying goodbye to her again, and it made him sad and afraid. He felt the anguish that she had never sat beside him there, possibly never would, and he felt all the strangeness of her – the fact of her being a stranger landed here as from another planet – with the nearness of a punishment, exacted, undeserved.

But there was something else, too, and he knew that the next time he went back to his place beside the river he would feel her there alongside him, as though he had planted her there, and he'd return to see how she had grown. She had left her scent upon his life and he had only to look out on the world to feel her presence there.

He slowed his pace and peered ahead where the shadows slanted thick across the way, leaning forward as he walked, as though trying to see round the corner of the approaching moment: she was there in everything; her life had rewritten his and he knew for sure that whatever he might scratch upon his future now, still she'd rise up to the surface of his days and he would see her there again.

His father keeps his back set to him when he walks into the firelit kitchen. Jack feels his shoulder muscles stiffen as though before a fight. But the man seems diminished in his refusal to turn round, impotent in his rejection, and Jack can see that in some way he has hurt him. The stovelight flickers and his father cuts the flame, shifting the heavy pan of soup on to a wooden board. A skin has formed, and there is a high-tide mark in the pan where the volume has diminished through being kept on the heat too long.

'You'll be hungry,' his father says quietly, although the quietness sounds to Jack like a withheld command. He takes a bowl from the drying rack and sits down at the table. His father hesitates, seems to struggle with something in his throat, as though a word is too large there and he might at any moment spit it out, leave it black and shining on the table between them. He also takes a bowl from beside the sink and Jack realises that he has not eaten – that he has been waiting for him to return home.

The kitchen smells of hot vegetables, and apples rotting ciderish upon the sill. They've been left there to ripen, Jack notices, and now are bruised, one or two seeming wormy, or nibbled at by wasps. But the lamplight makes them golden; he thinks of handing one to Elena and smiles to himself. They appear to have been left there deliberately, as though ready for someone to scoop them up and peel them, use them in a pie, cut out the bruises and wasp-tunnels, make them delicious again and good for eating. Jack glances at his father sitting opposite him, ladling soup into his mouth. He so seldom thinks of his father as ever having had a wife who did such things – although his father has mentioned that she used to make him pies; he has described the nutmeg-cinnamony scent of them, so vivid.

The old man's eyes are lowered but Jack can see that the lids are reddish as after overwork or tears. He assumes it'll be the hot day, or the dust that has made his father's eyes like this. He is on the point of remarking about the heat and the apples and how they've gone to waste, when his father looks up at him suddenly, almost violent with a knife-wound of disappointment. 'I saw you, earlier, with your woman.' He says the word 'woman' through narrowed lips devoid of blood, and his eyes slide back towards his soup. He sets his head down so that Jack cannot see his expression, but he dismisses him in that posture.

And although he never knew her, Jack can feel his mother some-where in the house, behind him perhaps, or moving about in another room, her industry of love and loyalty to her husband spelling out precisely the shame the man now plainly feels embodied in his son. Taking a woman up to the woods, what're you thinking of? His hunched shoulders are a mark of his disgust.

His father looks up, though not at him. His eyes seem to hear the sound of a train approaching, although the tracks are silent. He looks at the empty window as though anticipating someone's arrival there, their face against the glass. Jack feels diminished as a chastised child, exactly that height and tremulousness.

In that look, he can see how very little he knows of his parents' life before him. He has never felt his father's disgust before and it cows him worse than any blow. His father has never spelled out to him – he has not needed to – how directly his life contributed to his mother's death; the swap was almost direct: she died six months after giving birth. But he has never spoken of it; they have merely lived together with that fact dangling like a sword, hair-suspended, between them. Jack feels it now and hates the threat, because at twenty-three, in love, he suddenly feels assured of his innocence – love has assured him of it. There was no shame there, no wrong-doing.

He wants to tell his father all of this. That he has been given the chance in life to set right everything that he himself has been denied. But the equation is too subtle, too obscure and frankly mad-sounding for him to utter it. He says nothing. His father's eyes are fixed on the apples and Jack wants to take hold of his shoulders, tender and deliberate the impression he wishes to make on the man at this moment, and say, *I know, I know*. At the same time, he wants to bend his head and feel his father do precisely the same thing to him – the pair of them bent together in some act of contrition in the face of the fates that otherwise would lay them low.

His father's plate sits empty before him. 'Would you like more, Pa?' Jack asks him and the old man's face seems to cloud and clear, a storm of weather passing before he looks him in the eye. His face seems confused, very young suddenly, as though his son's question is incomprehensible.

He glances back at the empty window, and Jack has the profound sensation that his father has just seen a vision of his mother, maybe tipping apple peelings into the bin outside. He breathes in sharp. Can he smell cinnamon? And is this how it looks to have lost love?

Jack cannot bear the sight of it. When he repeats his question, his voice sounds choked, uncontrolled, and he half thinks that he might cry. His father hears the sound, and looks at him, startled. He sets a smile on his face, seeing that he has hurt his son and not at all wishing to have done so. He lets Jack take his bowl. 'Yes, more'd be lovely, thanks, Jack. Not bad soup, don't you think?'

'Like no one else can make it.' Jack's reply is the one they always use of each other's cooking. Tonight he wishes he'd not said it and finds himself looking up at the black window, following his father's eyes to where they, too, have swerved again.

The night outside is silent. The tracks are still. He wouldn't even know what to expect, had she emerged there. Perhaps he would not even have recognised her. And how can he care for her, but through some oblique compassionate yearning, a woman whom he never even knew? Jack frames this thought, sets the bowl of soup before his father's now-slight frame, touches his shoulder briefly to break him from his spell of reverie and remembering. That's how he'd know her, for sure, and in perfect recognition: through him, his father's memory of her now so palpable he seems to wear it like a second skin.

Anna throws the curtains wide and raises the sash window. The day rushes in with a sky of early aquamarine and a few small clouds running fast and high. Her lungs are still full of the city and she breathes in deep. Her belly is hollowed: she has not eaten since yesterday afternoon; a few thin sandwiches from a motorway service station. She is ravenous and happy.

Last night's rainfall has made the hotel garden shine with green, the dark box hedges glistening with raindrops not yet dissolved by heat. Just below her, pinned to the front wall of the hotel, an ancient wisteria is dripping. Leaning out, she can see that it is part of the same plant that last night had startled her as she watched it tremble and appear to smoke on the far wall that encloses the garden. It holds no menace for her now.

Directly ahead of her, a gravel pathway cuts across the lawns and gardens towards a wrought-iron gate in the red brick wall. Beyond this, scattered woodland divides the hotel from the town. She supposes that at one point in its history the hotel would have been a private house, and those trees part of its parkland. But the place has shrunk with time, its circumference narrowing until now it can be contained within the hotel's garden wall.

Either side of the path, the yew hedges would dwarf her, she suspects, were she to be standing beside them. They are cut into billowing shapes of uncertain design – as though they've stretched beyond sense whatever forms might once have occupied them. Almost hidden from view, a low privet hedge is squared off round a tiny rose-garden, the bushes dense but apparently well tended and all in flower. Closer to the hotel, an area of the garden is packed with herbs, which from her window appear to have run wild. She leans out of the window, noticing the uncut fennel, the knotted wood of a huge bush of rosemary.

Beyond the garden wall and the clustering of trees, the rooftops of the town are shining slick with wet. And beyond their furthest sprawl, on one side the land is farmed, with green and red-clay earth set to fields; the other side opens up to a vast monotony of green so dark it appears almost black, in places glistening obsidian.

Anna dresses fast, deciding to take a walk on the moor. She laughs to herself at her anxiety of the night before. She must have been half dreaming. There is no darkness here, she thinks, seeing how the pretty day outside has entered even into her hotel room: a red admiral has fluttered inside and landed on the chintz chair-back, perhaps mistaking the flat pattern of flowers for the real thing blossoming outside.

When the hinge of its wings stretches open, motes of pollen catch the sunlight where they fall on to the fabric.

6

'See, it's mistaken you for a flower.' Jack lifts the bee from where it has landed on Elena's hair. It is late afternoon, and the bee staggers in his cupped palm. Its hoard has made it docile. Elena laughs and thanks him. She touches her hair where Jack touched it, leans towards him to look at the bee. Her face and throat have been heated by the sun and when Jack kisses her skin it tastes sweetish, as though the bee has left footprints of honey upon her.

They have driven out of town to have a picnic on the moor. The main road is narrow, the banks steep and topped with stone walls of sliced flints and granite. Driving in tandem with the rim of the hillside on the west, they turned off down a track and suddenly were out in open countryside with the view cut wide and showing mainly sky – the moorland falling away steeply to the east, and the town half hidden by a rise in the land.

They left the car a few yards off the main road, and walked down the track with wild barley and brome growing tall on either side, the stalks bleached pale as dune-grass. They stopped when the track ended, and the earth grew springy underfoot. To trace a line from the point where they have come to rest would be to bisect two kinds of land: they are at the highest point of a soft ridge that, closer to the town, marks out the dark moor from the meadows. Along this ridge, in places, hazel and birch trees grow bent against the distant sea-wind, and at the highest point, a pine tree touched by lightning stands at the apex of a small triangle of soft grass – the place they head towards. The tree casts its shadow away from them, and the trunk gleams metallic in the late grey light.

The high air runs tight and clean around them, pressing them together. She wears a dress of thin yellow cotton and her brown eyes seem golden because of it. The wind catches her hair and he touches the tangles appearing in it, thinking that they look like gossamer, or make-believe cobwebs.

He throws the rug across the grass. They lie down on it and he can feel the warmth of her against him. Propped up on one arm, he notices how, further down the hillside, the trees grow closer together as though fertile in the wake of an underground spring. He imagines running a line from that point out towards the sea. Perhaps it joins up with his river, where it runs on the other side of the town. He thinks of it as 'his' river, and mentions it to her, tells her that he would like to go there with her. When she replies that she would love to, he is afraid that the phrase sounds abstract, or as though she might follow it with a condition already dishonoured, 'if only I could have remembered . . .'

He brushes the thought aside and holds her more tightly, kissing her throat, her hair. From this angle, he can see the rooftop of the station house, can guess also where the tracks must be, out of sight behind the trees. But he does not want to think of home, buries his face against her, shutting out the world.

Where she has lain beside him on the rug, her right arm crooked behind her head, her shoulder bears a minute indentation of the woven fabric that dissolves in seconds. He kisses her skin and watches the cloth-marks disappear. Dusk casts scant shadows upon them, as though the day ends more slowly in this place. She glances at her watch and when she stretches he takes hold of her again. This time stay with me, he tells her, knowing that she will not. Already, his love sounds more like a request to his ears, and not an offering – with none of that freedom left to it, only the desperation of a muffled demand.

He starts to look away, and this is the moment when the lone bee mistakes her for a flower. It had been foraging far from the hive and hopelessly, among the budded heather and clover. He jokes that even Nature wants her to stay. Look how you belong here planted beside me, you fit right in. He tries to ridicule his urgency, but can hear the sadness in his voice, as though remembering a moment already left only to longing.

He listens to the bee's hum. The noise is very faint and as delicate as though the sound itself has been caught in honey: even the noise is sweet to his ears. He listens intently to it – the diminishing thread of lost time – and tries now, as then, to gather up more of it than he is able. It slips from him, is lost, refound. He listens for it still. There it is. And then gone. If he could, he would give up everything in exchange for that moment's fixity so that he could take it out whenever he wished, and not lose it, as even now he is losing this.

There is one light burning in the kitchen window, and its gold beam makes a quiet river of light run from the house towards the greenhouse where he sits. The bee buzzes, falls silent. Jack is tired. But it is not his tiredness that is making him slip in and out of memory so much as his desire to see her again. He cannot have the whole of her. So she is delivered to him in parts. The bee trundles lazily about the finished flower of a strawberry, as though remembering the flower through the fruit now swelling there. Its wings flash glassy as an eyeball and he sees her lids slip down so that the lashes fall upon her cheeks.

With his face so close against hers, he could see the hairs as fine as the down that grows closest to the root of a sparrow's quill, colourless and impossible to detect unless wet, and his kisses carried faint dampness with them as though he transferred a vital gift of pollen to her, planting it inside the moisture of her skin.

A thin moon floats free suddenly from the mountain-banks of clouds, though still there is no starlight. The rain has stopped. Jack wasn't aware of its stopping: he supposes that he might have slept, been drowsily sung to sleep by its perpetual descent. The moorland is black, and he wonders, too, if he missed that boy returning? He didn't see anyone else going up there. Didn't see any more hideous search-lights, their bone-white beams flaying the land wide open. Discovering nothing, until now.

The bee finishes with the strawberry plant and swings a tight arc back upon itself to settle on a vine leaf, traipse around the sweet white Muscat grapes.

The strawberry leaf trembles where the bee left it – or perhaps it was the breeze that just skipped in. Jack pulls the plaid rug higher up where it has fallen down to his thighs so that his guts feel the night's chill. The same rug. He sets his hands flat upon it, smoothing it across his useless legs.

He can see her, the way she wriggled from him across the rug as though to escape, turning back to look at him, her eyes dancing, letting herself be caught. Something tickled her face, she told him when they stopped kissing. It had pricked her through the red wool rug. Lifting it up, there on the grass beneath were three wild strawberry plants in a tight cluster where they supposed a bird had transplanted them. She wrinkled her nose at the thought but peered closer as though they'd just discovered treasure.

The fruit was tiny, little green gemstones. 'It's a gift,' he told her, and dug them up with the flat edge of a stone, and with his fingertips for a makeshift trowel. The plants came away easily. Their roots were very close to the surface, and they were connected by strong brown tendrils running like a mathematical equation, criss-crossed between the plants so that the trio would not have come away separately. Had she not been lying on them, he doubted that they would have noticed them. The grass was long enough to offer concealment.

Uprooted, they were so small that they could sit all three inside the palm of his hand. Her head bent over them alongside his. Her hair swung against his face – a sheet of scented silk. He turned his face closer towards her to breathe it in. 'Will they live?' she asked him.

'Of course,' he reassured her. 'They can live through anything, and you only have to think that they've survived alone up here, so—' He took out his handkerchief and set the plants there, tying up the corners in a makeshift bag.

She laughed as she took it. 'You must plant them,' she told him, looking back at him as she headed towards the car. She skipped forward then, still laughing, and he ran to catch her, glad that she had made a joke of the strawberries – the trio of plants so ungrown and yet so tightly bound together.

The bee is silent as though drunk among the sweet green grapes and Jack sees her stepping out of the car where he dropped her at the end of the hotel driveway. By then it was evening, and he watched her disappear behind the screen of cedars. He drove away quickly, and they agreed that he would appear to be no more than a taxi-cab at this hour. She walked away without looking back. Indeed, why would one look back at a taxi driver? But her nonchalance scared him.

He passed Andersen's bottom field with the swollen-bellied cob wrenching at the long grass. A week later, and she'd have her first foal beside her. And he drove through the quiet town, past the George, and the ironmonger's where the lights were still on in the back room, reflecting yellow off the knives in the window and the tin buckets suspended from the ceiling like ranks of polished moons. The place had never seemed more beautiful to him. But its beauty spelt out his regret, as though he were looking at a snapshot taken many years ago, an image otherwise unremembered, from someone else's life: he felt his remoteness from all moments, and places, that did not contain her.

When he reached home, he went straight out to the garden. It was dark and the only light was from the kitchen window – just as now, similarly gilding him. He took a terracotta pot from his father's shed, mixed up some compost and earth from the flowerbeds, threw in some chipped pot to the bottom, a handful of sand, some straw and manure for heat, and made a perfect nest for the strawberry plants. He pressed the soil tight about them so that they were held firmly. He watered them and packed the straw about them. With their tendrils joining the three of them together, they seemed almost to be holding hands, he thought, smiling when he finished planting them, seeing the sign and ignoring it.

The fruit are just starting to ripen now – their ripeness hastened by being set beneath glass. Then, there was no greenhouse, and he'd set the terracotta pot outside the back door so that he could check it each morning. The fruit were small, when at last they turned pink, but very sweet – in the tangy sweet way of wild strawberries, dropped from the wing. When he offered one of the fruits to his father, he hesitated before taking it and his eyes misted with all the worry of which, by then, he knew. He took the fruit, ate it and complimented his son on its fine taste. He made a great show of relishing it. Too much of a show, as Jack remembers, underlining the fact that she had never tasted the strawberries, just pressed herself lengthways across them, with his added weight flattening the leaves hidden under the rug he'd set beneath her.

Jack stretches out his right hand, the left pressing for leverage against the red plaid. He plucks one of the just-ripe fruits and puts it into his mouth. Am I tasting her, to eat this cousin of the fruit that lay beneath us? He shuts his eyes and remembers everything. The taste is vivid on his tongue.

Walking through the rose-garden, Anna can feel the man's eyes upon her, and she does not linger. His gaze is no kind of threat but it is unsettling. When she came down into the hotel lobby a few minutes earlier, he had stepped forward suddenly, from behind the desk, as though he had been expecting her, or as though he recognised her. He had even bowed slightly, and his shoes made a clicking noise on the marble that sounded almost military. She half expected him to bark her name. But when he raised his head to greet her his mouth hung ajar, and she, too, stepped back in surprise. He apologised. She didn't quite understand what he was apologising for. And they stood facing one another for a moment, each waiting for an explanation. Then he seemed to remember himself and stepped back. Anna smiled at him, handed in her room key and left.

When she walked out of the hotel she was conscious that her feet made no sound on the carpet and it was an effort not to look round to see how he had managed to make so much noise – as though he had somehow been standing on an earlier layer of the hotel's history, touching marble and not the red nylon carpet that she had stepped on.

But she did not turn round, merely went quickly outside and into the garden she had been looking at earlier from her hotel-room window. As she walked away, she wished she had not left her copy of the novel on the bed. She had the sudden impression that the man might go up to her room and snoop around there. She could not say why – perhaps a fear of appearing gullible, or romantic – but she did not want anyone knowing her reason for being here: chasing the shadow of a story long since forgotten. By 'anyone' she meant only the girl of yesterday evening, and the man she had just seen. She quickened her pace as she remembered. No, not just seen, for he was the man she had caught sight of in the corridor the previous night. The memory returned the fear to her. What had he been doing?

Dampened after rainfall, the roses' scent feels like a wall of richness she can walk through. She touches the full-blown flowers, and the petals fall. She stands out of sight of the hotel behind a tall hedge of yew. Beech trees rustle in the wood beyond the high brick wall.

The rose-garden is arranged as a tiny, very rudimentary maze. She hadn't noticed it from her window. But it is possible to walk between the low privet that surrounds the rosebeds, along a narrow lawned pathway that forms a geometric spiral: the way out can be found just by taking an aerial view – even from her small height of five foot three. The way in and way out are at opposite corners of the square formed by the maze. To go right through is to divide the square into two perfect triangles, and on the far side, set deep into a hedge, there is a white wrought-iron bench placed in such a way as to suggest contemplation of both roses and the maze that contains them.

The metal is wet; she wipes it dry with a tissue and sits there for a few minutes, listening to the birds singing wild in the nearby cluster of trees. She runs her hand along the right arm of the seat, feeling its marks and scars. She glances down. One cut is much deeper than the rest, as though someone made it deliberately. It reminds her of a prisoner's way of marking time. A prisoner in a rose-garden? She is glad that she is out of sight of the hotel.

The yew hedge tickles the top of her hair and when she leans back into the dense cushion of needles, a twig scrapes the exposed skin of her neck, drawing a scratch of blood. She touches it away with her fingertip. It disappears with that one blotting. She forgets it.

Apart from birdsong, the town is very quiet and, screened by the high garden wall and the trees beyond it, she can almost imagine that it does not exist. She notices a gate in the wall, partly hidden behind a fir tree, its branches lifting and falling in the breeze, hiding and revealing the curled iron bars. Virginia creeper runs across most of this part of the wall, and when Anna goes across to try the handle she does not expect that it will open. But with her weight upon it, the handle turns.

The gate opens inwards. It moans as she swings it towards her. She closes it from the other side and looks back at the hotel through the ornate trellis of ironwork.

From here, the hotel no longer seems empty. Sunlight presses against its façade and the windows are aflame with it. She can no longer see the cracks in the plaster, the sunburned paintwork worn thin with age. Distance makes the cheap plastic urns at either side of the entrance look like the Italian marble ones they have no doubt replaced. From this short distance, the garden seems abundant and well tended. Shadows cut slantways across the grass and give the scene the appearance of order and design. Anna notices a movement in the shadowed doorway of the building and pauses: she is being watched.

She turns away out of sight and walks downhill through the trees in the direction of the town. There is a pathway but it is covered with a slew of leaves, as though the route is seldom used. Either side of the path, beneath the trees, the ground is overgrown with rustling ferns; beyond them, rhododendrons and the humpbacked tangle of briar roses. But looking upwards, still there is a narrow gap of blue in the canopy of trees, and this, better than the path, reveals the route ahead. Sunlight enters heavily here and the top of her head grows warm. Horseflies swim in the bluish light. She can hear birds jumping about in the undergrowth beside her, their movements snapping twigs.

Passing beneath the trees she remembers the scene: the lovers walking through a wood towards the town at dawn. She wonders if this is the wood the writer was thinking of. There were bluebells and wild garlic. A rainstorm had made the trees drip and they reached the town just after sunrise; it was May, and they had spent the night together in the forest. Anna remembers the description of the dark pines that shielded them from rain, and the pine needles that meant the forest floor was soft to lie on. She can smell the scent of pine now, although she cannot see the trees, and wonders if that is because they are out of sight, deeper in the forest, or whether she is imagining the smell.

It is windless and each noise is clear. Anna walks steadily downhill, seeing the scene unfolding equally around her and in her mind's eye. She can almost feel his hand around hers as they jog over the uneven ground, refusing to let go, holding her tight each time she stumbles. She almost expects to hear him speak to her. She is smiling to herself at the familiarity of the scene, humming as she walks. But although she breathes in deeply, she cannot smell either bluebells or wild garlic, and notices that, of course, she is too late for either, and anyway, by now the rhododendrons must have smothered them. Underfoot, the ground is slippery in places and she has to reach out to stop herself falling, her hands pressing heavily against the trunks of trees.

From time to time, she has to duck beneath an uncut branch that blocks her way, and every time this happens she is reminded that perhaps people no longer use this path. And thinking this she feels a nudge of anxiety, which she sets aside, until the next branch slices across her descent. She remembers the tune they sang together as they strolled home through the woods, but she stops humming it after a couple of notes because her voice sounds too loud and solitary, with no hand in hers and the forest very dark and tall, the treetops now meeting overhead in places, shutting out the light. She quickens her pace.

The path leads downhill to where the trees thin out and eventually the edge of the forest is marked by green: a short band of meadow before the first houses of the town, set inside the crook of the valley. Anna pauses on the edge of the trees, steadying her breath, glad to be out in the open sunlight. From here, she can see the old station house to the right, slightly apart from the rest of the town. With the tracks removed, it appears to stand sentry over nothing. She suspects that it is empty. Windows are smashed in the outbuildings. The roof of a greenhouse is visible behind a tall hedge and the mass of plants within it seem to press against the glass as though left there to grow wild.

Behind the station house, a meadow runs right up to the lip of the hilltop. Beyond this is the moorland visible from her window. It curves around the town in a dark arc, half enclosing it, seeming to encroach upon the buildings at its edge. Anna heads straight downhill into the town, deciding to take a look around, maybe pick up some food before making her way up on to the moor.

She squints upwards at the sky where already the sun is high and there are no clouds. There is a fresh wind now and the trees grow loud behind her. As she walks down through the long grass, she glances back at the sound the trees make and sees that already the pathway is swallowed by shadows. It is invisible now within the darkness.

She walks a little faster, pretending to herself that her pace is altered only by the angle of the hill. Looking back, she cannot believe that that is the way she has just walked. To think of it makes her neck go cold with nerves, and damp as though conscious of someone's eyes being fixed upon it. The shadows seem to conceal still more shadowy movements, the sense of people stepping behind trees to remain unseen. Had someone commanded her to turn round and retrace her steps, she would have refused. In fact, she would have been unable to do it.

She notices that burrs have hooked themselves to her clothes, and she cannot brush them off, as though she is carrying the forest with her in minute pieces.

She does not turn back again. She is glad to reach the edge of town. A car passes, returning her to herself.

'The thing is to try to keep it secret,' David rubs his eyes with tiredness, 'at least for a while. At the very least until we're sure what we've got.'

The five men are clustered near the place that – until last night's storm – was the finished dig. With the tarpaulins at last removed, rainwater and water from the overflowing spring have filled up the hollow where the remains of the boat once lay. A few yards away, just above the spring where the earth had been weakened by the excavation, the crevice opened up into a different stratum of time: with the discovery of the body, the landscape has been remade. They are looking at it with different eyes, or as though they've been handed a telescope when before they'd relied on natural sight. Measured in time, the view stretches back many hundreds of years more than they had thought.

It was an accident that changed everything: the number that transformed the logic of an equation, the single letter that reinflected the meaning of an entire language. David felt the significance of the discovery in his still-dark skin, as though he hadn't found a body but stepped inside one, inhabiting its shape so snugly that the sense of what had happened had become unavoidable to him, colouring everything he could see, and everything he could remember. He had been navigating just a few feet wide of true, and the accident had happened; knock a few figures off the structure of his mother's illness and she'd still be alive today.

But when would this haunting end? The closeness of everything he could see appalled him, as though he was transfixed inside a too-long moment of revelation, and the brightness of it hurt his eyes. He wanted the brightness to stop, and yet he felt the consequences of it, too: his own life is overdue and heavily within him now. He half expected to meet himself one pace ahead. And he would have liked this to be so, so that without effort he might fall into step with himself and hot-foot it from this place. He bunches his fists, repeats, 'Secret at least for a while, at least until we're ready to go public with it.'

By this, he only means 'at least until I've got myself clear of it, because isn't it obvious how far inside I still am?'.

'Don't know about keeping it secret for "a while",' one of the others says, screwing up his eyes as though estimating a length of time with a ruler. 'It'll be public soon enough. You'll probably be quite a celebrity. So will she.' His laughter makes David feel idiotic, and he is conscious of the older men staring at him in curiosity.

Just past first light, the day around them is pale blue with a few small clouds blustering low to the horizon. Someone has been back to the town to bring sandwiches and hot coffee in a Thermos, and they are sitting on the ground eating and drinking. Had anyone seen them at this moment, they would perhaps have assumed they were hikers, stopped at rest. But looking round the group David thinks they look like gravediggers, or robbers discussing where to stash their loot.

He looks away. He still feels lightheaded, not just through lack of sleep. To shut his eyes, even in blinking, is to be beneath the earth again.

No one has touched the body but him. Sure enough, they have flashed their torchlights into the crevice where it is buried in the peat, but they are waiting until it is fully daylight to go down – a purely practical suggestion, to wait for the best light, and for the climbing equipment to arrive. Now they scratch their heads, yawning, peering down into the gloom. 'We'll probably need to get an earth-mover up here.' No one is in any great hurry.

Earlier, when David suggested they should tell the police, the others fell about laughing, as though he had cracked a joke. 'Good idea, let's get Forensic on to it. Maybe they'll be able to convict someone,' and one of them had offered to take bets, 'Date to the nearest hundred,' 'Motive, anyone?' and 'A prize to Davey if he's right about it being a woman.' When they questioned him last night, 'Why did you say "she"?' he hadn't been able to answer. To say 'I just know', or 'Because it reminded me of my mother's death', would have sounded ridiculous, so he had tried to make light of it. 'Habit, I guess, like talking about a boat,' and this had seemed to satisfy them.

David looks at the group of men standing beside the hole in the earth, swaggering, he says to himself, while she lies there unknown to them but even so about to be trawled over, every bone unhooked, her flesh revealed. The thought horrifies him, fills him with disgust for his part in it. He is still in the underworld of his imagination, trying to claw his way out. But the difference now is this: he has one eye cast back at the body beneath him, and by comparison the light of the upper world seems false. He can almost not bear to look at it.

He wants to shout at the others, to tell them that they should let this go, not expose her to any judgement, but leave her secrets be, because who has discovered whom? He closes his eyes, opens them fast: he can see it all still; he has touched her; he has held her in his arms. More than anything, he wishes that he had not found her, as though that way her death might almost not be true. See, we do play a part in the past – he feels locked still in that argument with his father – and just by finding her I have had a small hand in her death.

But if I had said nothing, what would that make me? He rubs his collar-bone where his breath feels trapped, as though about to choke him. He feels the pain still throbbing in his head. Because it doesn't mean I'm good for the price that this has cost. This thought presents itself to him like a cloak – some kind of comfort in that understanding of his frailty: he just did what he could; he shouldn't expect the sense of it to clear until much later.

So he stands there, observing himself trying to look laughing and proud along with the others, while secretly he is goggle-eyed at himself, as though he were sitting at one remove, watching his behaviour, noting down his experiences. He sees himself taking a sip of black coffee, tasting only the bitterness of the soil that he is sure, were he to bare his teeth, would show black as liquorice along the line of his gums. He clamps his mouth shut fast. He is conscious of setting an expression on his face that he hopes will seem normal. But even as he thinks this a voice is laughing at him and at his thoughts. Normal? And then he feels the leathery wetness of the skin, and his forehead's crack against what felt like a skull. Was it that that knocked him out?

He takes a bite of sandwich and chews the grit of the riverbed. He sets it aside. Eyes shut, he is delivered back beneath the crust of turf and his fear at that sensation makes him tremble. He stands up, windmilling his arms as though to banish stiffness. But with every whirling motion he is trying to cleave the open air around him, steady himself by being able to move so freely without that hampering nest of falling earth. So he stands there whirling, but can think of nothing else beyond the sensation of being pinned there alongside a stranger's body with the earth for priest, scattering clods of peat on his unready head.

He walks off quickly out of sight of the others, behind a rise in the heather, and vomits. And when I sleep, he asks himself, will she be there? Will I lie this close to death for ever?

After the rainfall, the night seems to have been washed clean, with bright starlight and a fast wind scattering water-drops on the greenhouse roof. A small fir tree stands nearby and the tips of its branches just reach the glass, shuffling against it. The meadowgrass hisses as the breeze rushes through.

With the only light the gold beam from the kitchen downstairs, the darkness is almost complete and the night has become noise. It is too agile and rowdy with sound for anything else to seem to matter. The stars mean little to Jack: he cannot decode their patterns. And looking up at them they seem all off-course and jumbled, and he frowns to think of the significance that might be said to play there. As though *this* was bound to happen, he peers into the warm darkness, seeing nothing, hearing the night grow louder. As though all this black noise and emptiness lay inside the moments we were together.

He listens to the night and his head twitches as he falls in and out of sleep. The scattering raindrops seem to dance in a rhythm of loose syncopation with the shuffling fir, and the drip from the overflowing pipe falls flat and steady. He tries to see in the dark, leaning forward to look through the greenhouse glass. But he can see nothing. He feels as though he is sitting in a black tent, or as though to throw a stone at the glass would be to smash his way into the brightness of daylight.

The nightsounds pattern themselves about him until he feels almost like a flake of snow being built up to a design that he cannot understand. The wind flows swift around him, catching at him as it catches at the plants, making their leaves shudder, and he sees her similarly surrounded by sound, behind glass: she is dancing. There is some kind of dance at the hotel and, naturally enough, he has not been invited. But she asked him to see her beforehand; they have just been together, and he has lingered.

It has been a hot day, without rain, and the gardens have not yet been watered. The lawns are parched, already yellowing in places, the grass so tightly bound by heat it appears to be woven into the earth. It is just after eight o'clock – he heard the clock strike at the top of the stairs in the hotel – and he watches her walk fast up to the main door. A band has been pattering quiet melodies into the dusk, but at eight the volume of noise abruptly doubles and Jack stops mid-stride, caught off-guard by the sound. He was on the point of leaving. He has walked once round the garden, pretending to admire the plants, and now is strolling down the main pathway towards the gate at the bottom, meaning to go home through the woods.

But the weight of sound makes him hesitate, as though he is being told something, and when he turns he is surprised to see that she is gone: the sound seems to reach out towards him, like a stranger tapping on his shoulder in a crowd: you've dropped your wallet. Looking back, he expects to find some evidence of her having been with him, something left there on the grass – a scarf, perhaps, or even just a hairpin. But there is nothing. And without proof, some evidence of their being together, he cannot leave.

He watches the figures inside the hotel cast shadows on the lowered blinds. Every window along the ground floor is golden. The building seems to recede into the evening, as though at any moment it might lift a few inches from its foundations and hover there, weightless. It seems fantastical, something he could annihilate with one eye-blink. The sandstone of its façade he imagines scattering in fine grains, dissolving with the descending night. He traces her window and can see only a faint gleam of light emerging from around the drawn curtains and it makes him sad to think of her there, stepping into the room alone, the ceilings so high they make her feel like a child – or so she told him.

When she left him earlier, she had asked him to believe in her, which he took to mean that she was asking him to trust her, not to think ill of her in any way – and this was easy enough to do. He held her more tightly, telling her that of course he did, and always would. But looking back at the building now, he finds significance in her choice of words: believe in me. It seems almost impossible. As she walked away from him, her figure diminishing with distance and darkness, she seemed to be re-entering a world so remote from his own that he could not say with any certainty that it existed in the same way.

Of course he does not doubt that it exists: he is almost too conscious that it exists – that it is real and important – in a way that his world does not. Hers is the reality; he is an interloper. He has brought her only dreams and asked her to believe in them, to enter into them with him – to disregard one reality in favour of another, and that one less tangible. To ask this directly, he thinks, would be to ask for the entire world. It would be to restore life to someone on the brink of death.

He watches a small group of men emerge from the main door to smoke, their brilliantined hair making them appear to be wearing close-fitting helmets, their cigarette lighters snapping as though they were igniting fuses, with just that flare and fizz. Their laughter sounds like dogs barking, and standing that way, just outside the hotel doorway, they seem almost to be guarding the place. Jack imagines them blocking his path, were he to try to enter. There would be no violence, only exclusion, and afterwards they would laugh at him – discreetly, as they might also laugh at a madman or a drunk.

Jack sees her inside the hotel room, struggling with her dress: she told him that she was going to be late. She had not seemed to mind, then. But now he can see her tugging at her pale hair, almost whipping it as she runs her hairbrush through it until it shines. The softness of her face will have grown still, her movements strong and deliberate – not how she is when she's with him. Then her face has moods and pleasures running across it like changes of light and her lips and brow are agile as though a nerve kept watch beneath her skin. When she is with him, her body seems breakable, as though her own emotions might scupper her, exert such a force over her that her bones might shatter. The excess quivers in her fingertips, which are never still.

Jack thinks of her without him, the small tasks she will even now be performing that he will never know of, and then the way she descends the stairs – not with the light, hurried step she has when she is just about to meet him, but almost solemn in her gracefulness, expectant – and he cannot see where he might find the strength to believe that, at that moment, she exists *for him*. Her independence, the separation of her world from his, saddens him more than he can understand. He longs for her, knowing that his longing has on its surface the jealousy of possession, but that beneath it lies a depth of feeling multiplied in an infinite mirroring leading down into the core of all passion and all understanding. He thinks this quite clearly, and feels the thought's vertigo swing by him, making his head grow tight as though he might actually keel over with dizziness. He staggers slightly, as though someone has hauled him to the edge of a deep well, twisting his arm behind him, commanding: *Look*.

He has sweat drops on the back of his neck. Even in darkness, the day's sunlight is radiant off the earth. The ground feels warm beneath his feet and he glances down as though expecting to find his shoe soles smouldering. He looks up at the sound of a man's exclamation, and the figures in the doorway turn round in unison to look back inside the hotel. Jack sees a flash of silver behind them and tells himself that it must have been her, and that they were turning to look at her, at his love. He is certain that it was her, although he knows that it is impossible to say for sure from this distance, and with the night between them.

But he believes it was her, just then, descending the stairs. And merely to have seen her at that moment pulls him clear of the edge of the well and he stands more surely on the lawn, looking back at the brightly lit building bathed in sound.

He turns away quickly and walks down towards the gate, meaning to leave because only now does he feel free to do so: that was his sign, the evidence he had earlier longed for. But as he passes the rose-garden he hesitates – the scent distracts him – and he sits down on the wrought-iron bench, screened from the house by a yew tree. He smokes a cigarette and listens to the dry flutter of leaves in the nearby wood. From behind him, the sounds of the hotel dance band move in and out of focus as the wind shifts, as though it, too, were sounding out its music on the air. He listens as a car crunches across the gravel and there is laughter as people go inside the building. The wind is warm and, coming from the west, it brings the scent of flowers with it, and the powdery dryness of grasses scorched by sun. It is strong enough to shake petals loose from the rosebushes and they drift across the pale grass, snag in the dark yew and box hedges, fall torn to the ground, are blown away.

With his head tilted back, he can see the shivering leaves of ash and the larch tree leaning forward over the high brick wall. The night beyond is starless, as though fine clouds are veiling any light. His left arm is stretched along the back of the bench and he has shut his eyes for joy in being alive, in loving her, and in *this* – his toes curl inside his shoes as though he might break through them, his flesh transfigured –

when suddenly she slips into his outstretched arm and lays her head against his neck.

For a second he remains absolutely motionless, as though to move will be to dislodge her from his side. 'I knew that you'd want proof,' she whispers, kissing him. He draws her tight against him, disbelieving she is real, thinking he must have fallen asleep and is conscious of this dream only for it being so willed. She is laughing at him, telling him she is glad to have caught him here. Only when she leaves does he notice that her dress is the colour of ripe strawberries – deep pink, almost scarlet. Although when she turns to wave at him from the far end of the garden – by now he is standing at the gate leading out into the woods – the warm wind has run the clouds right from the sky, and then she does indeed appear to be dressed in something silver, where moonlight falls and covers her, making her a stranger to him once again.

He is through the gate and walking fast then, through the woods, the leaves overhead clattering in the hot night air and the high ferns fluttering like birds against his bare arms where he brushes past them. The scent of the forest floor and the press of silence seem to hold him, in his downfalling walk, and he feels as though he has been tested, found wanting – although the final judgement still hangs in the balance somewhere out behind him. He runs from it, his teeth clenched tight, and where the pathway twists he has the sudden desire not to obey it, but instead to forge on straight ahead, simply plunge on into the forest and away. He wants the night to take him in, absolve him by letting him dissolve into itself. He does not want the judgement he is sure is imminent, one pace behind him, its breath ready on its outstretched tongue.

He curses himself for asking for evidence of their being together, for wanting her to deliver him some sign that they were real, because when she came to him, knowing perfectly that he would be there, it spelt out the extent of his love for her in a way that now has made him full of fear. Running through the thickening pines, the elm trees encroaching, grand with rustles and threats, he looks ahead at his life and sees only the dark forest now surrounding him.

This is how it will be from now on – his eyes sting with tears and panic as he thinks this – with her, or nowhere. That is me from now on, and this my reality: a downhill plunge through the hot night like an animal's hopeless hunt and scavenge after uncertain reward. For the first time, even with her in his arms, he had felt the frailty of their bones' entanglement. He had seen them both, as from a treetop height, from the height of the canopy even now above him, and he had pitied them, and in all their eagerness he had seen the danger most of all in that close union – as though to love someone as much as they loved each other was a joy reserved for angels or the dead.

So he clung tight to her and when she told him he was crushing her, squeezing all the breath from her, he did not loosen his grip but whispered, '*Yes*,' into her ear, and she understood and he felt her take handfuls of his hair and grasp them tight, not like a girl but as an animal would to hold its prey or mate.

When he steps out of the forest, the waves of meadowgrass are glistening. He lies down, outstretched on his back in the long grass looking at the sky. He registers the fact that when a person cries lying on their back, the tears do not properly fall but gather in the corners of the eyes until two tiny lakes are formed. Looking up through these lakes, the black night astonishes him with its hidden prisms of colour, and he laughs for sorrow that she is not with him now to see it.

7

He is sitting in the café at the corner of the main street where it meets the town square. He has not seen her for two days and throughout that time the summer's heat has grown oppressive, the sky cloudless but heavy with thunder. Waiting for word from her has been like waiting for a storm to break, and when the boy from the hotel delivered her message he found himself shaking him by the hand in thanks, not knowing what he was doing. He felt like an idiot. He did not mind. The boy smiled at him over his shoulder as he left, and Jack thought it pretty obvious that it was a smile of sympathy – as though he suffered from an affliction, was someone to be pitied. But this thought only made him laugh: all that mattered was that soon he'd be beside her.

She asked him to meet her in the café. Only that. He did not understand why: they seldom arranged to meet anywhere so public.

He arrived there early. It is a busy time of day, around four o'clock. The radio is playing and each time someone comes in, a bell jangles, and a wave of heat seems to fall in through the door. The overhead fan is useless. The waitress grimaces up at it from time to time, tugging at her apron. Schoolchildren sit at the counter with ices. There is the babble of conversation, fluid and musical as a description of happiness, uninterrupted.

When Elena walks into all this, he almost does not recognise her: she is wearing loose cream trousers, a pale blue shirt, white tennis shoes and no makeup. Her hair is tied up at the back and pushed underneath a straw hat that sits tight across the back of her head like a skullcap or beret. Dressed this way she looks like a teenage boy just stepped off a tennis court. She carries a small brown-leather bag and swings it just like a boy might swing a racket after he's won a match. She walks straight up to him and her entire appearance is jaunty, carefree. But when she hesitates beside him just before she sits down, he notices the nerve flicker at the corner of her mouth and he can see that she is acting.

'Hi.' She smiles, slipping into the seat opposite him. She picks up a menu and uses it as a fan, her eyebrows raised in exaggerated astonishment at the heat. 'Do you think it'll break?' She tips her head towards the door of the café, with the bell still jangling and the heat seeming to have chased in here after her. No one looked round when she walked in. No one recognises her.

'Look,' she sets her hands out, fingers facing him on the table, 'don't be fooled by the disguise. I didn't know how else to do this. I needed to talk to you freely.' She's speaking fast and low so that she won't be overheard. Her lips are set in a smile as she speaks so that the words seem to come out thinned and bright. Her hands are shaking. He picks up the menu and tips it over her hands, taking hold of one in his own where no one will see it and gripping it tight so that the tremble leaves her voice when she starts to speak again.

'I want to tell you everything.' Her eyes are fixed on his. The waitress arrives. They order lemonade, and when it arrives in tall glasses she exclaims, 'Well!' and sips it quickly through the straw as though to stop the next thought from following. Anyway, he knows what it would have been: that they must look like children, drinking lemonade through straws. It makes her self-conscious as though her other self just walked in and laughed to see her like this. She shakes her head, repeats, 'Everything,' and looks down at the menu as though deciding what to eat. But her eyes move quickly across the words and he has the impression that she is trying not to cry.

'Look,' she starts again. 'There's a reason for my being here that no one knows, not even—' She does not need to say 'my husband'. The words are there as tangible as though she had spelt them out on a blackboard. 'The first point is this. You know I'm in love with you.' Jack grins to hear her say it and leans towards her so that their knees touch. He does not care who sees. He wants people to see. He wants them staring and silenced so that he can just slip into the seat beside her and admit everything. But she is not smiling and her brow is creased with anxiety. She looks away, as though expecting someone to walk in the door and haul her off, catch her and take her back to lock her up – exactly that kind of schoolgirl expectation of reprimands moves across her face.

Still with her eyes turned from him, speaking so quiet now he thinks at first that he has misheard, she continues, 'But he will not be shamed by me. He is stubborn, and he will not fail at anything. When he married me two years ago, he took a great risk. He could have left me where I was, playing to provincial theatres. It was not so bad. But I had no room there, no freedom to move about. He understood all about that.' Her cheeks pale as she continues, and she turns to look at Jack directly.

'For him, in many ways, the risk has not been worth it. He wanted children. I could not have them. It damaged things for him. I suppose he regrets what he did. But he is proud, he would never admit to that. So now he has his secrets, though he is loyal, after a fashion. And he knows very well I owe everything to him.' Jack holds her hands tighter. He wants to tell her that even if she owes her husband as much as she thinks, how could it be enough to keep them apart? But he cannot do it. She is too much in earnest and her seriousness at this moment prevents denial.

'All that he has he's made himself. Even his name, Greenwood. What did you think? His parents went to America with suitcases—' She frames the air. When she sees his disbelief, she merely looks away, shaking her head. And then she tells him everything, just as she said she would.

Sunlight is falling straight through the glass of the café window on to Jack's head, which aches with heat. At least, he tells himself that it is merely heat. But he is sure that it is really his heart, his thoughts, which are burning, and her self-containment as she delivers to him everything she promised – this is the thing that hurts most. She sounds as though she is reciting lines, or reading quietly from a novel. As though at any moment she might break off, turn to him and laugh, confirm a reality quite apart from the one she is even now insisting upon.

But nothing of the kind happens. The café's heat grows unbearable and sweat drops down between his skin and shirt so that his jacket hangs limp across his shoulders and his hair feels like a woollen hat he is forbidden to take off. Her hands are still on the table between them. His hands now rest loose against the seat.

She tells him about her family, and about how her husband went straight to them after he'd been in Vienna in the spring. 'He was there, in Heldenplatz, three months ago when Hitler arrived, and he witnessed what happened afterwards. My parents did not believe him, even then. Of course they, too, had seen things, but not enough to be certain of the danger. It was he who insisted they go back with him to America. He has made it look like they are taking a long holiday, just a pleasant visit to see the new life he has made for me in Hollywood – just until we can see what will happen, he told them. He has made it seem very natural. A visit from their American son-in-law. A trip to see their daughter, the first time in two years. They have been there for a few months now. He has rented them a little place up in the hills. He will see that they are secure there. But they left everything behind. Still they talk of going home.'

'Perhaps it will be possible. There's no proof it isn't safe.'

'Proof?' Elena frowns. 'There are stories. And he did not tell them everything he saw.' She glances around the café as she speaks. 'He has done all he can, and he has made it possible for others too. He has given them jobs at the studio that even the studio didn't realise might exist.' She looks at him, and tries to smile, but he sees that she cannot. 'So much of what he risked was because of me. I was the reason.'

As he watches her, he has the impression that her husband might at any moment walk into the café and, with no kind of contest, she will merely leave. 'I owe him everything. This is what I mean when I say that.'

He cannot bear it. He tells her loudly, 'No. You are free to live the life you want.' But her quietness confuses him. This is only the first part of what she has to say.

She touches her hair, her collar, the gesture light and regretful, almost as though she is taking leave of herself. 'No, I am not free in the way you think. There is more. The reason I'm here – looking at the place for that film, and—'

'Was that a lie?' he asks her now.

She shakes her head fast. 'For him, of course not, his work goes on. This was always part of his plan, and I am part of that. But for me it was also an excuse.' He is trembling now to watch her. He is afraid. The schoolchildren sitting at the counter break out laughing and Jack wants to shout at them to be quiet. He leans closer towards her.

'I had to come to England because there is a doctor I need in London, a specialist, disorders of the blood. I'm told there is a war being waged, the good against the bad cells, who are winning.' Jack

—
147

says nothing, and she looks at him as though he perhaps has not heard or understood. Her voice is very quiet, very patient. 'I am unwell.' The three words emerge on a cadence that might have been 'I love you'. He can hear her saying the phrase again, and he half thinks that he has lost his grasp of language. The mediocrity of the phrase does not match the expression in her eyes, which seems to tell him so much more. He is angry with her for being unwell. It is outrageous. He feels his neck grow cold as though he might throw up.

He can see her exactly as she was on the day she arrived. He tells himself that he should have known. That her appearance of fragility should have warned him off – warned him away from her as a pack abandons the weaker animal. He can see her gestures, the way they suggested someone used to caring for others, or for sick infants – he had had exactly that thought and it had made him love her. He had not thought then that the sick person might have been herself. He looks down at the table and feels his spine go numb as he listens to her continue.

'I wanted no one to know until I was sure myself, until I had proof. Now there is no doubt. Still, there's a chance that everything will be fine. There is this chance.'

He hears only 'this chance' and it is not enough for him to cling to. Even the phrase sounds remote with foreignness, strange to his ears as though, were he to translate it, it might come out more hopeful than she has made it sound. He is indignant with her for giving him nothing he can grasp hold of. He wants to shake her until she gives him more than 'this chance', more than 'unwell'. What does she even mean?

Of course she tells him exactly what she means, and he sees plainly how little hope she has. 'So, you see, I am not free. What choices do I have?' She frowns, rubbing at her forehead as though to dislodge an answer. 'Now the doctor tells me it's all a matter of timing. New treatments just some way ahead. Only not quite yet. So.' She bites her lip. 'But he is more right than he can know. It *is* about timing. Because how can I tell my husband all this, now? He will not believe me. Or he will think that I have tricked him, that I have always known, and have used him, that I knew this when I married him, that even my parents are part of the bargain. And isn't it true?' Her voice seems to gutter and break as she asks him this, and he can say nothing.

'I am their guarantee. Nothing is settled for them yet. They also can be very stubborn, very wilful. They are not happy in America. Without me there, they might try to return at any time.' And then he sees the world without her, and her parents suffering because she, his love, was no longer there to be their guarantor – to sacrifice herself on their behalf. He sees this, and he feels sick at the realisation that he does not give a damn about her parents. Why should he? It is her he cares for, no one else. He would swap his life for hers if she would let him. A fantasy. He sets it aside and looks at it in distaste.

'So it is all a matter of timing.' She repeats the words quietly, and he cannot meet her eye. He notices the thinness of her arms, that until this moment he has seen only as slender but which now seem to reveal plainly all the signs of illness to him. He cannot believe he has not noticed them until now.

The café bell is jangling loud as people pass in and out. Alongside the ringing, he hears the first sound of thunder, and hearing it, swats a black bug from his shirtsleeve. 'So, you are going to pretend that nothing has happened here – for how long? For ever?' He sees her wince. He hates his cruelty but he cannot stop it. He feels cruel. He sees himself stepping over a line between his youth and adulthood and he finds the transition unbearable. *These people*, he thinks, looking around as though finding himself in a world composed only of adults. He has words he'd like to hurl at them. *Scheming. Cold. Calculating.* He thinks that they are all mad. And, for a moment, by 'they' he also means her. He wants to say, 'And you let me fall in love with you, knowing this?' But that far he cannot go: he would have fallen in love with her with one second of their lives left to live, or if loving her had meant an eternity. It had nothing to do with time. It was outside and far beyond the minutes that otherwise contained them.

She touches his hand and he looks at her face, retracting all his hatred like a setting-down of arms. What was he thinking of? He is exhausted. Elena smiles faintly, and he realises that all this time she has been following the pathway of his thoughts. 'You understand that that's it, that's everything,' she says, her breath no louder than a whisper. He has the impression that her life is balancing between them. Only its brevity meant he was not conscious of it until this moment.

A cold sensation of fainting gathers around his temples, and his flesh prickles with nausea. In full view of whoever might care to see, she suddenly takes his hands and holds them, like a mother taking hold of an injured child. 'I owe him this explanation. He was good to me.' He winces to hear her speak of herself in the past tense, until he realises what it means. 'I must be sure that my parents will be safe, without me there. But I cannot go back. That's it.' She tries to smile. 'And because there is this chance I will get better, I must cling to that because I love you so——' Her shoulders fall and she seems to descend through generations until she suddenly sits there hunched and tiny-seeming as a small girl, and he does not give a damn who sees but stands up and scoops her into his arms, cursing her softly against her ear where no one else will hear.

'There is more than a chance, there is every chance.' He holds her so tight he can feel the breath being forced from her as he grips her, noticing the weakness of her bones and finding it unbearable. 'We have every chance because we've found each other, do you hear? We go together, so nothing bad will happen now. You don't owe him your life.' He sits her down and now he settles close alongside her. He makes her tell him everything. He feels like a farmer, she his only crop that needs tending every hour: his life depends on it. His adulthood he draws around him like a heavy coat, seeing too that he can lay it at her feet, offer it to her as something she might walk upon.

He has his arm around her shoulders and their heads are bowed together like sudden orphans, plotting schemes for their safety now that the whole world has abandoned them. The bright café disappears. The clatter of sound becomes the wild call of birds at dusk. He has a flood of tears inside him and with every breath he's vowing not to let them fall, not ever once again in front of her. He can see how she needs his strength. He can tell that it might be of some use to her. He rolls it up and feels as though he can feed her with it until she grows lustrous with health again. What else can he do? So he goes through every detail of her life and of her family, and of how things can be simplified so that she can extricate herself from her marriage and come to be with him. Nothing else will make sense and he can see that she sees this now, the vision of how they will have to be hovering just ahead of them – almost within fingertip-touching reach.

He presses her head against his chest so that it fits and he can hold it safe there. 'There is a chance,' he tells her, as though he has more news about her than she does of herself. 'And we must take it. It's all we have.'

The thunder rumbles on and he holds her close. They sit that way until the café closes and the waitress brings them their bill with a look of curiosity. She will recognise him, the station-master's son, there is no doubt of that. But the girl she seems to stare at as though she belonged to some implausible other world. She looks at her slyly, just as someone might watch a public performance or the progress of an auction, as though she, his love, might imminently be her property. He cannot bear it, as though pieces of her are already being borne away, leaving her diminished.

He rushes her from the café, shielding her from the woman's gaze. The sudden rainfall comes hissing on the tarmac, and she stands shivering in it, despite the heat. He runs with her back up to the hotel and does not care that people might see them there together. It no longer matters. But he does not go inside with her. He sees her back to her separate life like a brother seeing his sister off to school – all happiness and play now vanished from their house.

But now we have a plan, he tells himself, as he turns for home. My God, he staggers as he leaves, fears he might fall down, we have a plan but what chance? He turns back to see that already, just as on the first day, she has disappeared inside the hotel.

Anna walks down the main street and the sunshine falls square upon her. Her step is light and hurried: she wants to get up to the moor while the good weather lasts. She swats black thunderflies that fall upon her bare forearms like ash motes around the time of autumn bonfires. But she does not mind them. For the first time since arriving here, she feels carefree. She can breathe in the good air and feel the strength that comes from it. The air is close among the buildings, and she longs to get out into the open countryside that is visible above the rooftops and between the building-backs of the small town square.

She notices a café, its yellow blinds half drawn against the sunlight, and she steps off the pavement into the road to cross over to it to see if she can buy a sandwich there, when a man's voice calls out just behind her – not loudly but near, 'Elena!' Traffic carries the voice, scattering the first syllable. Anna swings round to see if she is the person meant, and as she turns a car passing too close and fast clips her rucksack and she is knocked to the pavement. The car does not stop; the driver had no idea she was there. She falls heavily, her head cracks against stone, and the blue sky shifts overhead and darkens as with the sudden advent of a storm.

When she wakes, she is leaning back against a warm body. Arms are holding tightly to her, supporting her round her shoulders. She looks down at her hands and they are grazed, covered with grit. Long trousers have saved her knees, although she can tell that later the flesh will be swollen with bruises. She knows that she has cried from the salt taste on her lips. Faces are peering down at her and she recognises no one. Did she imagine the voice calling out that aberration of her name?

She corrects him, 'Anna,' and he replies, 'Of course, Anna, I'm so sorry. This is all my fault.'

His voice is so near that she can feel the breath against her ear as he speaks and she leans back into it and rests her head. She hears someone ask if she needs an ambulance: 'Shouldn't we get her to hospital?' And she tries to sit up to prove that there is no need. 'Hang on, let's see how badly you're hurt.' And she is asked to inventory each limb to decide where the worst pain is. The people watching start to move away. She wriggles each foot and leg in turn and shakes her arms, saying, 'Look, I'm fine, nothing broken.' But when she moves her head she feels the dizziness come again and thinks that she might faint. 'It's my head, all in my head,' she tries to joke, but winces, feeling sick as she lifts her hand to touch her forehead to see if it is bleeding.

'Let's just sit here for a while,' he tells her. 'Don't try to get up right away.' She feels him settle back and she realises that they must be supported by something, a lamp-post maybe, and she has a vision of herself propped up on the pavement like a noonday drunk. 'So how do you come to be here?' he asks her. And it seems like the most natural thing in the world to tell everything, speaking aloud but quietly, as though she were at confession, or as though she were piecing together the last few months of her life to set them down in a diary in the right order.

She feels that she has told everyone but no one about herself. For months, doctors have insisted that she relate each minute change in her body to them and they have taken note; her friends, not so numerous at any time, have disappeared with neglect: she did not want to discuss herself with them. She wanted no one's pity, or concern. Most of all, she did not want anyone looking at her and seeing her illness first. She was never attached to it. It was a parasite and she wanted to be free of it. Once free, she didn't want people observing her with that expectant, hesitant look - as though, healthy, she would be lacking something, and her illness might at any moment trot up to them like an errant dog, the picture of her only then complete.

She tells him all this. But she is not conscious of speaking. She is conscious only of listening, as though her own thoughts echoed up to her from a great distance. There is no restlessness or unease, either in her voice or the man's voice behind her that murmurs from time to time, seeming to understand - precisely in that encouraging, deliberate way a priest might mutter from behind the confessional curtain, hopeful of neither gain nor burden, leaving judgement to someone else; and it is nothing like the doctors' hunger, their eagerness for news of every change in her 'condition'.

She laughs, not happily, but with the remote anger that has come of being able to regard her own hopelessness from a distance now that she is through the time of danger. 'My condition and I—' She tries to sound lighthearted but her chest is tight with tears and the relief of having spoken so freely after such a length of time.

'Idiot,' he says, very kindly. 'You sure we shouldn't get you to hospital?' He lifts her up, but without impatience, just shifting her into a more comfortable position.

'Never again.' She tries to keep her voice light. 'Haven't you been listening?'

She feels ridiculous, but full of relief, as though knocking her head has unplugged a cork from herself, and from her fear about what has happened, and about the future. For the first time since her illness she has a sense of what recovery might mean, and she can see herself being healthy – which only means that she can see herself being free.

From the low angle of the pavement, the sun slants into her eyes and she watches high clouds blown across the sky. But down here the day is windless, very still, and there are few cars or people. She can almost imagine herself in a park, sunbathing, and she does not want to move. When she says this, he laughs and tells her that that's a sure sign that she's ready to go. Supported from behind, beneath her armpits, she is lifted to her feet where she sways, and is held tight so that she does not fall.

'Let's go to that café,' he tells her, leading her across the road with one arm around her shoulders.

As they go in, the bell above the door makes her jump, it is so loud. 'Cowbell,' she says, 'Tyrolean.'

She is shown into a booth, and hears the man laugh. 'Are you OK?'

He is sitting opposite her with his arms outstretched to hold on to her by her upper arms, as though to keep her balanced. 'You don't *look* ill,' he tells her, smiling. She smiles back at him, seeing his face clearly for the first time. She tries not to stare. It is as though the voice she has been listening to has merely taken shape: he is the embodiment of all its kindness and warmth. She finds him very beautiful, and very definite. His dark hair is an almost exact match of her own, and yet it makes him seem incredibly clear, as though he is composed in perfect focus. He makes her feel as she did as a teenager: convinced that beauty would always stay distant from her, be taller than her somehow, and belong to someone else. But here he is, and she recognises him – as though she has seen him from far off, and admired him, and considered him utterly beyond reach, as impossible as being in love with a photograph of someone long since dead.

She feels exhausted suddenly, and her breath seems too large in her throat. She is conscious of crying but makes no noise, and is aware that she is crying mainly because of the way that his face seems to crumple with anxiety as he watches her. And to see this stranger's sadness, on her behalf, moves her more than she can say - as though he has just offered her a gift. He slips into the booth beside her and holds her against him.

With her head resting on his chest, she feels as though she might stay there until she falls asleep, and that he would not mind. Her dizziness settles, becomes a kind of profound tiredness covering her limbs. She listens to him telling her that actually they have already met - almost. She smiles at 'almost' but certainly she can't remember ever having met him. She is quite sure that she would remember.

'But how else would I know your name?' he asks her, and she has to admit the logic of this. 'Maybe you didn't see me,' he tells her, 'but I saw you. We were looking for the same book in Foyles, the book that's set here, and you had the only copy, from the second-hand section. I still haven't found it. I tried to order it but it's out of print. I was behind you in the queue, and I saw you sign your name. I thought you might think I was following you. I didn't dare approach you. You seemed very self-contained. I didn't want to disturb you.' He touches her hair and tells her that she has a bump and that this proves she is a real invalid, and had better look out and not go around answering any other strange men who call her name.

—

'I guess now I've made up for not wanting to disturb you before.' She imagines him frowning with annoyance at himself above her head, and when she feels his lips lightly brush the top of her hair, so light, as though he almost hopes she might not notice he has done this, she suddenly remembers that of course she has seen him before: she has dreamt him.

Anna does not tell him this. How would she explain such a thing? It would sound absurd. So she stays very still, her cheek against his chest exactly as it rests against her pillow in sleep. The intimacy of this image makes her breath catch, as though he might also have seen her lying nakedly in bed. But it is true, he has entered her nocturnal secrecies. She sees herself sitting on the floor of her flat with the contents of her bag tipped out before her, the pieces of her life scattered in torn fragments as she tries to fix them back together in her mind. And she remembers the day she found the book, how glad she had been, and how eager to read it.

So she had followed the thread of one of those scraps of memory, and it led her to him. But before she was able to find him, she had passed so close to death that it left its thumbprints in her blood, smudging out so much that had been her. When the illness left her, it was as though she had burrowed miles deep within herself in order to survive, as though the strength that she had drawn on was a labyrinth of other people's lives all speaking loudly to her, urging her to stay awake. People she had not even known had murmured to her, touched her, pressed her forward, entered into her most private place of sleep, just as he had done, and she had been lifted by a tide that first had fallen, taking so many with it.

She wanted to thank someone. But who? Her gratitude was for everything that tended towards life; her debt was owed to many long since dead. 'If I'd been born fifty years earlier, there'd have been no chance. It's all a matter of timing.' She whispers this, and is not sure he has heard until she feels him draw her closer, his embrace telling her that he knows.

And yet she had imagined that her dreams of him came because of the story, for no other reason. But he had so definitely inhabited them, and now here he is. Anna clasps the side of his torso with her left hand and feels the heat of his skin beneath his shirt. She feels as though she has been physically moved forward through her life - like someone switching to an express train in the night. Until now, she had imagined that, once healthy, she would discover herself somehow ahead of herself, solidly, like meeting a friend after years of separation. She would be very changed, but complete; perhaps she would recognise fragments of herself, but it would be the whole person that would matter, that would make the most sense.

But now, thinking of the day she must have first seen him, in the bookshop - as though in spite of herself, refusing to see him consciously, knowing how seriously she was ill - she sees that perhaps this is merely what she is: someone composed of just such scraps of memory and imagination, nudges felt from out of other people's lives, half-dreamt things that in her waking hours she can sometimes barely see, but which emerge, suddenly, in flesh and blood, just as now.

The bell rings as someone enters the café, closing the passage of her thought. She is returned from her reverie. But she does not leave the dream: she is not asleep. Her head hurts too much for that. She does not mind the pain, and smiles to think of it because it tells her she's awake; it has a purpose.

'I'm not asleep,' she tells him.

'Me neither.' He laughs, and she hears him ordering two glasses of lemonade from the waitress. 'Is that OK? I think they still make it here themselves. I imagine it's delicious.'

Jack watches the rain from beneath the cover of the station canopy. With the sulphur lights burning beneath the eaves, the raindrops fall golden, dissolving into the gravel between the tracks and sleepers. When the freight train passes through he can smell the coal, and the hump-backed containers glisten in the wet half light. He'd like to throw a match there as the freight train thunders past, and make the thunder burn, watch it devil its way down through the valley with a cargo flaming and unforgettable.

He hears his father rolling up a window in an upstairs room, and he imagines the carpet drenched with rainfall, seeing it ruined in a flash of malice. He stands up, physically shakes himself and walks along the platform. The softness of wood-pigeons now makes him want to cry: its fragility will outlive their brief conjunction. But he is done with crying and he tells himself this, afterwards wonders if he didn't even say it aloud because the thought came out so stern.

He thinks of her in her room at the hotel, and he wonders if she is looking out at the rain. He sees her doing different things – sitting beside the window, taking a bath, getting changed for bed, sleeping. He wonders what she is doing with a kind of ferocity and indignation at the fact that he does not know for sure. It strikes him as absurd, utterly pointless, and now he wonders only how long it will last. He wonders when it will merely slip back into the past and become an idiocy – with the status of fantasy, almost, or dreams – that once the two of them endured. That's the only way through. He squares his shoulders with this thought, trying to see it as something he could set upon his back, a great rock that he might somehow find the strength to bear, and shift around and uphill if she wants him to. Anywhere, but certainly to a place where she does not have to bear it on her own frail shoulders – shoulders frailer than he'd ever thought they might be.

Already, he is looking at the last few weeks and dreaming of them as though they were a lost and happy time. The last few weeks, he reminds himself, that were in such a great part so great a torment. She was not mine then, either. And soon enough she'll not be mine again. So then can I say that she was ever mine? When? Where? At what point in time? Her doctor had been right. It was all a matter of timing. Timing and the fullness of coincidence, trying to catch at ghosts, because even a shadow speaks of a life that *was*, so *might be* once more in the future. Now he has to pray for that shadow-time to come again. He has to haul the past into the future and make it grow there, too.

But what was the exact moment where we were really together? Jack runs through them all and they all seem equally dear, precious – and equally impossible, as though he dreamt the entire thing, or was deluded, or merely mad. No. It was all real. He must wish for the impossible again.

He leans against the station wall and the cold stone feels good against his back. The freight train does not burn. He flicked no match. It passes on black into the greater blackness of the night beneath the trees that hide it now from view along the inverse spine of the valley, and then right out of sight. He remembers standing in more or less this exact spot and seeing her step off the train into the heat-filled afternoon. He remembers how he had looked at her and seen her so apart from everyone else, as though she didn't even for a second belong there among the crowd on the platform. He had thought: a star, a chosen person, and he had seen her glamour, and noticed the contradiction of her vulnerability and loved her without question.

Jack watches the darkness where the freight train passed. He looks after the empty space between the opposing masses of land where silently – at least from here – it passes on into the night. The rain still falls, and the tracks, so gunmetal clean, make the drops bounce back up into the air again. He sees her and knows that he understood perfectly, even then, that she was an impossibility for him, as impossible as though she had passed him by on a fast-moving train, with him able to do nothing but stare, and yearn, and possess her only in his imagination. But what had happened? How had it been possible? He rubs his eyes, unclenching his hands that were two fists beside him. Stupid of him to ask these questions. It was possible. Somehow, it did happen, it is true. And now it is the only thing he is sure of.

He listens to the sadness of the wood-pigeons and wonders if she is listening to them at this moment, and similarly loving the sound. He imagines its sadness as a silver thread that runs between them. He traces the line towards her, thinking: the line that joins us is as slender as that — a silver track cutting its way through two huge weights of time made manifest in earth, and to look along after it is to look only into darkness.

His father is calling to him. He turns and goes inside the house.

8

'Patience,' Elena can almost feel her mother's touch against her forehead as she tells her, 'slowly, *langsam*, time enough for everything,' and the clock's tick like water from a tap – an abundance of duration she was no fool to doubt. And my God it could almost be the same clock. Elena averts her eyes from it as she goes up to her room. The same clock, and me the same girl I ever was in everything but this love.

When she reaches her room she turns back to look along the empty corridor and the clock-sound seems to linger there – as though it is waiting, not rolling forward; as though she has jumped ahead of it and by her own overreaching of herself has gathered more of life than her allotted share. Patience. You're the same girl you ever were, she tells herself, hating the thought now, as though her future was written in her from birth – that she should find love, the desire to live, only in the nearness of death.

She opens the door to the dark room and breathes in its crowded odour – too much a sum of other people's intimacies – and tells herself that she steps gladly into the dark of selfishness, if this is what it is, to care about her own life more than any possible future sweetness for unknown others, a sweetness that can come only as a residue distilled from the pain of excess wonder now, too much of love.

I'll take selfishness. She holds her breath to steady herself as she shuts the door behind her. Selfishness and any charge of cruelty, carelessness, lack of foresight, bother about other people's futures, anything – I'll be worthy of the worst insults if this is what it takes to free me from my body's obligation to sickness. I'll take the blame for unmentionable wrongs, give no thought to anyone but me and him, anything on earth if it will make the slightest difference. Because to hell with patience for I have none of it, just for God's sake give me time and I will gladly then be damned for ever.

In the darkness she hears the sudden rushing of the freight train, cutting through the country on the other side of town. The sound is enough to tell her that she can't forget, and that forgetting would be a kind of violence, as sure as her own hand on whatever trigger, switch or blade even now being whetted, primed for silence. She can feel the land's divisions at the sound of that train, as sure as though it were the earth itself being divided, shifting beneath her with tectonic rumbles, remapped to alien countries.

Elena crosses to the window where the rain falls loud on to the gravel and against the glass. Drops bounce off stone on to her face. The train runs on. Its sound reveals its shape and she can almost see it slip like an underground river through the earth, scaling distance with weird stealth, its potency masked by darkness. And in her mind's eye she sees the freight dump at the far end of the tracks – a coal-heap, perhaps, soon enough turned to cinder, vanished to smoke.

Seeing this, all thoughts of selfishness, and of her separation from any out-of-sight crowd of nightbound people – all this disappears. She feels the hand grow cool upon her brow, her mother's 'Patience, langsam' now a balm and not a barb to mark the quiet of suffering. Because this cannot remain secret for ever, she tells herself, love cannot be gagged for ever: it is too loud to remain mute and buried. Something that reaches out and draws another into this charmed loop of love cannot be silenced. It's a fraternity of feeling far beyond all naming and possession. It is too loud. Kill it, and the echo will remain.

She has a sudden vision of him calling out to her from beyond the wood and the building-tops, the vision so sudden and forceful that she leans her head out of the window as though to catch the note.

But there is only the train whispering now as it passes away through the evening, and the rainfall steady as the clock's tick muffled by the tunnel of corridor so that, if she is honest, she would not be able to swear that she can hear it still. Though when she sits down, certainly enough, in thinking of her parents' now abandoned house in Saalburgstrasse, she is able to say that she can hear it quite clearly then. And so it is no longer the sound of the clock itself that she can hear, but the subdued tides of childhood, drifting in and out of memory – the things borne also upon the sound of the clock that stood alongside her childhood in the hallway of their house.

Silly things that I can hear again, she tells herself in thinking of them, silly things that mean nothing to anyone but me. Digging potatoes with my father in early autumn, his knack I never learnt for sounding out the earth with the tines of the garden fork. When I dug I'd spear the secret whiteness of potato flesh so they'd emerge run through, imperfect. He'd laugh and tell me, 'Quiet, listen as you dig.' And I have never known if he really meant that. Did he mean that he could hear where the steel cut earth, and divine that unseen difference between the soil and skin? She remembers the trick of digging potatoes so clearly that she can feel the knee-grit she'd be left with after rummaging elbow deep in earth to retrieve them – and her haughty walk, triumphant to her mother with potatoes caught up in her makeshift sack of skirts held out in front of her so that they'd jump about all trampolinish. And even this thought sunk and irretrievable beneath earth the very second I am gone. Elena shivers, her clothes damp with rain, and cold against her skin.

—

Camphor and eucalyptus follow just such coolness, running along the tick-tick of the hallway clock as she is rushed upstairs into a hot bath after dawdling in the rain, 'You will catch your death,' making her see even then how plainly some people might bring upon themselves their own demise, running after it as though it were of little consequence beyond the victory in a game of tag. Dipped in the scented water run so hot she would be dizzy within seconds, though her mother wouldn't let her leap out until she was 'cooked right through', heat and hunger twining now about her thoughts as though she'd been a little loaf alive with wriggles – something to be watched over until risen to a height appropriate to being left out by herself. Then lavendered sheets stretched cold and tight so that beneath them she'd feel swaddled and play at being readied for death by lying still there, fixed flat to the mattress until her mother came to release her, sitting beside her on the bed to read her menaces from *Struwwelpeter*, the deep green fringe of her chenille shawl tickling Elena's sleepy skin and making her think of the dangers of dark pinewoods circling her dreams.

Rainfall now sounding so like the clock's tick that the two are indistinguishable. Both run away into the hidden caverns of the earth, that she thinks must now be belly-full with forgetfulness. It is this Elena kicks against. She wants to remember everything. She wants nothing to slip from her but to be held, and given to her love in the ripe fantasy of a shared old age. She knows she will not see it, but surely they will have some time of dreaming on it – some time, even if not much? And she tells herself to take a pride in that faint stubbornness, since at least it offers some resistance to the drip, drip falling-off of time that's left her.

But it is so hard to do. Stubbornness is not enough. How can it be? she wants to know, since it's a kind of digging-in of heels when all her instincts now are to rush diving forward on through life. And yet this is the very thing that's disallowed. She has never felt so light – almost luminous, airy as a firefly or a cindered scrap of paper floating skywards for a wish – and yet neither has she ever been so conscious of the heaviness that binds her to her curtailed future so that, however violently she shakes and wrestles with it, it'll not be thrown off. It's a cloak of armour against everything she wants.

Evening is all about the hotel room now. It is darker than the hesitating light outside, attenuated but not extinguished by the multiplying mirrors of the rain. She stands up, goes to the bathroom, turns on the light, runs a bath. Breathing in the steam, she breathes in a sweetness that returns him to her. Perhaps he left some part of his scent upon her. Perhaps the brief tattoo of his lips against her face left the imprint of his skin there, and it's this that she is breathing now. She leans against the white tiles of the bathroom. 'We have every chance because we've found eath other.' She remembers how, only hours before, he had held her, saying this, and his arms about her confirmed his words. Patience, Elena, and courage too. Love will not stay silent. It will emerge even in the svelte shapes of dissolving bath-steam.

She smiles. Her love, her boy, her life. He feels very near to her, as though he might step towards her through the steam, just as on the first day that she saw him. The engine-smoke cleared and there he was. It was as though the smoke-veil had lifted to let her see far back into her past. Her first thought had been: do I know him from my childhood? He reminded her of something she had no idea that she had lost.

She touches the water. It scalds her fingertips and he disappears. I must hold fast to this now. She rubs the mirror, looks at her face that seems so changed, no longer her own but belonging only alongside his. It is unnerving to her that she does not see him there beside her. I must hold fast, wait just a little longer until the moment brings us properly together. I must dive deep under the approaching time until the danger has passed, hold my breath for love. Patience and waiting. Quiet only for a time.

In the mirror her reflection hangs pale and indistinct: the steam quickly clouds across the glass. If only there was time to wait, to be patient and quiet in. But there is none. She splashes her face with cold water to stop her eyes burning, swollen now with tears.

When she comes back into the main room of the suite she notices a small square of white paper that someone has slipped beneath her door. She must have stepped over it in her earlier blindness. Surely if it had arrived while she was in the room someone would have knocked. But she heard nothing, and this makes her feel already vanished: why knock on the door of an empty room?

She reads the note in the bright-lit bathroom. It is a message from the hotel switchboard. Her husband, Harry, has telephoned to say that he has changed his plan. He will not travel directly from Europe to America, but will come to England first. He will arrive shortly after lunchtime on the following day.

The bathwater falls thunderous, drowning out the drip of rain, the ticking of the hallway clock where perhaps it even now remains, between the coat-stand and the mirror, both so full of ghosts.

'That's my room, there,' Anna points, 'second from the end on the right.'

'And mine, second from the left.' He has known her only for a day, but when he thinks of her going to that room without him, already he can see how he will miss her.

She turns to him, and he notices that she has so many different kinds of smile. This latest one he finds the most lovely yet, and he thinks how rare it is to encounter someone with so deep a love of surprises. She is happy just at the thought of any kind of newness or revelation.

That is what illness, her nearness to death, has done for her, he thinks. It has made her long for change and for surprises of whatever kind. Because she has dipped her toe into death and felt its monotony. She has understood in that toe-dip just the thing that I have struggled to dispute. Because sometimes when I look over my shoulder I see only the flat shadow and not the gemstone glitter or any brightness at all. Sometimes I see only the endless falling into shade and this alone propels me forward.

He watches her face, imagines himself tasting that smile, considering it better once it has sat on his own lips for a while. Already he has told her so much, and he wants to tell her this also. He feels sure that she would not mind. But his hesitancy is a kind of admiration.

He touches her hand lightly near the plaster, where her skin is grazed. 'Is it very bad?'

'Not so bad.' She smiles, wriggling her hand as though for proof. 'Nothing, really.'

He wants to tell her that he can feel her courage like static in her fingertips.

They both look up at the hotel, seeing themselves in the rooms that are an almost perfect mirror of each other. To fold the hotel down the middle would be to impress their rooms one upon the other. David imagines himself asleep there: would even their beds be layered then? And he wonders which side she sleeps on; he frames the question as 'Mine?' or 'Hers?' and glances down at Anna to find her watching him.

'I can't believe we haven't passed each other in the corridor.' She shields her eyes from the sun as she looks up at the building. 'I didn't even think there was anyone else staying here but me.'

'We just keep different hours, I expect.'

'But we could have gone on like that for ever,' she smiles, 'if you hadn't caught me in the street.'

'Caught you? Is that what I've done?'

She looks away, her answer lost beneath the sound of an approaching car – 'An old Austin?' Anna wonders. 'When were they around? Forties? Thirties?' They both turn to watch the olive-green car crunch slow-moving over the gravel, pull up outside the front door of the hotel, which bangs shut in a sudden gust of wind, as though someone leapt out and ran inside the building too fast to be seen.

The engine is cut and no one emerges from the car. Sunlight reflects off the windows. It is impossible to see who is driving, or if there is a passenger. Noiseless, it looks as though it might have sat there for years.

A figure emerges suddenly from the hotel and stands hesitant upon the step, holding the door open as though expecting someone to pass through. He is not a tall man and, though listing a little with old age, his slight build makes him seem youthful, his bright white hair, from a distance, appearing almost blonde. Anna tells David about the first time she saw him, at night in the corridor. He laughs. 'That wasn't a knife, it was a key. I think it's his main job now, to wind that clock.' David waves at him. 'The time-keeper of the Grand Hotel, not such a bad life, but lonely I guess. He's quite harmless anyway.' But the man appears not to have seen them when David raises his arm. Although he is looking in their direction, he seems to be watching something else.

'You know, he's been here since he was a boy.' David settles himself more comfortably on the grass. 'They took him on because his father and grandfather both worked here when it was a private house. I got it out of him last week. He's full of stories, though he was very cagey, and there's a lot he wasn't letting on.' Anna glances up at the man. He is still standing in the doorway. In the few moments of his standing there, the shadow from the portico has edged towards him, covering his expression so that it is now impossible to say in which direction he is looking. He seems to be waiting for something, or expecting something to happen, his weight canted forward on to his toes.

'He's a very kind man, no one to be afraid of.' David tugs Anna's sleeve gently so that she tips towards him. 'Though I think it's fair to say he's not all there,' he murmurs, laughing softly.

'That's mean,' Anna chides, leaning close.

'But it's true,' he tells her. 'Something bad happened here, way back when he was bellboy just before the war, and he holds himself responsible in some way. I don't think the place has ever quite recovered. He's a very sweet man, but sad, too – just look.'

Their heads draw apart for a moment as they look back up at the hotel, expecting to see him still waiting there. But he has gone. And this puzzles them, as they both remember the loudness of the door when, only a few minutes earlier, the wind caught it and rattled it in its casing. They assume that he was merely careful when he turned to go. Perhaps he did not wish to disturb them, seeing them together on the lawn.

But the greater puzzle is that the car, too, has disappeared, as though they were so wrapped up with one another that they left no space for hearing anything but what sound the other made. But it is enough to make them look hard at the empty space in front of the hotel, and both are thinking how vivid, in fact, the last few moments were – the loudness of a blackbird's song from the yew tree, the rush of wind through heather and pine, the subtle clatter of sycamore leaves crisped by sun; even the rub of hair and skin seemed potent with significance. How could they not have heard the car?

But they do not wonder on this for long, just as a warm dream slips through insignificance and meaning, leaving nothing but a residue of almost-memory – a thing the dreamer does not properly possess.

'What's the word for that?' David understands perfectly what Anna is asking him. 'Is there a word for this kind of thing?' He smiles at her, taking her hand in his, saying nothing.

Two days of rainfall and now suddenly the sky is a cloudless wash of blue. There's a warm wind blowing fierce and steady off the moor, and when Jack walks up the hotel driveway the swallows are diving in loud clean arcs around the rooftops and the tall trees are rustling with open leaves turned sunwards.

He has had no word from her for two days. But he has stayed away for as long as he is able. This morning, as he washed and dressed, he was conscious of the care he took over himself. Deciding on a pressed blue shirt, he knew that the decision to go to her had already been taken, although for the rest of the day he pretended to himself that perhaps he'd wait until tomorrow.

Now, approaching, he can hear laughter and the delicate snap of glass and china. Fine weather has turned the hotel inside out: all the windows are open, and a canopy has been set up to provide shade for the terrace that runs along the front of the building. On the terrace, a number of chairs and tables are arranged. Most are occupied. And in front of the building, on the lawn, a white canvas pagoda is flapping where the wind catches it – again, chairs and tables are set out beneath it, in the shade. It is around seven thirty in the evening.

Jack slows his pace as he approaches the hotel. The scene that faces him is nothing as he expected. He has the impression that some kind of party has either just ended, or is soon to begin. Either way, he has not been invited. Were his approach less obvious, he would turn round and leave. But he is half-way up the drive and to retrace his steps now would seem ridiculous. He feels people's eyes upon him. So he strides on uphill, wishing he had not come. He feels conspicuous and too young; he is certain that people will notice him and expect to see him at any moment greet an aunt or grandparent.

As he walks into the hotel, the sound of a man's high-pitched laugh makes him jump. Was he laughing at him? He looks down at his clothes and finds fault in them. He dislikes the hang of his trousers, is ashamed of his shoes, over-polished to compensate for their cheapness. He curses himself, deciding that he'll just sit in the hallway for a few moments, pretend he is looking for someone, and then go. He should have waited for word from her, as planned.

He glances at his watch, barely registering the time, conscious that he is acting a part, trying to appear invisible, so that when someone approaches him, he moves aside to let them by, not expecting that he might stand a chance of being recognised.

The man stands for a second in front of him before Jack realises who it is. The station cleaner, smartened up, but still holding a dustpan and brush. His face is red with heat and effort; his collar presses into his neck. His eyes alight on Jack with a look of gratitude, as though he might ask him for his help, 'Be a pal and sweep up that broken glass?' The man blinks at Jack in surprise. 'Didn't expect to see you here.' He grins at him, leaning towards him with relief. 'Come here to spy on the girls?' he whispers, nodding in the direction of the terrace. Jack starts to move away, but he is trapped. The man thinks that he is moving into a better place for them to talk.

'If I'm caught hobnobbing like this there'll be trouble.' He grimaces, and Jack tells him not to be caught out, please, on his account. 'Maybe they'll let me off if they know you're not one of them.' Again, he nods in the direction of the terrace. 'Hotel don't like me to fraternise,' he adds darkly, moving closer to Jack.

Jack is forced into a corner, just inside the main door. With the loudness of the music, people flow out from inside in ever-greater numbers. Dancing has already started beneath the pagoda. The cleaner is looking at Jack expectantly, and he knows that at any moment the man will ask him why he is here. He looks at his watch and the man leaps on the gesture. 'Meeting someone?' Jack looks down at his face and feels enraged at his tone of insinuation. But it is the truth. He had hoped to meet her here. Now he only wants to get away unseen.

The man raises his hands and laughs. 'Don't tell me.' He shuts his eyes. 'We all have our secrets.' He tilts his chin in mock grandeur and Jack cringes, noticing a woman's raised eyebrows as she passes them. He tries to curse her. Why don't people mind their own business? But he is more angry with himself. He finds his embarrassment loathsome. He cannot stand to be so easily coupled with this man still giggling beside him, his shoulders pumping with enjoyment. What does he find so funny about his being here?

He turns away, looking for a means of escape. Perhaps he can just let himself be caught up in the crowd, hope that the man will let him go. But he is tugging on his sleeve – 'Now that's special!' – when Jack sees her walking in the opposite direction to him along the terrace, out into the garden. 'No, not over there,' the man corrects him, nudging him to get him to look at a group of girls sitting together at a table in front of the hotel.

Jack takes a pace back, hoping that the shadow of the doorway will conceal him. Even with her back to him, his recognition of her astonishes him, as though she is standing so close that they are touching. He knows her walk, and the structure of her bones and flesh, the weight and shapes of her – her exact dimensions that are unmistakable, lodged in his mind's eye like a precise mould into which only she can fit. But suddenly to know all this fills him with panic, as though his knowledge of her were stolen, an intimacy he has no right to.

He looks around. If he tries to leave at this moment she will notice him. But now he has a very particular reason for not wanting to be seen: she is not alone.

He watches as she hurries across the lawn towards a man whose back is turned to her; he barely moves when she goes to stand beside him. If anything, he appears to angle his body still further away from her, seeming to draw back as she leans towards him, her naked shoulder pressing against his black-suited arm. When the man starts to walk away, a half-pace ahead of her, she gives the impression of following – of 'chasing', Jack describes it to himself, of chasing after another man. He can see her hand resting on his arm, and the way she has to take rapid steps to keep up with him makes Jack's throat tighten with shock. The man bends to speak into her ear, and Jack watches her raise her hand to touch his shoulder, a light touch that appears more than merely willing. Can it even be true?

He is aware of the breath seeming to dissolve out of his body, as though it has run right through his limbs, transforming them to nothing. The clarity of the image before him – of her alongside another man – seems to eradicate even the possibility of his existing in the same frame. It has weight and substance. He belongs to a lighter world. He could hurl a rock at them, shout, rampage through the garden – it would make no difference. The trail he left would be cleared away like a painting being restored with a dab of white spirit. But he cannot look away.

He is conscious of the cleaner beside him, saying something that he hears only as a quiet stream of ordinariness, something he might paddle in while the heavy wave thunders harmless in the distance. He feels shot through with pain and massive tiredness. He has the wild idea that he ought to offer to help the man still bobbing about beside him. Perhaps he will wrench that pan and brush from him and go over to her, sweep about her feet to prove the extent of his humiliation. He imagines the way she would react were he to do this. He can see how she would pretend she did not even recognise him. But he would make sure that she did. His presence beside her would be so loud that even she would not be able to feign deafness.

'You should have a glass of water if you feel unwell.' The man is giving him instructions, and he realises that he must have spoken. But what did he say? He follows him inside the building and takes the glass of water that is handed to him. He thanks him, and says that as he is not feeling so good, perhaps he will just go home and not wait any longer. The man smiles at him, as though they were sharing a joke. But Jack cannot smile back and he knows that he has offended with his rudeness, so he tells him that it was a pleasure to have run into him, and that no doubt he will be seeing him very soon around the station, and that the water was a kindness, and he hopes they don't work him too hard here, and thank you thank you.

He is conscious of babbling, words running senseless into each other, and he turns to go, horrified by the force of his imagination. It has made him believe that so much was true, when in fact it was in so great a part his own invention. Nothing was fixed. Dreams were spoken of as though they were real. He sees her hand upon that other man's arm, the way her body leant towards him; a few slight gestures that have now changed everything. He pushes his way outside past the people lingering in the hotel lobby, and grouped in idle clusters on the terrace and the gravel driveway.

He heads across the lawn in the opposite direction to the one he saw her take, trying to keep his eyes cast down. A large group of people has gathered, and their slowness makes him want to fight his way through, kicking and cursing. His politeness sickens him. He hates the language of manners that has failed his emotion so entirely. Each time he apologises, 'Excuse me. So sorry,' he is conscious of the lie of his disguise. As long as he can keep apologising, keep the lie in place, he runs no risk of being recognised. He understands now the remoteness of the imported crowd. Apart from the cleaner, no one from the town will be here.

Pushing his way through, he feels a hatred he has never before encountered. But it is not for her, or for anyone in particular. It is for the imminence of all things changing, when he had imagined that at least one thing had been caught – their hearts, coinciding. Now he wishes that he could scrub out everything that the last ten minutes have brought. Were it in his power to do so, he would. He would erase this crowd, the black flood in the garden. It signifies the onrush of the minutes, and all the darkness of his disillusion. He wants the brightness to return, and cannot yet look square at the idea that it might never come again.

Jack is almost at the far limits of the garden when he glances up, and sees her instantly as though she had waved to him to attract his attention. But she is not even looking up. She is beneath the pagoda, dancing with that man, and he cannot help but watch.

Seeing her from this distance, he has a sudden image of his future – the moment when he will catch a similarly common glimpse of her. Miraculously, she will be alive and very well. All her talk of illness, and that story about her parents being in danger – all that will have been a lie. He has never seen her looking quite so pink with health. He wonders what flash of inspiration made her think of it – to extricate herself from what? What can he call it? For him it was his only shot at love, and absolute. For her, what, exactly?

He feels his heart race in his chest. She will not remember him. He will be an anachronism, long forgotten. He will no longer exist for her. She will not even turn her head as he passes. The certainty of this future moment makes him feel nauseous and faint. He presses his hand to his chest where his heart, unreliable, seems to swing and lurch. He wills himself to go up to her and tell her that he knows everything now, and has she any idea what she has done? His feet stumble heavily forward. But the sight of her gleaming there in the soft light makes him hesitate.

He tries to steady his breath. If she has lied then she will live, and nothing else matters. The realisation affects him like a falling-off of clothes in the night. He feels light, and utterly without self-regard. He is conscious of swaying slightly where he stands. Has love meant only possession until this moment?

A waiter offers him a tray of drinks, and he takes one. He feels like a thief. He is astonished that it was offered to him. He has only to smile, to lie, and drinks are handed to him gratis, as though he has a right to be here. He cannot believe that he has not been found out.

He tries to summon up a vision of her suddenly turning, seeing him, and running through the garden to find him as she did before. But he looks at her, sees the curve of her spine held beneath another man's hand, and knows it will not happen. His eyes sting and he blinks hard as he watches her, praying that he will not cry. He sips his drink. Champagne. He feels more than ever like a thief. How long can he keep this up? Any moment now he expects to be accosted, very quietly expelled from the garden. But no one comes and he steps further away into the shadow of one of the massive yew hedges where he can watch her without being noticed. Anything is better than nothing, he tells himself. Even these moments of watching her with another man. I'll even take this rather than the horror of things without her.

Glancing upwards, he can see the sky's dark dish of night, unbroken, as though only this small sphere of the hotel garden has been blessed with light. And when I leave this time? He drinks, drops his glass behind him on the soundless grass, reaches to take another from a passing tray.

He cannot properly see the man she is dancing with. He moves stiffly, and Jack assumes he is quite old. His face is unclear. He has dark hair, and while Elena seems so brightly lit, her gold dress catching the light, the man's silhouette seems to gather darkness, as though he stood in perpetual shade.

Jack looks down at his feet. He cannot even imagine them stepping into the same circle of light that she appears to move in. He imagines setting them beside her delicate gold evening slippers. He can see the ugliness of that contrast like a statement of his foolishness, his error in believing such things might co-exist.

—

181

When he looks up, even from so far away, the other man's back looks like a velvet door shut in his face. He can see himself being handed money, very quietly. 'Please, will you just go away, there's a good chap.' He supposes that it is the man's wealth that suggests his attitude of impartiality and separation. Jack watches the way he barely seems to acknowledge Elena's presence beside him. Wealth is his trick, his way of deflecting all claims the world might make on him. Unlike me. Jack finishes his drink, reaches for another as the tray passes by. I have no trick. I am claimed so entirely by my love that I cannot even see myself now. He feels as though he could smash the glass against his forehead and register only the muted tinkle as the pieces fell. I am not here, I am only eyes, he tells himself, steadying himself, setting his feet more firmly on the lawn.

He watches them. The shade of the pagoda washes Elena's skin in a soft white light and her hair appears luminous and cool as platinum. Even though he is standing in the shadows, Jack feels too hot by comparison, as though were he to touch his own hair his fingertips would come away burnt. It is a disappointment to him that this does not happen.

The band is playing, and the conversations around him seem to lull and swing in time to the music. Jack feels the champagne work in his blood, and the remoteness it brings is welcome. He leans back against the yew hedge and fantasises that this is a nightmare he will soon wake from. A twig digs into his back. Because if not asleep, then what? He tries to tell himself that his faith in her was a madman's faith in a lunatic god, a rogue aberration of which now he can see the wildness. But he knows it is not that. He watches her, the smoothness of her limbs making him want to run to her and hold her, very quiet and steady, and say nothing, just wait until she sees their logic. How can she believe that something else is more true? He wipes the wetness from his face with his sleeve.

—

182

A couple, standing nearby, distracts him. Something in their posture is familiar. Their heads are bowed together as though they were hatching plans. Eagerness to be together runs right round them, and although they do not touch, they seem impossible to separate. But they caught his eye for a different reason: they are a tableau of memory, as though for the last few weeks two actors have been shadowing him and Elena, copying their gestures, reading what was written secretly in their hearts. And now here it is, exposed, and mimicked with an exactness that is startling.

A sound escapes his throat. Somewhere between a laugh and a sob. The two young people look up and walk away, frowning. He wishes that he had been able to take hold of them and haul them over to her, ask them to repeat what they just did, and perhaps that way she would remember. He can recall exactly what he and she were discussing when they stood like that together, only two weeks ago. They were discussing her reason for coming here. At least, they were discussing the reason that at first she was prepared to give him. The preface of their conversation had been love, just as it has run ahead of all their conversations, inflecting even the barest words with meaning.

He remembers that it was then she told him about the novel: 'The studio is interested in the story for a movie.'

Now this excuse shines with the significance of gemstones rattled in a prospector's sieve: the story. Two young people in love in a small provincial town not far from the sea, but bound by land sufficiently to warrant the critics' descriptions of it as 'pastoral sublime'. He wonders if she would even remember that this was the reason she first gave him. Was that, too, a lie?

He tries to picture her curled up beside him on that red plaid rug on the hillside, her hair knotted by the wind, with grass stains on her yellow cotton dress; the way he joked that it wasn't quite the Ritz, handing her a doorstep sandwich with a kind of flourish, and she had set it aside and pulled him down beside her, kissing him to keep him quiet. She had whispered, 'Foolish boy, I love you,' against his ear, and he had been happy then, believing her. Now he supposes that she had meant something else entirely – that even at that moment she was seeing him in contrast to her real life, and insisting on a preference for him that she did not feel.

He is conscious of crying, aware from the soreness of his eyes that tears must have fallen for some time now. Her dancing seems to stamp itself across his memories of her until he can barely believe that they are real.

He backs away. But we did fit to that story, that idyll, he wants to shout at her, although he dares not trust himself even to remain within earshot, so certain is he that the words will any moment leap out from his mouth. It was true. But no longer. This jealousy and hatred was not part of that. He is glad that she and that man are not standing close. He is overwhelmed by feelings he does not know what to do with, as though someone had just handed him a knife. If that man comes within striking distance – Jack clenches, unclenches his fist, looks away.

Evening has descended on the garden. He should have left a long time ago. He watches the figures scattered and gilded in the trembling light, sure that when he walks among them he will douse each person out as he passes, blacken them with the darkness of his grief. He braces himself for people's stares as though he were on fire; it sickens him that no stares come. He feels reduced to the substance of a harmless spirit that no one can even see, still less be inclined to mind, or to remember.

He drains his glass, and raises it, thinking he might hurl it into the crowd so that she will notice him by the chaos he creates, but it is lifted from his hand as he turns to go. He stumbles, is tipped slightly off balance. He wishes he had that excuse to fall. He has no desire to remain upright, or act like any kind of man.

He looks back at her, and imagines that, even from this distance, he can see the red scratch across her throat, although of course this is not true. But he can see its cause again – the intimacy of a briar rose that marred her vulnerability as she lay there on the forest floor beside him. It must have drawn blood, Jack registers. And will she bear a permanent scar? He has the fleet vision of himself striding over towards her and pulling aside the neckline of her dress to reveal that scratch, asking her directly how she came by it, forcing her to lie. That scratch would be sufficient evidence of guilt.

The music stops and Jack watches the man draw back from Elena, and go to stand a few feet away from her beside a table where drinks have been set out. He is hidden by people gathering there after the dance. She does not follow him immediately, but stands by herself, looking for something inside her evening bag that she appears not to find. When she bends over, her hair falls across her face and she pushes it back. She seems to hesitate, caught in indecision. He has never seen her looking so old as she does at this moment. He tells himself that this sets her further apart, but he knows that it is a lie: it only makes him love her more, and want to care for her and live his life beside her.

He cannot believe ill of her. Whatever she has done he would forgive her. He takes a few rapid paces towards her, snagging his trousers on a rosebush, cursing, his legs weak beneath him and his forehead damp with the sweat of nerves and drink. A group of people walk black-backed in front of him, and when they move aside he stops, seeing that the man has once more rejoined her. He stands very still, watching her from the distance of thirty or so yards. She appears to glance across the darkened garden towards him. *Now, come to me*

185

now, he wills her. As she looks in his direction, she half-raises her hand, as though understanding that he is there. Then the man takes her elbow, and once more she is hidden by the crowd.

Knowing it is impossible that she should hear him, he whispers, 'Goodbye,' to her and feels heartsick at the thought that this word could be true.

He turns away, his life seeming to flow cool and faint behind him. Walking down the garden through the flickering evening he feels the vertigo of his departure, as though their story is run through with too old a truth for their thin lives to sustain with any dignity or difference. The old story. Longing and waiting and impossibility; and beneath everything, time's frantic burn.

When he looks back at her and can no longer see her in the failing light, her absence from him comes as no surprise. Already she seems lost inside the mirror of a dream, their story weightless as the tale, unwritten, of two familiar ghosts.

III

Still there are still the seeds of energy and choice
Still alive even if forbidden, hidden,
And while a man has voice
He may recover music.
Louis MacNeice, Autumn Journal XVIII, 1938

9

Always – at least, for as long as he can remember – Jack had imagined some kind of future for himself. In the same way, he would sit on the station platform as a child, looking out for trains, anticipating the steel hum of the tracks, the way the sound would seem to gather far off and move towards him with the weirdness of tides – so that when the train itself arrived glistening and palpable, its nearness would be a shock.

Snorting beside him, angry as a prickled colt, the train seemed unreal, and he could quite understand the daring of those movie clowns and maidens who strapped themselves to tracks: why not? The metal craziness was too vivid, too manifest, surely, to be real.

Only when it was gone could he see it. And then he would miss it. He'd wish he'd paid more attention. Wish he could believe in it while it was in front of his eyes.

In just this way – contemplating his sceptical love of trains – he would think of his future. He'd imagine the quickness of ageing. He'd anticipate all the things that he might miss, that surely he would miss if those trains were anything to go by. This thought would make him sad, oftentimes even mournful, and he would go around – mope around, his father called it – wide-eyed and with an ache in his belly so huge that people laughed at his skinny self's capacity for food.

But it didn't stop him dreaming of all the times that might be his, and of all the things he was sure enough to miss out on if he was for just one second inattentive, too incredulous to notice what was inches from his eyes.

For this reason there had never been a moment, in his experience, when he didn't regard his future as a kind of buzzing hive of possibility and chance – as though he only had to hook himself up to a stripy-backed chariot and it would carry him humming off to somewhere or other more or less unexpected. He knew the vision was silly: he told no one. It did sufficient job of explanation in his mind's eye – a gift of wondering for himself – and that was enough. It meant that the sadness fell from him. He passed through his teenage years unscathed and softly happy – more or less content. If he failed at something, he turned to something else. It became a kind of motto for him: always to see the alternative.

The certainty that there would be an alternative, like the suddenness of nocturnal freight trains, was his article of faith, and it meant everything to him. For him, thoughts of the future were inter-changeable with the persistence of his longing, his heartbeat's tap-tap on the half-shut door of time. Yearning for the future was merely his way of being alive.

He remembers all this on the night he saw her at the hotel, dancing with that other man. The alcohol has worked its way round his blood and he feels the lightness of it still, and the acute watchfulness of disbelief. He left the party, walked down through the woods intending to go home, and found he could not do it. He saw the light inside the kitchen and its loneliness appalled him. So he walked straight past the house, and through the town to the river.

Now he is sitting in his secret place beneath a willow tree. The sandstone is still hot after the sunny day. But the river is roaring now, so that he knows there must have been great rainfalls higher up the land. The last couple of weeks can't have brought this much weight of water, can they? He peers over into the slipstream. Where have I been not to notice this much rain?

He asks this only to torment himself, to make him answer his own question so that, steadily, he will have to think of her. He will have to see her alongside him, hiding from the rain beneath the tall trees of the coppice. He will have to think of the delays caused in their meetings by the unpredictability of rainfall. He will have to remember her joy in sunlight, her 'Look at the clouds going so fast', as she pointed out high cumulus casting shadows on the burnt umber of the exposed peat.

So many things to mention to himself. So many things running by him for him not to be thrown back right into the astonishment of childhood: his platform shock at the immediacy of trains, too real to be seen for anything that they are.

Still, he cannot believe ill of her. He wonders for a moment if it is his vanity that will not let him think that she is anything but lovely. Is it just that he cannot believe he was so foolish as to trust someone not worthy of his trust? No. She could be anything and he would love her still. He likes the roundness of this idea. He feels its wildness. He marvels at its distance from everything he has known. Can a person be so free? He knows that this is what it is: freedom from all normal codes of conduct, rules of behaviour – he runs the ordinariness of sentiment by himself on tame wheels, seeing himself push away all familiarity in that gesture. A child cutting itself free of its guarding reins. Laughing even at the hurt of grazes.

The air is close, specifically honeyed: trumpets of honeysuckle have emerged from their sheaths since he last came to the river; the plant grows rampant along the riverbank, skeins of it festoon one side of the bridge and it hangs indolent from the lower branches of an elder tree, whose blossom has already turned to green bullets pre-empting ungrown fruit.

Freedom, sure enough; he leans back, resting his head in the long grass on the bank, seeing the stars flash gaudy through the leafy sky straight overhead. Freedom with its price: isolation. He presses his right hand to his temple to hold his sorrow tightly there. I have lost something I did not possess: he slips the equation of his love into that tight phrase and thinks on it for a long while.

The town is very quiet; few people are still awake at this time, after the hinge of midnight. He wonders if it is swallows or bats making that sound like the etching of his torment, scraped there with such elegance in the darkness. Do swallows sing in this much night? The leaves are forever shuffling, reshuffling about him, and he imagines the sweetness of nesting birds peering down at him from the branches beneath their half-cocked wings.

But he cannot think long of sleep. Thinking of it at all is to think of her. He sees her in another's arms and feels only madness – no rage or grief even at that vision. Just the terror of misplaced objects. The knife in the golden meadow. The villain at the window. The lunatic antic in the quietness of a crowd. The meteor's strike at the cocooned atmosphere; great ages rent by accident; the river running wild off-course by a beaver's subtle dam; or an ice-floe gone awry so that right now, in the early part of his life, he comprehends the anguish of the heart's exile when it has been shut out of the only place, he's sure, it can belong. He peers up the track and sees only a whispering curtain of green that cuts the light; he can see no future, can believe in no new life now he has lost her.

But he had wanted their world to be everything, the only one she cared for. He had wanted to be able to wave their love around like a voodoo talisman to ward off evil and potential trespassers; for people to back off in awe just at the sight of them. He had wanted them to be the indestructible figure in the amber. Something that anyone, in any age, might see.

He curses as he cries. He feels the dull ropes of adulthood bind him. He would like to wriggle free and swim back to his youth to find her waiting there, and new.

Letting the night into his lungs with gladness, he sees a world composed of accidents and ghosts; he sees no chance of meaning in that meeting-place of flesh and spirit. He wishes, prays, that she will return to him and that what life is left them will be theirs, with no more nonsense of their separation, not now. He holds his apple love for her in his hands. Even in the night, he can feel it shining there. But without her love to match it, how can it be enough? I cannot make her feel a thing she does not feel. I can only wait until her memory trips her up, returns her to the time, now past, when she did love me. But he sees her moving swiftly away from him, hurrying to catch up with that other man.

He shuts his eyes and hears the swollen river still run swift and furious: higher up and out of sight it swarms through broken banks.

Elena steps into the corridor as though on to new ice. The room behind her seems lit with noise, as though her movement through it was a passing point of darkness, certain to be heard. But as she hesitates in the doorway, looking back, her husband's figure is motionless and silent on the bed.

This evening, at the hotel, she half thought she saw Jack leaving the garden by the bottom gate. The figure caught her eye because he had been running – at least, walking fast enough to be eyecatching in the middle of a party. Straight away she thought she must have imagined it: she had sent him a note the previous day, asking him to wait for word from her. That she loved him, and if he could wait for a very short while then she promised him all would be well.

But the impression of him looking back at her through the crowd at the hotel will not shift from her mind, and she cannot sleep. What if he decided not to wait, but to come to find her? He would have seen her with her husband. No, she cannot sleep, thinking that this might have happened. He has no reason not to trust her; the truth would give him no cause for doubt. But his searching for proof of the truth is liable, she knows, to have offered him only falsity. Now she has to get to him to see that he understands.

The door's click-shut is muffled by baize, and her bare feet are noiseless on the carpet. She wears her tennis shoes strung round her neck by their laces so that her hands are free. She anticipates the blindness of night.

Even at this hour – around one in the morning – even in the silence, the hotel seems taut with life. Elena has the impression that to open any door along the corridor would be to reveal a scene of vivid wakefulness, as though the doors all open on to day, with only the corridor observing the rules of night. She imagines people leaning close to their hotel-room doors, pressing their ears against the wood to listen out for her as she goes; she feels just that vulnerability and attentiveness of acting. But when she reaches the head of the stairs, she looks back down the corridor into silence: the doors are all still closed.

She pauses beside the lilting clock that swings on through the night, returning her to home. She sees her father lean towards it as though whispering secrets into its walnut belly; the long-fingered way he'd twist the brass key to keep it tightly wound – the key she now owns, carries always with her, the only physical remains of that childhood clock: the wishbone relic of memory.

And even these small things, she thinks, I must set out before him. He knows nothing of them. This thought causes her pain; that she is unknown to him in any way fills her with anguish. It makes her see herself multiplied by the camera's power to transfix and distribute, scattering herself to the air, when she would like to be a smooth, small stone that she might hand him, watch him press with pleasure to the flesh of his palm. She would like the two of them to add up precisely to that simplicity. A unity fierce-bound, and composed. She wants their secrets to be future gifts; she would like to delete the rogue shocks that signify her illness, erase them utterly; she would do anything to have more time.

She looks back at the clock, can hear its pendulum-hunger throbbing in her blood. She imagines the finite calculation of its swings, a definite and near number before it, and everything else is of as little consequence for her as though it had never been. She feels this as acutely as though the date were already known to her. She thinks of the things she longs to do within the limits of time, sees herself cramming the seconds full of her love for him. But she hates the vision: her love is all leisure and expansiveness, lingering and steady joy. The mantra runs again: I would do anything to have more time. She peers ahead in the gloom as though searching for the test – the 'anything' that she will happily suffer in exchange for seconds, hours. She tries not to think 'years'. There is no guarantee of years.

She treads the stair-carpet on naked feet, her soles flattening the scarlet wool, which springs back instantly after.

The lobby is empty; only one light burns, behind the reception desk. The armchairs and sofas have their backs to her. She imagines people crouched in their wings, waiting until she has passed before resuming their conversations. The front door is shut, and Elena has the sudden fear that perhaps it is even locked. She has the ridiculous premonition of crawling out of a ground-floor window, like a thief, and her heart is hammering in her chest when she tries the handle, finds that it sticks but then turns, when behind her suddenly she hears someone clear their throat and she looks round to see that it is the bellboy, only a few paces away from her on the red hall carpet.

They face each other in the half-light. He holds something out to her. She takes it: a flashlight. She notices that his hands are unsteady. He whispers to her, 'He wasn't there. I tried. I'm not certain he will have seen your note. I had to leave it. I'm so sorry.'

She shakes her head and feels her blood seem to slow down in her veins. 'I understand. Thank you.' He leans past her to open the front door and she slips by him and out into the night.

So few words. She imagines them sinking heavy to the ground, weighted down by their significance. Then it must have been him in the garden. Elena feels her throat tighten with fear. Unless he found it, read it, and still wanted proof?

His doubt, even from this distance, seems tangible. She understands his wish for a fixed point, for stone and a fixed face to time; but she can give him none of this. She can give him only love's quicksand, the fragment-memory of a childhood clock, the high, thin sound that its ticking made as it echoed against the stone-flagged hallway in a disputed street. She wants herself to be sufficient proof. Don't ask for proof beyond your heart's knowledge, she wants to tell him. It is far cleverer than your mind, doubting, patching up its straw house of logic. Don't doubt my love – she wants to grip him by the shoulders to impress her words upon him. Because then you doubt me.

So he came to find her, and saw her dancing with another man, a stranger he would not even recognise as her husband. She imagines what he will have read into that sight. 'For friendship's sake,' her husband had said to her. 'And as it will probably be the last time.' He finished his sentence through gritted teeth; she did not know whether in anger or sorrow. She was ashamed of all the trouble she had brought to him. So she danced for shame, and for farewell.

The grass is damp underfoot. She bends down in the deep shade of one of the chess-piece yew trees to put on her tennis shoes. She touches the grass and the cool blades are dripping with nocturnal dew. When she looks back up at the hotel, three or four lights still shine from the rooms. She tells herself that she was right to be anxious about people catching her out: she can imagine them in the hidden bedrooms, speculating, sneaking clues and tip-offs to betraying strangers.

She counts along the windows to her room, second from the right on the first floor. It is in darkness. The glass reflects starlight. She walks down through the garden to the iron gate. She is careful to walk in the deepest shadows, fearful of being seen. The night rustles about her. The air is warm and she can smell each scent as she passes it, as though each one is sparked by charcoal.

The gate is loud beneath her hands; the sound disturbs something on the other side, which shuffles, rattish, in the long grass. She imagines Jack watching her setting out to find him in the darkness, the way he would hold his arms out to her to help her find her way through the louring trees. She can see his shock that she would risk such a thing for his sake. The way he would measure her up, as she is at this moment, with the woman he first saw stepping, suited, off the train into the fine June sunlight. He would try to lift the person she now is back into that image of self-containment, saying, 'You don't have to brave the darkness for me, I believe you, Elena.' He'd laugh in protest, take her arm and link it through his, she is quite sure.

She strides on through the hushed grass. The surface of it is moonlit. Where the wind catches it it appears to be running smooth in one direction swift as a gathering tide. It flows downhill, snags among the trees as on black rocks. She hears the hotel door bang closed and looks back up at the building. She can see no one. She supposes it was just a draught that took it, but the shadows on the garden seem unsettled from this distance, as though someone has moved among them to push them off balance like a hand swirled in inky water, raising the quiet sediment.

The ground underfoot is wet with the outbreath of the hot day's green. As she goes beneath the trees, she slips on the mud, her hair falling loose, tangling in the undergrowth. She rubs her eyes, dirtying her face.

Elena imagines the earth's breast rising, falling. When she turns on the torch and flashes it into the forest, the tree barks gleam pewter. She enters and the air is humid. She feels it close around her throat. Fallen branches crackle underfoot.

Can you not see me now? She hesitates. The trees seem to make a sound like their two breaths intertwined, and she leans closer into the darkness, straining to listen. She fears that to reach her hands out now would be to grasp at nothing.

At the station house, a figure passes restless through the downstairs rooms. Hearing footsteps on the gravel outside, he stops to listen. Not Jack's footsteps, but someone else's, a stranger's. Elena knocks at the door, knuckles on wood, too nervous to use the bell at this late hour.

The house is silent for some minutes of indecision, before Jack's father opens the door to find a young woman standing on his doorstep. He recognises her instantly as the woman he has seen with Jack, although close up her appearance is nothing as he expected. She looks half wild, he thinks, noticing the smudges of dirt on her face, the twigs stuck to her unbound blonde hair, as he waits for her to speak. Her chest rises and falls as though she has been running, and with the light from inside shining on her, concealing him, he feels a momentary advantage. But he has never seen anyone with skin like hers. It fills him with indignation. It looks luminous as washed silk. Her lips are trembling, her eyes wide as with nerves or excitement. She has rolled up her sleeves so that her arms are naked and bear the thin red scratches of scandal on pale skin, as though she has lost track of her own gestures, has not been conscious of what she was doing.

He backs away as though she had pulled a gun on him. She is too bright for this place, and he feels the danger of her, as though behind her in the dark a secret army was waiting for her sign. She opens her mouth to speak, but he holds up his hand to silence her. He does not want to know what she has to say. Her appearance alone tells him enough. She pushes away a strand of hair that is floating loose, touches her mouth briefly, and he is sure that now he can see everything that must have happened.

'I have to talk to Jack.' Her voice has trouble beneath it.

He shakes his head. 'He isn't here.' They must have had a fight. Jack must have ended things, and now she is pursuing him. He finds her presence unbearable. Even though she stands in darkness, he has the impression of her shining a bright light right the way through the house, exposing everything. He cannot stand it. The thought of his son being with her is horrifying to him, as though he were being forced to witness an intimacy he finds obscene. 'No. You can't. He's gone away.'

It's true, he tells himself. He does not know where Jack is now. He had thought he must be with her. It is not a proper lie. 'You shouldn't have come here.' He starts to turn away into the house. 'You should go back, go away.' He watches her raise her hands to her face, and tells himself that it is right she should feel remorse. He does not want such dangers as this for his son. He does not want him chasing about the dark nights with a look like hers upon his face, without dignity or shame. She does not move away. He shuts the door.

Hours later, he is woken by a noise outside on the gravel. It must be Jack, returning. He goes to the window to look out. No, not his son, but still that girl, her pale shape obvious against the fir. She must have been waiting for him all this time. He watches her lean heavily forward against the gatepost as though trying to stave off sleep.

He sits back down on the edge of the bed, now cold. He runs his hand across the empty space behind him. Too dangerous to love at all. He slips beneath the blankets. Still less someone like her, with that famished, wild look about her. One life should not depend upon another that way. She should find her match in someone else, he tells himself. In anyone but my son.

His lone outbreaths are unsteady in the silent room. When he readies himself for sleep, he does not turn to either left or right, but lies stretched out flat on his back, his hands bent against his chest. Even after so many years without his wife beside him, he is surprised to find his hands, by morning, perpetually empty, with no sign whatsoever of the sweat of his nocturnal struggles to retrieve even the very smallest part of her.

'That's bloody good.' Jack remembers how the girl who introduced herself as Katya had reddened as she laughed. He remembers the face, but not the year. When did they ask him for that drawing? Around ten, maybe twelve years ago? Some time in the eighties maybe?

Blushing, she held out the piece of draughtsmanship. 'Look at this, Jane. He's got it just right.'

'Made it look a lot better than it is.' The other girl looked rapidly from the drawing to Jack as though for clues. 'Don't know how you did it. Never seen the place looking quite so—'

'Swish!' Katya finished her sentence, lifting one shoulder, her eyebrows raised. 'Very posh.' She twisted her mouth to pronounce the last word as 'poesh', nodding her approval. 'Ought to do the trick at any rate. Don't you think so?'

'Absolutely. On the money. Amazing you did it just from a photograph. It's almost spooky.' Jane frowned then and looked down at Jack for an explanation.

He leant back in his chair. The things he could say at this moment. The tales he could tell them. He imagined doing it. Imagined the way they'd run screeching from the house. 'Blummin' nutter!' All thought of the job vanished as though he'd played some kind of elaborate trick on them. Lured them in some way. He smiled to himself for a moment as he contemplated doing this, although he decided against it: he needed the money, after all. This irony was not lost on him.

For most of his life, since the war, he has worked as a draughtsman. Buildings and commercial properties, mainly. Illustrations, from time to time. Sketches for brochures and catalogues. And sometimes things like this: a drawing of the

Grand Hotel. 'I'm sure you know it?' one of the girls had asked him.

'Oh, yes. I know it.' He tried not to sound too confident, and to keep his voice steady. But he knew that he could have drawn an accurate picture of the place there and then. From whatever angle. Blindfold, probably, if they'd asked him. 'Yes, I know it pretty well.' He looked away.

The day they asked him he got 'plastered', as he described it to himself, after they had left, finishing off the best part of a bottle of Laphroaig that he had been saving for an occasion of some kind. He decided that this was certainly one of those. In the end, he showed the girls only the worst of his drawings. The best ones were too close to art for them to be able to use.

But he had been the obvious choice for the job. It was a small town. He was, to a modest extent, known for his work. He had fallen into it in wartime when, unable to fight, 'work' had meant reconstructing 3-D landscapes and cities from flat maps and plans. Or by guesswork and clues, he had rendered impressions of the possible interiors of enemy buildings. He had dabbled in drawings of military equipment. But in the end, he lacked the nerve for it. He wanted at least to offer some kind of frame for the human form. A trigger says nothing about the shape of a man's hand, he had realised. As though all men are equal in their innermost dimensions. Of course this is not true, and something in him balked at the lie. The crook of a man's index finger and thumb, with its arterial plunder just beneath the surface, being, after all, a very intimate part of the body, and very seldom known. He would rather draw corpses than guns.

Jack looked up at the two young women. They were hesitating in front of him. He thought 'like flies' before he could stop himself: their eagerness bothered him. He still had the urge to say something. To cast a stone down the well to see if, even now, there was the chance of an echo. He could not believe that his words would find no purchase, even in their oblivious minds, entirely ignorant of everything about him. All they knew was that he was the man to see, locally, about draughtsmanship. He'll be 'just the ticket', as he overheard them saying when they thought he was out of earshot. I'm quite cheap, too, he had wanted to add, but thought better of it.

'Go there quite often, did you, before?' He'd known they wouldn't be able to stop themselves asking. The other girl leant forward as though to egg on her friend.

They were kind girls, he could tell. But they seemed to him to possess a quality of smoothness, a kind of indifference of the soul that left him speechless. He had nothing to say to them. It was more than their belonging to another age. They seemed so free of anguish, or any sense of danger. Perhaps it was simply because they knew nothing of the war. Even their parents would be too young to remember. But they seemed so incurious, and that he couldn't understand.

He knew that when they left they'd hop into their neat soft-top car and drive too fast along the lanes, heedless of the land around them. He felt that he could yell its secrets in their faces and they'd merely whoop and cackle, swear at him, shrieking, 'Let's get out of here. He's effing mental!' Though he knew, also, that they were not uncouth. But they were modern in a way that Jack knew spelt out his own redundancy. Their expressions were undisguised in their pity – which he did not mind. They seemed to bounce and lounge by turns. The one called Katya wore trainers, for which she apologised when she arrived. 'Had to get to the gym!' she exclaimed. 'Did I need it after last night's blow-out!' She sniggered at the other girl, Jane, who blushed. Her blushes were meant to silence Katya, who chewed her lips suddenly as though to prevent more revelations.

He heard them giggle as they left, revving in his driveway, spraying gravel as they took the corner on to the main road at speed. One of them waved goodbye to him out of the open roof. They seemed glad to get away. He was glad to see them leave. It gave him a chance to gloat over all the pictures that he had not shown them.

The picture they'd decided to use was a simple drawing of the hotel as seen from the garden. The girls argued over whether it would be better for the 'cover option' or for the 'double page spread bang in the middle'. They wanted it for a brochure they were making for the hotel, part of what they called 'a PR job'. They had their own business. He had only given them three choices, and they chose the one with fewest people. 'You can see more of the facilities.' By this, they meant the coach-house, which apparently now contained a mini-gym, although he had not been aware of this.

In the drawing they settled on, he had imagined the hotel some time around dusk towards the end of summer. He had seen the day's heat reflected as gold in all the windows. He had even made the brass doorbell shine. There were parasols set out on the terrace so that the figures might sit in shade, out of the burning sunlight, still hot even at the close of day.

He had made a copy of the picture he knew they'd want, but he need not have bothered. He could see it as clearly as when he'd decided to draw it. He could see her sitting with him – not with that other man, but with him – and they are taking drinks together on the terrace, so quiet, unhurried, as though they had done such things a hundred times before, and would continue to do so for many years hence.

He had only ever had one photograph of the hotel, not taken by him but by a reporter, coincidentally on the last day that he saw her. He guessed that it had been taken shortly before he arrived, when the light was still good – perhaps around six o'clock. The dancing had not yet started; there was no band. A number of people figured in the picture, but only one looked directly into the camera's eye: the bellboy – as it were, an extra – who, naturally enough, was excised from the photograph whenever it was used. Indeed, when it appeared in the papers, Elena was the focus of the shot, although in truth she was only one of many players thus caught.

Jack bought a copy of the photograph from the local newspaper. He paid sixpence for it, including p&p. No one asked why he should wish to have such a thing – as though the reason were so obvious they didn't even need to ask. Jack remembers how he paled to think this, his palms sweating as he put his request in the evening post. No, they did not ask because he did not exist in that world. He was just another bystander, spying on the scene from the outside.

He decided to look at the photograph again before doing the work. But to do this, he had to piece it back together again. First, he had to find the parts of the photograph that did not include her. He had kept them in a Coronation biscuit tin, concealed by a row of books on a shelf in his sitting room.

The tin contained various other 'relics', as he called them. They were not happy objects: clippings from the newspaper bearing bad news; receipts for drinks they had shared; a label from her dress that had fallen out – she laughed when he kept it, saying, 'Put it in the bin, you idiot.' But he remembered how she kissed him when she saw him slip the label – Lanvin, Paris – into the ticket pocket of his Harris tweed jacket. He even remembers how the jacket had itched. It had been his father's, reserved for 'best'. He had often worn it when he was with her. How could he not when it had been thus set aside for life's most important times? He had suffered itches gladly.

So he took down the tin, rummaged out the pieces of the photograph, and matched the ragged fragments with a trembling hand. Years before, in the violence of his despair, he had ripped the thing apart. He hadn't wanted to see her with that man for a moment longer than was necessary. Of course, *he* had been in it: it had been a pleasure to destroy the image. But the pleasure was short-lived. Even now that he has usurped him in the drawing, putting himself in the dark-haired man's place, he can see him with her still. In his mind's eye, the two impressions seem to hang one on top of the other, like two prints glimpsed together in the developing tray, matching, unmatching, fighting for precedence beneath the wet red light.

He contemplated these images in the moment that he heard the girls' car hum away down the silent lanes, the sound eventually dissolving in the afternoon. He wondered if there would ever come a time when one of the images would float emphatic to the surface. Until that moment, he was without doubt, he would be haunted. 'Not entirely there.' He supposed that that was the expression for it. But thinking this, he imagined the girls tapping the sides of their heads with meaning, smirking at one another, trying to stifle their giggles.

He put his hands over his eyes. He saw himself sitting so close beside her that when he leant just one inch further forward, as he did then, the kitchen table pressing against his chest, he could feel her warm arm against him, smell the hot, clean-leaf scent of her hair where it brushed past his face. It had been too easy to draw that picture. As though it had been etched on to his retinas. All he had had to do was reiterate an image too often seen. It had been like taking dictation. He had only set down what was already there.

Now, with the night still thick about him and the star-light seeming to spark up close against the greenhouse glass, Jack remembers this scene, although the year it happened still eludes him. He presses his forehead, trying to remember.

He thinks about how when you shake a tray of soil the stones and largest pieces of earth come up to the surface. The mind, and memory, is just like this, he thinks. Any kind of unrest or disturbance brings to the surface all the heart's unsolved hurts, and deep love can re-emerge even in the middle of confusion. He remembers a line he once read somewhere about rubies at a man's fingertips. Where had he seen it? Perhaps it was in that American novel, the book that started everything, and that is why it comes back to him now. He felt the scratch, the pain that raced round the surface of his skin. But it was the heart that pumped the blood, reminding him of that pressure to live. The result was gemstones, *her* – how did the line go? – rubies at his fingertips.

Would I have had the rubies without the soil? He frowns at his mixed logic, but it doesn't stop him wondering. He runs his hands through the years without her, the dry earth flowing through his fingers quick as sand. He remembers the way those two girls laughed at him, clearly thought he was a decrepit fool, another species; as though age were not a continuation of youth, but a different form of existence altogether.

But they were probably about the same age he was when he met her. Perhaps they were a few years older – so then her age. And he sees how clearly that, for him, it is them – everyone else in the world – who is a different species, a different kind of thing entirely when seen in the same light as her. Everyone else is cut out of the picture. It is immaterial which man sat beside her at that moment: neither possessed her. She was not either of their property. She was not liable to be owned. It was folly ever to have thought such a thing was possible. He is glad merely to have been her witness: to have known her transfigured him. 'Glad' contains the debt of his life, with all its grief and longing after an impossibility.

He visualises the photograph, presses his hand to his breast pocket so that he can feel its faint elevation through the fabric of his jacket.

His chest rises and falls with his breath. He imagines his flesh insignificant as the soil that lodges the gemstone, and he smiles. If that's all I've amounted to – he rephrases the equation – if I've amounted to that much, then I have not waited for her in vain. He peers out into the night. The eastern sky is paling before dawn.

By the time they reach the dig, the afternoon has filled with heat and light, and all the clouds are vanished in the blue. They bought food from a deli they discovered just off the town square. At one time it had been the ironmonger's. Now, marinades and cheeses are kept in the remaining steel pots. Kettles hang for ornament, not sale, on chains suspended from the ceiling. Where the hand-turned knife-grinder once stood, there is an electric cutter used for Parma ham. An espresso machine occupies the space that before had been the counter where the nails were kept in deep wooden drawers – a merchant's chest worn black with use, its heaviness now vanished in a jet of steam.

They bought bread and olives, three different kinds of cheese and two large peaches, deep orange in their ripeness. They had elderflower cordial to drink. David had never tasted it before; Anna described how when she was small, a neighbour used to make it from the flowers of the tree that grew in her garden. He agreed to try it. He mentioned the elders that ran wild along the riverbanks near the house he lived in as a child. He drank, and exclaimed in pleasure at its taste. His eyes looked at her in soft astonishment – the body's capacity for surprises.

She imagines him as a boy. He reminds her of the girl she has forgotten how to be. Illness has clouded more than she thought she stood a chance of ever remembering. When they talk of their childhoods, she feels like a gardener replanting stubborn seeds for a future season. Until recently, she had closed down this faculty: she had not thought she would see much more of her future; she had deliberately stopped looking out for it. It had been too painful, as though it had given her an emotional crick in the neck. Too much time spent angling and squinting after something she thought she'd only ever see in her imagination, never discover for herself in reality.

He nudges her as they walk uphill in silence. 'Where are you now?' he asks her gently. She is glad of the intrusion. This, too, comes as a surprise. For so long now she hasn't cared for company in her thoughts. He takes her hand. 'Here it is.'

They reach the dig to find that the others are hard at work. It is two days since the body was found. 'Out of my league.' David shook his head, when she asked him why he wasn't going to be working on it.

'But you found it.' She was puzzled that he looked away when she said this.

'It's too important for me. I'm just an underling.' He had grinned at her. 'Anyway, wood is my area, really – that's why I worked on the boat. I could only guess at something like this.'

'So how's it even possible?' Anna had pressed him.

'Before she's radiocarbon-dated, we can't say. But she's preserved in sphagnum peat, and the aldehydes and organic acids act as a kind of preservative, though the skeleton is pretty much dissolved. There've been hundreds of this kind of thing found, maybe thousands that haven't been recorded.'

She looked down. 'We're probably walking over them all the time.'

'Preserved or not, they're there.' He touched her arm and she straightened up, returning to him.

That was yesterday, and he had not been sure that he should take her to the dig. He laughed at himself when he had thought of asking her. Do you want to come on a date to see a prehistoric woman? 'I was hoping you'd ask me,' she had smiled, 'but I didn't want to pry. It's your thing.'

'Used to be,' he replied, only then realising that the decision had already been taken without his quite acknowledging it: he would quit archaeology, quit following his father, discover his own life now.

She didn't seem surprised. In fact, she had seemed excited when he told her. 'I trained for a few years, part-time, as a carpenter, but it came to nothing.' He handed her a photograph of a rosewood cabinet he had made 'just for fun'. 'See, it's inlaid with hazel.'

She had looked at it in pleasure. 'It's beautiful.' She pointed out the small insignia engraved on the corner of one of the doors. 'A bee. Is that your signature?'

He was embarrassed, as though she had spotted some vanity. 'It's just my mark.'

'I love it, really, it's perfect.' She changed the subject, as though there was much more she had wanted to say.

Later that afternoon, he had caught her looking at him as though trying to decipher something. 'What? You look very thoughtful.' He kissed her as he waited for her to speak.

'I was trying to understand how you could bear to do anything else. That cabinet was so lovely. But I think I've worked it out.'

'Go on then, your verdict.' He had felt a rush of happiness at her liking what he had made. Until then, it had felt like a secret, or a hobby he was foolish to indulge: his father had looked at the cabinet and commented on how it reminded him of 'those odd proportions' of an Egyptian funeral chariot, 'look' – he'd fetched the colour plate for reference, as though David had done nothing but copy from a textbook someone's earlier invention.

'Well,' she wrinkled her brow as though catching the words

there, considering them before speaking, 'it's very like archaeology, only from the opposite direction. It's a reversal of all that. You're not stepping backwards, trying to squint ahead to see what it all might mean. You're just walking straight ahead and this will be your trail. You can be free this way, isn't that it, not weighed down with other people's lives? Making things will be your own evidence.'

He took her very tightly in his arms so that she had to stop speaking. 'That's it exactly.' He was full of love for her for understanding him. There wasn't much. It was really quite simple. But she could see him, she understood, and she liked him still. 'Don't say anything else,' he told her. 'That's it exactly.'

Now they are at the dig, and he feels its remoteness from him like good air rushing through his lungs: the haunting is gone, he has stepped outside the body's shadow and the crowded past, and all that that entailed. Anna's arm is pressed warm alongside him. When she moves, her shoulder brushes him and her cheeks are pink with the climb uphill.

He waves to the others as they stand beside the dig. Anna can see the figures moving in and out of view beneath a grey plastic awning that conceals the body. The course of the stream has been diverted away through a large section of yellow pipe. 'The water came up so fast that she was almost washed clean,' he tells her. 'You can see her quite clearly now.'

They look down together at the fissure in the earth, shrouded by the awning. Sunlight reflects off the plastic. Shielded from the wind by the lip of the hill, the air is motionless and heavy with heat. 'She has cropped hair, and there's some kind of necklace that's maybe jet and amber.' Anna touches her own throat where she wears a thin string of coral.

'Do you have any idea how she came to be here?' Anna steps back on to the soft turf, away from the edge.

'It's way too early to say.' He glances sideways at her; she meets his eye.

'Tell me.'

'Well, this raised bit of land here was most likely a low promontory that stretched out into the sea. That much we know because of the boat, the silt, sea-snails, kinds of pollen. The peat would've been laid down in the Mesozoic period, perhaps a hazel wood, fallen to wetlands over a stretch of time. So this area here would've been bogland, with fresh water from the spring. She was maybe at the water's edge when she died, and quite remote from any significant settlement.' David shields his eyes from the sun. She fidgets beside him: what is it he's not telling her? 'OK, a few things they worked out yesterday, clues to what she's doing here.'

He shifts away from her slightly, looking down. 'There are possible signs of a violent death – the way the skull area is caved in, the throat split, other breaks over the skin, and a large stone placed over her – where I cracked my head in fact.' He tries to laugh, rubbing his forehead. 'That'd fit with a Celtic sacrifice – it's called "triplism", a symbolic killing three times over. And that could help date her to a few hundred or so years around the start of the millennium. But it seems she was also bearing a child. So it's more complicated.'

Anna is frowning, peering down into the opaque plastic sheeting as though trying to see through it. Her face is pale when she looks back at him. 'You're not convinced it was a sacrifice?'

'If it was a systematic, sacrificial killing, it's unlikely it'd be a one-off. And she was pregnant. So what would've been the public motive? Was it part of some kind of genocide, an attempt to wipe out the next generation? We just can't say. It's inconceivable without more evidence. If it did happen, it's been erased from history. No one like this, pregnant, has ever been found before. She's the only one. Alone, she's not proof enough for that kind of speculation.'

Anna has started to turn away. She rubs her forearms as if to warm herself, although the day is hot and close, the air very dry. 'You think it's more likely it was personal?'

'Someone taking justice into their own hands maybe. So part private ritual, part a kind of crime of passion. Maybe a husband discovering she was carrying another man's child, or at least suspecting that she was. But it's just story-telling, trying to make sense of things. It's all we can do.'

He puts his arm around her shoulders, 'Come on, I'm superfluous here anyway,' and, as happens each time he does this, is alarmed at the smallness of her bones. He cannot imagine them surviving long beneath the earth. He hides this thought away quickly as though she might see it if he thinks it for too long. She looks at him anxiously and he holds her tight.

The breeze is gathering as they walk up to the high point in the land. Clouds run swift across the open moor, the shadows chasing downhill like a fast-flowing stream. They wade uphill through the purpling heather, glad to get away from the dig. Neither confesses to this, but both of them, in secret, would swear that they heard a voice, very faint inside the noise of gusting air, seeming to call out to them as they left.

They do not break their stride. As they reach the hilltop, they are laughing and out of breath. They pause there, looking back down towards the dig. What had the voice said? Both of them are wondering this at that moment. But it is impossible to say. No word was formed. The voice was nothing, just a reminder. And looking down the way they have come, already the crevice where the body lies is entirely hidden from view, obscured behind a raised point in the land.

10

The men have been working since first light: they needed the cool of morning. Now the heat of noon is amplified in the shade. There is little talk. They work on steadily up the tracks, cutting back the willows, alders and beech trees that have leant too close.

It is not a busy line. The first train to pass was the six forty-five up to London. Then every ninety minutes, or thereabouts, the men set down the saws and scythes, the one at the end shouts, 'Track!' and they all take a breather as the train thunders by. Not too close. But close enough for the inches to matter. Close enough to feel the whip of the slipstream after the train has passed, in its wake a billow of heat and speed, with the aspen trees dancing full of rustles and the willow flicked up like marabou.

The job will take two weeks. 'That's the estimate. Not all the track needs clearing,' Jack overhears the man telling his father. 'But it's thick enough to be causing worry. At any rate it'll be some work. The problem is I'm one man short. I've been let down.' He looks at Jack uncertainly. College boy: Jack can see what the man is thinking. He seems to take in his pale face, his skin almost greenish as though he were unwell, his eyes blackened so that the man leant sideways to look at him and Jack could tell that he was wondering if he'd been in a fight. Are those black eyes really shiners? 'It'll be some work,' he says again.

His father glances at him, and looks away. You think I'm strong enough to work? he wants to ask them. You don't know, but a minute felled me. One second was all it took to do this damage. Now years will go dropping from me like dead leaves since I'm without her. You don't see it, but I'm an old man already. I'm not good for this life any more.

Since he saw her with that dark-haired man last night he has not slept. He returned home as the sky began to fade to dawn. He lay down on his bed without undressing, and rose at eight as though it were an ordinary day. But catching a glimpse of his reflection that morning in the hallway mirror, he had to run outside to breathe cool air for fear that he would faint. He was the same but changed in everything that mattered. His reflection was a lie, a close impersonation, as though someone else had slipped inside his skin.

He tried to write a letter to her. But he saw her opening the envelope, glancing at the signature and throwing it aside without reading what he had written, so he tore it up. He despised the look of his anguish, yet could find no disguise to conceal his devastation. But disguise was all he wanted; a protective measure of artifice to lull her back into the right memory of him. Anything would be better, he thought, than this flayed pain to which he could see no end.

So Jack took the torn pieces of his letter out into the yard and burnt them in the brazier. The fire consoled him: he was sure he was in hell. He watched the ash motes rise skywards in the heat. They turned to soot where he caught them in his hands. And then the wood-pigeons made their song up in the eaves and he cursed them for making him remember her in a time before the hell began.

He stabbed at the ashes with a stick, watched the embers fly and deaden. He could not catch hold of her. It was as though everything past and present was still hidden in tomorrow. So little had happened.

He longed for so much. *It is my life I miss.* He gripped the side of the brazier, which was not hot enough to cause him pain, and so he cursed this, too, for he could see how tightly his life would shadow him, and that from now on he would live with the ghost of his life keeping perfect step beside him. I will never meet myself again, he swore aloud, because that would be to meet her, too, and that cannot happen now.

He looked down at his palms covered in soot, and was angered by the illusion they offered – as though his flesh had suffered pain.

'I'll help,' he tells the man, who stands upright to look at him. Trying to pretend he hasn't been sizing me up for the job for the last few minutes, Jack thinks. 'If you're after an extra hand, I'm sure I can help.' His father smiles. Jack notices the look of relief, and wonders at it.

'You'll start tomorrow, then.' The man seems uncertain suddenly at Jack's eagerness. As though he can see the weakness in me, Jack thinks, standing up and squaring his shoulders, trying to look sturdier than he feels. The man seems satisfied and turns away to continue his conversation with his father.

This is how it will be now. Jack leaves them, goes round to the back of the house, cannot stop his eyes flickering up at the line of trees: behind them, the hotel stands out of sight. It will be just like this from now on. People will look at me with that same expression. As though I were sick, or mad. Or as though I were badly wired, with a botched job somewhere deep inside me, liable to give them shocks if they come too close. Well, it's how I feel. He stares at the ruffled pines, imagines her behind them, cannot help himself concocting just the vision that will hurt him most.

He imagines taking a swing at that dark-haired man. He swipes the top off a delphinium with a flick of his hand, watches the petals scatter and the pollen colour his fingertips bright yellow. I'll be a pariah. I'll be exiled from normal life. Everyone will read it plain as day just by the merest look at me.

He thinks foolish thoughts then. Ways he might change himself. Anything so that he does not resemble the person he was when they were together. He grits his teeth to think of the madman's beard he'll try to grow. He imagines himself living in the woods apart from everyone, or in a city he's never been to where he'll talk to no one and take his meals from tin cans, not setting foot outside his room for weeks, leaving post unanswered, bills unpaid, until at last someone comes to take him away. He thinks of the hurrying chance of war, the relief of it cresting over him. He thinks of the work he'll start the next day with a relish that is vindictive, imagining the hardship of manual labour, hankering after bruises and cuts.

So rapt in this vision is he that he does not hear his father come round the side of the house to find him. 'You're sure about that work?' He stands in front of Jack. 'He was let down at the last minute. But it's his fault for being one man short. I'd understand if you had other things you'd rather be doing.'

His voice bears no malice, but Jack bristles at his meaning. 'There's nothing else for me to be doing now,' he tells him.

His father looks at him for a few moments, nods slowly, and starts to move away as though their conversation is closed. But then he stops, and Jack hears him breathe out heavily before he speaks, although he does not look back, as though not wanting to be party to whatever effect his words might have.

'When she came looking for you here last night,' he speaks very quietly, 'I could see it was because you had ended things, and she wasn't happy with that. I was proud of you for having seen sense. It's no way to be. It's a trouble you shouldn't get into, and in a small town like this—'

Jack does not move. The air seems to grow silent about him as before rainfall, even the aspen hushed and no wind moving in the long grass. 'She came here last night?' His voice is tight as though the air were thick enough to exert pressure on his throat.

'I assumed you'd been with her. She looked—'

Jack feels his mind blacken at his father's meaning. He clenches his fists. It was not him who had caused her to look like that.

'It was past midnight that she came, and I told her you were out. She waited. She didn't think I knew but I watched her waiting for you just outside the gate. When you didn't come, she went away, up by the meadow and through the wood.'

Jack sees her doing these things. His mind feels crammed with visions of her coming here, being turned away, waiting, going back up through the woods alone. He cannot believe it is true. How had she dared do such a thing? He sees her spurred on by shame, and by too-late remorse at her treatment of him. In the dead of night, the second that that other man was sleeping, she must've come down here to salve her conscience. His image of her is shot through with conviction of her guilt. He feels sick, wishes that already he was working, sweating over something with his mind switched off. Right now it holds him too tight, almost strangling him with the horror of her betrayal.

Like a thief, he thinks, appalled at what he feels to have been stolen from him.

His father hesitates, turning round to look at Jack's expression. 'It's not over, then.' He frowns.

'Of course it is, that's why she came here.'

His father shrugs, walks away. Heat blanches the paving stones so that even the dust seems to vanish in the sunlight.

Night-time brings some quiet to his thoughts of her, although again he cannot sleep. His mind is choked until the morning's effort, clearing the tracks. He works with a ferocity that is self-hatred, unadorned. He reassures himself with each swing of the blade that he was mad ever to have thought she might love him. She was from another world. He was nothing to her. He made her up. He spits on the gravel of the tracks, stubs his boot against a sleeper in his rage.

Sweat pours down his face. He feels thin with so much sweating. Each time the aspens tremble in the faintest breeze, inwardly he curses them for making him look up, with an impulse of anxiety, and glance along the tracks: is there a train approaching? And he remembers his father's words of the previous day. 'It's not over, then.'

Each time his head lifts in expectation, peering through the gauzy green, he hears those words whispered there: it's not over. Soon enough, they sound like the easiest of prophecies. How could it be over? How could it ever?

'I want you to have this.' Elena touches the bellboy's arm. She had been about to pass him on her way downstairs.

It is his job to wind the hotel's grandfather clock, and most days she has noticed him doing this around five. She holds out the engraved brass key to him. 'I have seen the thing you use.' She smiles. 'It is no good. It does not belong with this clock at all.'

He looks down at the key and shakes his head. 'I can't possibly take this.' He holds it back out to her but she pushes away his hand.

'You must. This key belongs here,' she lowers her voice, 'and I have wanted to thank you. This is best. I would have left it here as a gift for you when I went away, anyway, but as I've seen you now – here, you must take it.'

She presses the key into his palm, her fingertips brushing for the last time the grey silk ribbon that hangs from it. 'I used to use it when I was quite small,' she withdraws her hands, 'and when I wound the clock I'd say that I was winding time. I think I almost believed it, too.'

He looks behind him, as though expecting that they will be caught out. But they are doing nothing wrong. In itself, this gift is innocent. But what if they were to be seen? He knows that her guilt, his complicity, both would be revealed, her secrets instantly made known. This gift is sufficient evidence, he thinks, sufficient proof. It's louder than I will ever be.

He holds it as though it were hot. There are voices on the landing, people approaching, the muffled thump of a door swinging shut downstairs.

'You have been very kind,' she says, her voice still quiet for fear of being overheard. 'You made a good deal possible.' She tries to smile but he can see that she cannot. 'Think of us when you wind the clock.' It is a plea, and he answers her, 'Yes,' with his eyes.

She turns from him. It is the first time she has used the expression 'us' in public, or to another soul.

Twelve men worked on the tracks. The late June heat peaked around midday. Everything after was a kind of falling-off of clarity. Clouds gathered low to the horizon out of sight of where they worked, although the oppression of them was felt: later, everyone could tell, there would be a thunderstorm. Bluebottles clung to the fur of the willow leaves. Only horseflies darted through the filtered light. The tracks gleamed dark as oiled lead.

Seen through the widening canopy of leaves, the blue sky faded until it seemed that fine rain was falling all around the sun, steaming up the high atmosphere.

Thinking of that day now, Jack remembers how, at any point, he could have set down the machete he'd been given and, with or without a word, he could have turned about and gone back up the tracks to find her. He could have broken ranks to do that one small thing. He was obliged to no one. He could do as he pleased. His will was free.

Even at the time, he was aware of this. He was aware of the smallness of the decision – simply to walk in a different direction at a given moment – that would set everything along a different course. As though he had only to glance to left or right to discover a multitude of alternatives. Instead, he kept his head down and did the job as he had agreed to do.

With every breath, he was conscious of what he was doing, conscious that in a small or significant way, he was cutting himself a path that led away from her. He meant her no direct harm by it. But he wanted to absolve himself of his past; he wanted to break himself free of the thread of longing that led only to her, that bound him so tight he could think of nothing but that. So he pressed on with the eleven other men, down the tracks.

He knew what he was doing. But that is a very different thing from saying he knew what was in his heart, or what thoughts in his head were really his own. He felt the conflict in his bones, which ached more with that tension than with hard work. He felt as though his state of perpetual inner war was possibly the only true one. That every other condition a person might find themselves in was little more than self-delusion, or the will to believe that one fact might override another, when really – as he now saw it – no fact was dominant, and no solution final. There was only this: a person in conflict with himself. He felt like many men rolled into one. He was conscious of no longer coinciding with himself.

Sure enough I knew what I was doing, he thinks now. But I did it only by shutting out a crowd of other voices that I might equally have heard. He remembers his rage. His stubbornness and spurned pride. His inability to believe that she had deliberately wronged him, only that he had wanted something she had never meant to give. And he remembers the quiet voice he set his back to, the voice of doubt, gently tugging at him to turn round: are you sure this is the right thing to do?

The blades seemed to slice the light. The men walked forward through a broken kind of darkness. Ahead, the tunnel of green was beautiful. Hacking through it, Jack felt possessed by a coal-miner's dream of diminishing certainty, and the weight of it pressed too tight about his head. By early afternoon, it was hard to think of much beyond the task in hand.

So he worked on, alongside the others, leaning into the banks when the trains roared by, their wheels screeching furious as gunfire on the sweltered metal tracks.

I will only look. He presses his foot down hard on the accelerator, racing through the town in his father's car, an olive-green Austin. I will not even try to approach her, he tells himself. I'll be able to discover all I need to know by looking, just by seeing how she is. She can't be so good an actress that I won't be able to tell what she's feeling from the way she behaves.

Arriving back at the station house at dusk, he had stood by the back door for a few minutes, taking off his boots, which were covered in mud and oil and the yellowish sap from the cut-down trees. He had been heading inside to take a bath. His face and arms were pale with dust that had clung tight to his skin after a day spent sweating in the heat. His back felt unbending as iron and the pain across his shoulder-blades was unbearable, as though someone were pressing a hot blade there.

He lingered at the back door, wrestling with his boots, wondering how he'd go about cleaning himself up, trying and failing to have her everywhere in his thoughts so that whatever door of progress through the minutes he might open up, there she'd be, waiting for him. Thinking about taking a bath, sure enough, there she was, naked and smiling, her body exposed and vulnerable with washing.

He shut his eyes and opened them to see the terracotta pot of strawberries, the fruit just turning rosy now like rubies shining up at him.

He cursed aloud, shouted into the house to ask his father if he could borrow the car. There was no answer. He must be working, Jack realised. I'll only be five, ten minutes at most. Just one look and then I'll know. I can't go on with not knowing. At the very least, that's the reason I have to see her.

Now he hurtles uphill towards the Grand Hotel, the only car on the road. He thanks God there was some petrol in the tank, a reserve kept for emergencies. His father will be mad at him, but he does not care. The place is almost deserted: everyone must be indoors eating dinner; he glances at his watch. Seven o'clock. He drives faster, across the cobbles of the square, past the pub, up the high street and out of town towards the hotel, just beyond the tied cottages and Andersen's bottom field.

In his haste, he almost knocks a man over as he turns off the main road too fast and speeds up the driveway. He notices only the clean-cut flash of his evening suit and the faint green blur of his companion although, if he's honest, he isn't sure that there was anyone with the man. It could simply have been the fir trees dancing in the wind caused by the nearness of the car as he drove by.

He pulls up in front of the hotel and jumps out, cursing the way he looks but no longer caring. He anticipates the way people will stare at him, stand aside in shock at the sight of his filthy clothes, his sawdust-caked face. He has twigs and leaves stuck to his head. He knows this because when he rubs his hands through his hair, distraught, he dislodges bits of the trees he's been hacking down that day: they fall to the floor like evidence of the inappropriateness of his being here at all. A wild man from the woods in a place without nature; without admitting nature's existence.

Jack's heart is pounding as he strides inside. Dusk has filled the hotel with shadow, and all the doors leading off the hallway are closed. The place appears to be deserted, as though the guests had obeyed a command to hide and hold their breath at the sound of his arrival. He stands just inside the entrance and peers into the unlit hall.

The baize door to his right clicks shut, although no one enters or leaves. He can hear the sound of laughter at the head of the stairs, and the muffled song of voices in the dark, indistinct but real enough, as though he could strike a match and everyone who had ever passed through the hotel would be lit up, revealed to this moment by the hunger of his search for her. But no one is there, and he cannot quite catch hold of what the voices are saying, as though out of sight someone is gliding through the airwaves of an ill-tuned radio.

His breath catches in his throat, and he can feel his heart hurry against the cage of his chest. Where is everyone? What has happened? He wants to stand there and bellow out her name until someone brings her to him. He does not give a damn about humiliation. He must set his eyes upon her, stand in the same room as her, be somewhere near her, even if no more than that.

From the far end of the hallway, he sees someone approaching: the bellboy, carrying a storm-lamp, his small figure become a giant's shadow on the walls. 'A power-cut.' He speaks softly, waving his arm wide to take in the entire hotel. 'It should be over soon.'

Jack takes a pace towards the boy, meaning to take hold of him and shake her whereabouts from him. But as he draws near, Jack can see that he is trembling. He pities him. He bears no ill-feeling towards him. He half turns, but the boy touches him lightly on the sleeve and, as though afraid of being overhead, in a whisper tells him, 'She's not here, sir. She's gone, you just missed her.'

They are sitting together in the hotel bar. It is the first time either of them has gone there. It opens directly off the main hallway, on the opposite side to the dining room, and is behind a green baize door, which David commented on, guessing that at one time it must have been the library. Now, one wall of shelves is full of bottles and glasses. Facing it, three long sash windows look out on to the garden at the front of the building.

Anna is telling David a story about how bees made their nest in a dead elm tree. She was seven when it happened. The trunk had been hollowed out by Dutch elm disease, so was redundant in a way, she explained, and the bees used it as a surrogate hive. 'You reminded me of it the other day,' she told him, 'when you showed me that picture of your cabinet with the bee signature. I think I'd actually forgotten all about it until you showed me that.'

He kisses her when she tells him this. 'So it wasn't so idiotic of me to sign that bee, I'm glad of it.'

The story went on. 'Listen, let me tell you.' She returns his kiss, leans closer towards him so no one will overhear. One day the tree had to be felled: it was leaning dangerously over their garden, liable to fall over at any moment. Being so tall, it would have crashed straight into their dining-room window. So tree-surgeons came along and chopped it down – in segments, she explains, like hollow cakes where *mafiosi* lurk with automatic rifles. Well – she laughs again – something like that.

Anyway, they started to hack it into bits. But about half-way through, where they chopped, honey started pouring out. She remembers how she stood and watched, too little to understand about the bees at first, but suddenly it all made sense. Until then, she had oftentimes sat with her back to the tree and heard some kind of hum. She'd put it down to her own contentment at sitting there in the leafy sunlight. But on reflection, emotions maybe don't have sounds to accompany them, she'd realised, laughing at herself again – and then there was the honey.

She describes how it flowed out into the dust, and she ran about the place with buckets to scoop it up. Much was lost. She was stung three times, though most of the bees had already left. But the honeycomb came away in hunks as big as turkey serving plates – squiffy-shaped where they'd fitted snug to the tree's innards, but still, as big and robust as plates. She frames their hugeness with her hands.

David's thoughts wandered as she told the story, which is not to say that he was inattentive. But he made his own connections, ran her descriptions round his own memories to find their counterpart. He remembers a swing he'd built in a tree that stretched out over the river that ran along the bottom of his garden. They called it a swing, but in truth it was only a knotted rope.

One day when he'd been dangling at the end of it, the branch it was suspended from snapped in two, landing him in the river. It was deep water, and ran heavy with all autumn's swiftness. He came ashore by luck a few hundred yards downstream: a fisherman's wooden jetty caught him in its stilts. Had this not happened, he would have been carried the mile or so down to the lock – the place they went to scare themselves at night, peering over the edge into its bright white thunder.

He remembers this because that tree also was an elm, rotten with the same plague that had affected Anna's. His friends ran away when he fell into the water. To help him was to risk blame falling on themselves. So they ran away and hid, until later that afternoon he met them in the street. 'You all right, Davey?' Their eyes were wide with worry. Had he told his parents they'd abandoned him?

'Don't worry, I know why you ran.' He had meant to reassure them, but they only backed away. He had mentioned the unmentionable, exposed their guilt. They'd wanted none of it. So he grew up, understood new things, learnt what guilt might look like, and how fear engenders secrets.

He sees Anna with her back to the huge elm and leans forward to kiss her.

'It's not my earliest memory,' she finished, 'but it's where I count my memory as beginning.' Her voice dropped to a murmur as she mentioned her parents' divorce a year later, how she had known on that honey-day that it, or something like it, would one day happen. That sweetness, even when you try to catch it, flows out into the dust and is lost, however clearly you remember the hum of it, can place yourself right back into it in a moment, still, you'll remember the loss right there alongside the pleasure.

As she stops speaking, she realises that they are no longer alone in the bar. A couple, middle-aged, are sitting together talking in low tones in the far corner, their faces erased by shadows, their shoulders hunched in happy, confidential unison. At the end of the bar, a young man – who must have been here for quite a while: his glass is empty, his cigarette burned out – frequently checks his watch, although he pretends he is just flexing his fingertips.

Drinks are served by the one-time bellboy, his back turned to them as he polishes glasses with a linen cloth. When they first walked into the bar Anna noticed the way he seemed to steady himself against the counter, as though they had given him a shock. He faced them then and smiled, but she could not meet his eye. She could still see him that first night in the corridor, with what looked like a knife clutched in his hands. It was her strongest impression of him. It fought its way to the surface of everything else she now knew to be true. She could not quite believe that that knife had been a key, that he was doing something as innocent as just making sure an old clock kept good time.

No music plays. The lights are faint without being soft. The last of dusk spills in from beneath half-lowered blinds at the windows. Anna leans towards David and takes his hands in hers. They had come here to talk. There is so much she wants to tell him. But even the air inside the bar feels oppressive, as though the place were full of people all trying to drown each other out with shouting.

He smiles at her, whispers, 'I can't even hear myself think in here.' Anna smiles back in relief and they finish their drinks.

As the sun falls down behind the town, the last of its rays catch the hotel rooftop and façade. Looking back at it as they walk together down the driveway, David thinks it looks as though the building is lit from within, as though the sandstone is translucent resin shot through with artificial light. The garden is dark by contrast, its green turned purple in the dusk.

Anna looks back with him suddenly. 'Can you hear that?' They stop for a moment on the gravel, listening.

'The wood-pigeons?' David can hear nothing else.

'No. That. Can't you hear it?' She squeezes his hand, leaning forward slightly. 'Oh, it's gone. But it was so clear.' She frowns. 'Probably a radio, or one of the guests with a . . .' she mimes, holding her hands to her ears 'you know, Walkman thingy with speakers.'

He laughs at her as she insists she heard something. 'Don't look at me like that.' She nudges him. 'It went—' She starts humming.

'OK, I believe you.' He smiles as she marks out a tune in the air.

'*Where there's you there's me* – I think it went.' She shrugs.

They walk on beneath the cedars at the foot of the driveway. Rooks fly up suddenly from the tops of the lime trees. He glances back at the hotel just as it disappears from sight, as though the trees had cut dead all the lights that burned there.

'We've escaped.' She grins, taking an exaggerated step out of the driveway into the road. At that moment, a car passes close enough for them to feel the rush of air as it travels by them, too fast, up towards the hotel.

David curses, gripping her by her wrist to pull her out of its way. 'Christ, there's a car somewhere with your number on it.' He puts his arm round her shoulders and says nothing more. He can feel that she is trembling.

'Third time I'll be lucky.' Anna keeps her head down as they walk towards to the town.

'Idiot,' he shakes her gently, 'really, you're an idiot, after everything—' He does not need to finish the sentence.

'You're going to have to take more care.' He bites his lip. Now I've said too much. He looks away, feeling her move more closely beside him so that when they walk her hip presses against him. He wonders if she has understood what that admission of concern meant. He only just realised himself.

Wild pink geraniums tip over the stone walls that line the road. On the right-hand side, there is a line of beech trees with an open field beyond; on the left, a short row of terraced houses that could be derelict, the mullioned windows dust-caked with the residue of cars.

Dusk is falling fast into evening, and when they walk past the field, an old cob lumbers up, snorting in the heat, switching yellow flies away with its tail.

'There's a pub in the main square—' David tells her as they enter the town.

'The Chalk and Bone. Across the road from that café.' Anna finishes his sentence.

'It used to be called something else. The George, I think.' They walk through the empty market stalls set up in the cobbled square. 'But they changed it because of the burial pit found over in the Chase. It was discovered in the seventies by a farmer – Andersen, I think his name was. Part of his field started to turn rank and he wondered why. His family had farmed the same area for generations. He knew a bit about soils, and couldn't work it out, so he mentioned it to an archaeologist, and when they started to dig to see what was going on, there it was – one of the largest burial pits ever found.

'About 4500 BC, the chalk surface collapsed, creating a huge hole. Our Neolithic cousins must've thought it was an entrance to the underworld, something of that kind, because when it was excavated, a number of skeletons were discovered, curled up in the foetal position as though their bodies had been wrapped up in swaddling bands, waiting to be reborn.

'Sorry,' he holds the door open for her as they go inside, 'lesson over.'

'No,' she turns to him in the entrance, 'I want to know more.'

So they buy drinks, and find a seat in the corner by the window, set apart from the rest of the bar by the height of the chair-backs, angled as though deliberately meant for just such privacy. The whisky warms him and makes red spots appear at the top of her cheekbones. As they talk, he notices her habit of gently rubbing her forehead with her index finger and thumb, as though a thought hovered there and she meant to keep it still, or pinch it to keep it quiet. He likes the gesture. It makes him smile to himself whenever she does it.

They talk until closing time, about all that's hidden in the land, and about their childhoods, both wanting to start out together from some formative time and find the match with one another there.

And it was true: there were similarities, and near-accidents of circumstance that might almost have brought them together. By coincidence they grew up on opposite sides of the same town in the north of England. 'On opposite sides of the river,' Anna said. Because although both had moved houses a number of times, to different parts of the city, or the countryside surrounding it, it had always been the case that when they moved – if one traced it precisely on a map – the river had divided them. Both saw significance in this. Both admitted to the other, without quite believing it, that of course there could be no significance in this whatsoever.

As a young boy, David had worked alongside his father – 'shifting soil to the spoil heap only, chancing on the occasional arrow-head' – at an important dig in the centre of town. Later, as a teenager, Anna had visited the same site when it had been made over and turned into a tourist centre, 'with gimmicks galore, special rides, that kind of thing'. David grimaced. But he liked the thought that, years earlier, he had grubbed about in the mud where later she had slouched by, scuffing the displays with teenage trainers, no doubt. He is happy to think of her like this. He wishes he had known her.

He even told her about the time when he'd been allowed to join his father's team to tunnel for about a quarter of a mile beneath the city in the Roman sewers. 'So I've probably even walked over your head.' She laughed.

He looked away as he imagined it. He thought of her legs scissoring over his head in summer skirts.

There was much more: large parties as children that surely they had both attended. Her description of one friend's house, a party involving a clown and a monkey. The party spilled out into a square somewhere, and there was face-painting, and a man on stilts. The parents were hippies, the father had a Ginsberg kind of beard, was this the same family? They lived half the year in Spain, or was it Morocco? Yes, something like that.

Neither wanted to prove the other wrong. They didn't want to discover that, after all, it was unlikely that they should have met, that everything about their meeting was owed to the fluke of her stepping out into the path of a car, and him pulling her clear. The idea of him saving her life was too huge to look at square in the eye.

As they left the pub he took her hand and drew her close towards him and kissed her until someone keeled out after them saying, 'Yah, the pair of you!' and sent them scampering away across the square into the night.

—

The canvas of the market stalls flapped where the new wind caught it. 'Like being at sea.' She made a tipsy swooshing noise.

'All aboard.' Similarly boozy, he drew her back into his arms, and now no one could spy upon them kissing.

The air about them was warm, balmy. The small provincial town, whose heart, more or less, they stood upon, was almost silent. The night was very still. There was a half-moon, just on the cusp of fullness.

The girl calls, 'Darling,' after the man's retreating back. He turns round, holds out his arm to guide her alongside him through the crowded hotel bar. The gesture fills Elena with apprehension. The ordinariness of its intimacy appals her – just a man's chivalry towards his wife. But his black arm clamped about the pale waist of the girl looks to Elena like a kind of funereal ribbon, binding them together.

She looks at her husband. His face is inscrutable. His remoteness chills her. He appears to her to be wearing a mask. Its familiarity is what disturbs her most. It is the same face he has always presented to her. Only now she can see the rage beneath his skin. Her hand trembles as she takes a sip of her drink.

The words she has tried to use seem to jostle about her in the crowded bar, as though they are held tight in other people's hands and she cannot wrest them free. They have talked all day. She has told him that she cannot go back to America with him. She has told him the reason why. But he seemed baffled by it, and appeared to be waiting for her to go on, as though her telling him she is in love with another man was somehow not enough. Now he seems impatient to know what she intends to do. He wants her to tell him everything. But she is caught: what does it mean to tell him everything, now?

One day has passed since her hopeless run through the woods. Beneath the long sleeves of her dress, she still bears the scratches, and her bones are stiff with sleeplessness and waiting: she stood outside the gate of Jack's house for three hours. His father told her he had gone away, and made it plain enough she was not wanted there. She is certain that Jack must have said something to him to make him react like that, with such unambiguous hostility. 'Away' must have meant to London, or perhaps to the relatives he mentioned in the North.

There was a gleam of light rising over the hilltops to the east by the time she gave up hope. She walked back the way she had come, and as she struggled uphill she felt lightheaded with fear. But the fear did not overwhelm her. It seemed to keep step with her. She almost felt that she could turn to one side and address it directly, tell it that it meant nothing to her now that she knew the far greater reality of abandonment first hand: he did not return; he had lost faith.

He had believed his eyes and they had offered him an untruth. Not a lie, and not an illusion, but a scrap of evidence wildly misinterpreted. A distortion of the facts, like someone mistakenly turning two pages of a book at once, missing out the soil of the story, holding up only the flint of action for their evidence – a relic of an event that did not even happen.

Stepping through the iron gate, Elena hesitated at the sight of the white seat in the rose-garden. She went across to it and sat down. Only days before she had come to him there and found him waiting. Now she could hear only her own breath, too loud after her struggle uphill. She sat there for a few minutes, listening. Before she left, she picked up a stone and in one swift movement brought it down on the outline of wrought iron, making an indentation in the metal. I was here, and I did wait for him and he did not come. She turned away. It was a meaningless sign. She did not feel angry but bereft. His loss of faith imprisoned her. She was powerless to remind him of herself. That mark was an empty souvenir.

When she returned to the hotel she looked in on her husband, sleeping in the adjoining bedroom that opened off the main room of the suite. There was no indication he knew she had been out. She went to the bathroom, and cleaned off all traces of mud and leaf mould that had stuck to her as she fought her way up through the trees. She looked at her bare arms in the yellow light and they seemed entirely foreign to her, as though she had just found them beneath a bush: the veins ran blue beneath thin skin that was laced about with scratches. If Jack saw me now, she asked her reflection, would he still doubt me?

These marks are traces of my love, and surely he'd believe me if he saw them.

She felt a loneliness she had never known before, as though she had entered into a world that meant nothing to any other soul alive: now that Jack had left, she was in isolation there, looking out for someone who would not come again. His doubt seemed physically to have broken something; the pieces that were left were airless and without illusion – like a child tearing down a magician's curtain, revealing the trick beneath, the trapdoor, the cache of rabbits, the crouching girl. Now, she looked even at herself in profound doubt. Her reflection seemed like the silver bromide attempt to catch a ghost: the certainty of the image obliterated in a dazzling flash of saltpetre.

But her throat, exposed, still bore the trace of them together – little more than a slim pinkishness of the skin – where that briar rose had caught it in the coppice. No, she was not mad; she had not invented him.

She slipped into a nightdress and went back to her own bed, lying still beneath the covers until it was properly light. She did not sleep.

Now, looking back over the day that has passed since then, she cannot see the logic of it. She and her husband Harry have talked for hours but she feels as though they might as well have babbled in untranslatable languages. That afternoon, when they were in private upstairs, and he had turned to her in disgust, telling her that she was his wife and she belonged to him, and that for this reason he had expected better of her, she told him that she had, of course, always known about his mistresses, but had preferred to believe that it was not true, and he had struck her – for the first time, little more than a slap with the back of his hand against her cheek, as though swatting away a nuisance, something he did not wish to consider or be bothered with. But his gesture explained something she had not understood before.

'That is incomparable,' he told her, almost in a whisper, leaving the room the moment he had spoken. Both were astonished at all that that admission meant.

But she has not told him about the seriousness of her illness. He knows nothing of the specialist in London. She cannot tell him now. He would think it was a trick and demand proof. Doctors would be summoned. She sees the effort of that humiliation, and knows she would not be able to bear it.

'So, as a dying wish you want me to let you go, on the off-chance he might come back to you?' She can see his reaction as plainly as though she has already told him. He would not believe her. Or he would think she was insane: he would force her to go away with him, send her to an institution to be cured of the excessiveness of her emotion. Why would she wish to devote herself to a man without any guarantee that he loves her, and who anyway has vanished? To give herself to someone without proof that she was wanted? It was ludicrous, the behaviour of a madwoman.

When he arrived, he told her she looked 'wan', and frowned at her in reprimand, his voice indignant as he reminded her that she was supposed to be taking a rest here, as well as thinking about 'that novel'.

Elena looks about the bar. The pianist is playing – what is it? A Fletcher Henderson melody maybe. She can hear the words and notes but the sounds make little sense to her, almost as though she were newly deaf, watching the silent playing, feeling only the confusion of unreadable vibrations.

She puts her right hand on the table between them, presses her fingertips against the black lacquer surface. Her husband's hand, which rested with his cigarette against the ashtray, inches from her own, is violently withdrawn, as though she had made an attempt to take hold of it – although she had not done this. His hand retracts in revulsion, lingers about his mouth as he takes a couple of short drags on his cigarette, puffing smoke like venom.

I deserve all that, Elena thinks, looking down at her hand, removing it from the table top. But the evidence remains that it was there: damp spirals of her fingerprints on black.

The noise in the hotel bar seems to grow louder every moment. Through the dusky windows the hot air enters, offering no relief, only a kind of stifling dampness.

It is just approaching seven o'clock and daylight is leaving the building, running up the sandstone and over the slate rooftop. At this moment, sunlight still falls into the room beneath the three-quarters raised blinds. It shows up cigarette smoke and dust motes, giving the impression that people move through banks of steam or smoke that linger up to waist height. Then, much higher above their heads, the smoke whirls and eddies, settles in a fog that gathers, hesitates, and seems to descend.

Only people's heads and faces seem clear-cut, as though caught up in sharp focus. Elena has the impression that at any second they will all realise the imminence of danger; the fact that the smoke will meet and cover them, rising from the floor, descending from the ceiling. They will rush for the green baize door. It will be bolted from the outside. They will scramble for the windows; the catches will not budge, the antique glass will prove too strong to shatter beneath their fists.

'We must go somewhere else.' Elena stands up. She can bear it no longer. Terror haunts her, matches her every move like a watchful double. She cannot believe that no one else can see what is so plainly before her eyes. Her forehead is cold and she is conscious of sweat beneath her hair, tiny drips of it at her temples. Her dress feels absurdly tight and she has the sensation of her chest being wrapped in tight bands that she cannot shift loose. They seem to constrict the vertebrae of her back, and as she walks away she feels as though she is wading through fast water. She does not think she will faint, but that she runs the risk of drowning if she does not get out of the bar straight away.

People part to let her through. She keeps her eyes fixed ahead of her, but is conscious of being looked at as she leaves. Of course, the door is not locked, and she is aware that the bellboy stands beside it, holding it open for her. She thinks that it is him. She knows him only by the familiarity of his uniform. Her mind is glazed over as though she looks through dull glass.

She walks straight out of the hotel and on to the gravel driveway. She tries to walk slowly, but when Harry comes alongside her, he seems to be out of breath: 'Can't you wait, Elena?' His voice is furious. She has the impression that perhaps she was running as she left, and that is the reason for his annoyance. She wants no more talking between them, although this is what she knows must happen. She wants him to disappear. She wants the fantasy of his vanishing, removing the need for any more seconds of this terrible too-old, too-hard grit of explanation, when nothing of what has happened can be set in words that either of them will recognise or find acceptable in any way.

She would like Jack to stroll towards her at this moment up the driveway, smiling to see her because she'd be alone. But he has seen her with her husband and he has lost his faith in her. He has disbelieved she is who she says she is. He has disbelieved that *she* exists. She has the sudden idea to grab her husband by the arm and haul him off with her to find Jack and demand that the three of them see the logic of love that hovers above them, shining its light so partially on her and Jack that they will have to obey it. To disobey would be to walk in darkness. It would be a form of evil.

They pass beneath the cedars at the foot of the driveway. At the sound of the band suddenly striking up in the ballroom Elena glances back at the hotel. Rooks fly up as they reach the gate. She glances back again at the hotel: something caught her eye. A flash of gold on a uniform just inside the doorway. Perhaps it was nothing. But a figure does seem to stand there, concealed by shade, as though the lights have all been cut inside the building. From this distance it is impossible to say for sure whether the shadows are for this reason, or on account of something else, perhaps the weight of clouds.

She looks up. The dark trees rustle overhead and the cool air is pleasant on her face, as though Jack has just placed his hand on her brow, kissing her, telling her that she should not worry. Whenever he said this to her in the past, she believed him. And she remembers the time he dropped her off after their picnic, when he left her on this exact spot. Since then, a pink rhododendron has bloomed. She notices it, and can almost feel his lips again. Her love. He drove away so quickly that day that he did not see her turn back to watch him go, or take a pace back towards the car so that she could tell him how much she loved him, how much she was born for just that purpose so that her whole life has fallen quiet behind her now, insignificant – as though obliterated in the formation of a new-shaped world.

But he had already gone, and she stood there alone on the driveway and registered the fact that she had never before felt such happiness as at that moment.

Now she feels suddenly calm, and fears what this means: somewhere very far inside herself, she feels the edge of hope slip from her. She has asked for so much – to love and be loved back, and within the limits of a narrowed time, when she would have been wise to want nothing. She shuts her eyes. If I could somehow get back inside those seconds, find some way to exhume them from the past, I would not stand there wishing that he'd turn round. I would run to him, and tell him everything so there could be no doubt.

—

She glances back at the hotel, but it is already hidden by the overhanging trees. So she steps into the road just as a car swings by, speeding fast on its way up the gravel driveway. Her husband grabs her roughly by the arm so that she is thrown into the shadow of the fir trees, out of sight of whoever is behind the wheel. The driver does not even know how close he came to knocking her over.

'Idiot!' Harry puts his hands on his hips as he looks down at her struggling to stand up from where he pushed her into the covering tree. 'Come on, let's go. If you want to talk, we'll talk.' He turns his back on her and walks to the left, out of town. She follows.

When she looks back from a high point further along the road, it is impossible even to say that the hotel is still there: unlit, it is concealed by darkness.

11

They pass no one on the way back to the hotel. The horse is still stamping in the field, its eyes flickering sleepily upon them as they go by. There are no cars; the birds are silent; the gateway to the hotel is unmarked, and with the sign covered by the overgrown rhododendrons, their pink blooms spent, they might easily have missed the entrance.

They stumble as they walk uphill. The night crackles after the day's intensity of heat. When they speak, their voices are magnified as though hot weather has desiccated all obstructions to their hearing, so that noises bounce back off the flat surfaces of the buildings and the road. The tarmac smells faintly of liquorice.

David's arm is around Anna's shoulders as they walk. They sing a bit, laughing at their off-key voices, and at a number of other things, without much reason – the cock-eyed moon, or so he describes it, that looks half-cut, she says; it is tipped over on its side, as though poured full of lemonade so that it glistens, shimmering in the night.

The driveway is steeper than she had imagined and he walks ahead of her, hauling her along behind him. The building is in almost complete darkness, with a lamp burning over the main entrance, and one light visible in a ground-floor room.

At the doorway, David takes her in his arms again. From inside, they hear the sound of someone walking towards them across the marble floor. They pull apart just as the inner door swings open and the old man stands there in the shadows, leaning forward to see who's there. 'I'm so glad,' he murmurs, peering at them as though they were pale images darkening into sharp focus. 'Good evening, sir, madam.' He stands back a pace, letting them through. When the light touches his face, they can see how broadly he is smiling – a wide grin of relief. He nods at them, calls after them to say, 'Goodnight,' as they go inside together.

As they walk upstairs, the grandfather clock catches before midnight, whirring on the mechanism of seconds before falling to the hour.

Behind them, the man sits down heavily in one of the armchairs as though he had risen only at the sound of their arrival, as though he had been waiting for them to return all evening.

Anna is woken from sleep by what sounds, at first, like thunder. She does not move, except to open her eyes. David's arms are wrapped tightly about her from behind, and she faces the window. The curtains are open a few inches and instead of darkness between the pale cloth, there seems to be some kind of light burning there – not steady like starlight, the moon, or the start of dawn, but tremulous like heavy rainfall, or distant flames.

Her eyelids droop. She is very tired, and probably still drunk. When they came back to the hotel, they fell upon his bed exhausted after the climb up through the town, and even making it up the stairs seemed to wear them out. So they collapsed on to the bed and talked for hours, fell asleep, woke up again, slept, clambered fully clothed beneath the sheets, and now she feels as though she's been asleep for days: her limbs are hot with a depth of slumberous exhaustion as though she'd be incapable of moving them even if she tried.

She hears the sound again. She shuts her eyes, opens them to see the same faint flickering between the curtains. Rain, she thinks, it must be rain. But the sound is less like a rumble than the far-off roaring of a forest fire. She does not question it further, in the way she would not question a dream but would let it run through her, leaving its residue for her to decode on waking, peering at the lees of whatever had fermented in the secrecy of sleep.

She hears David sigh, without waking, and it is a sound like relief, as though he has been dreaming his way through the night to find home. She feels his breath against the nape of her neck. Their feet touch. She feels the soft skin of his toes. It is their only patch of nakedness. They giggled as they took off their socks and shoes, sitting side by side on the bed like obedient children. She smiles again to remember it.

Still the roaring sound, the hesitating light. She sleeps, wakes, remembers being similarly woken in the night a few weeks ago when she'd made the decision to come here. That time, it had been rain for sure – a massive downpour that dominated the city with its noise, transformed it like a dropscene. Waking that morning, it was as though sleep had been the last dry scraps of mortar, holding her together. The lightness she felt then was a kind of devastation. But it was also freedom, for she saw that the boldness she had had was worn right through:

in its place was nothing but a love of life - the clandestine reason for all her courage.

Now the danger of her illness is in the past, although she had been told at first that her chances were fifty-fifty - a pressure of life against death too stark to contemplate. Running between, like the line of a horizon lit by dusk, she had discerned the silver thread of that novel's story, an inscription of love in spite of heartbreak, which she had clung to, and followed to this place.

She moves in the bed, feels David's lips brush her hair. Earlier, he had asked her about the story. 'Does it have a happy ending?'

She paused before she answered. 'You know it doesn't really end. There's no way of saying for sure what comes after the last chapter. So I suppose, yes, it is happy.' She did not tell him what she knew about the author. It did not matter; anything might have happened next.

She remembers how she felt when she arrived here - her first impression so much a part of the book's conjuring. Now that town in her imagination has dissolved behind the stronger picture of the place where she first fell in love; the hotel, the surrounding land, both bear traces of her upon them now.

Turning in his arms, she can see herself as she was on that first day. The same girl in everything but this love. And she can still feel his hand in hers as they leant into the gradient of the hillside, ploughing their way uphill, constructing a tangible future out of what, until recently, she had thought was nothing.

She thinks these things on the edge of sleep and they are little more than wordless nudgings at the sense that she is right back at the beginning of herself, as though she has not been cured so much as burnt down to her base material, to let the new season start again as it should, after flames.

She hears the burning thunder-sound again. It seems to ebb and flow as though just held in check by a bank of guarding rocks, a rainstorm passing harmless by the shoreline, the fury of the sea held clear of where she lies. She can feel the danger of it, but cannot draw back from sleep sufficiently to wake and try to find out what it is. In her mind's eye it is the dark wing-tip of a storm, ruffling the surface of the ocean mid-Atlantic – and then gone, the surface unbroken glass again, while the danger lifts and levels in another place.

Her head sinks further into the duckdown pillow, which smells of her love, sleeping tight behind her. Like a spoon, she smiles as she swings towards sleep, and what is that song about the dish running away with the spoon, and then something about the moon and jumping over it, or lassoing it to bring it down – or is that something else? I'll bring you down the moon. If she was still awake, she'd ask him if he knows anything about this, and perhaps he would.

But there are no answers now, and no final truth to be discovered as she lets go, trusting at last and absolutely to the alchemy of sleep.

They are wading upwards through the knee-high grass, breathless with effort. He walks a few yards ahead of Elena, and she struggles to catch up. Her shins ache with walking so fast through the long grass. Dusk is gone. It is properly evening now, and the hillside is thick with shadows and the first heavy fall of night. Darkness is quickened by the density of clouds. Where the last pallor of daylight should remain, the horizon is black. Stormclouds are gathered and the air about them seems filled with smoke.

Elena calls up to her husband, Harry, 'Have you seen there'll be rain? We shouldn't go further.' But he moves steadily upwards, and she supposes that he has not heard her. She tries to walk faster but the grass snakes about her ankles, stifling her movement. The first thunder comes, sounding like a soft yawn, far in the distance. The sound is so unlike itself that Elena looks back at the town. Perhaps it was the engine of a car.

She stands for a few moments, catching her breath. 'Damn it, listen to me. There's no need to go further now,' she shouts, but again he does not seem to hear her. She watches his moving figure, black against the shadowed grass. The breath billows upwards in her chest, ballooning, too great to be contained. She clutches her sides, rubs her palm across her belly. She feels sick with tiredness.

But her exhaustion is more than physical: she has come this way before, with Jack. Her love has made the riptide she now struggles in. Each step uphill seems to insist on the precedence of a lie, as though to continue in this direction will be to trigger some danger of massive consequence, each step shoring up a dam to send a river miles off-course.

Elena hesitates and looks down at the town. From here, it is mainly rooftops. The slate could be no more than a layer of the earth pushed to the surface. Only the blots of electricity show at what point in time it is being observed. The circuits of electricity, she thinks, are like a fragile spider's web, networking across the skin of the land. Broken, the skin will fall back beneath the earth, and there'll be no appearance of anything particular to now. When all those lights are cut, I might as well be spying on a different layer of time.

Looking upwards, away from the town, she can see that her husband has reached the brow of the hill. He is a totem of darkness like a half-felled tree, or a tree that's been struck by lightning with its insides hollowed out. She feels as though she might get close to him and he'd turn to powder where she pushed him. His darkness seems obsolete. She is not afraid. We are the thunderbolt, Jack and I, she wants to make him see this. See, too, that the choice to be with her love was made many years ago, long before she was even born. 'All this is just talk,' she says aloud, 'and I would love him any number of times again if the choice were offered me.'

She stumbles as she walks, cursing her shoes as she takes them off, carrying them in her right hand. She calls out after her husband, 'Will you not stop?' She knows that he will not, and with the thought of having to chase after him, the humiliation – for what? To convince him of something about myself that he does not see by daylight? – she hesitates, and is conscious of the madness of the situation, and tells herself to turn back and to hell with him. But then she thinks of her parents. She must get his assurance before everything.

Elena walks up through the field towards the lip of the hill. She can no longer see Harry. He must already have started to walk down across the moor. When she reaches the hilltop, she sees that she has come out at a point she's never passed before. There's a broken-down stone wall that she mistook for a shape in the ridge of land. The sudden whip of warm wind catches her by surprise and it is hard to breathe. She leans against the stones. Her fingertips graze granite.

Looking down across the moor, Elena widens her eyes to bring the darkness into focus. She realises that she must have come out about thirty yards or so off the course her husband took. She spots him tacking steadily downhill some way over to the right. She takes a diagonal path down towards him.

The peaty earth is soft underfoot, and dry after days of sunlight. It is like walking on a well-sprung ballroom floor, she thinks, as though there are devices hidden beneath her feet. The ground seems to bounce back to its previous shape as she passes over it, leaving no trace, no footprints.

But she can smell water from somewhere – the scent is almost wineish. She fumbles for the word – brackish? She breathes quickly, and is reminded weirdly of eating chowder, and a sudden image of Coney Island and the boardwalk bleached by salt. That's it. She can smell the sea. From how many miles away is it brought to me? She remembers Jack telling her: fifteen miles as the crow flies, but not flying, the walk would run for almost twenty with the whalebacked monuments of the hills to navigate. By road, it's further still. These are just medieval routes, he laughed. Fifty miles to the west the Romans cut a straighter line, right through from coast to grain-rich arable land. They had no business on the moor. It was off their map.

Downhill, the smell of sea diminishes. The salt gives way to the sweet of underground streams and the ground grows marshy. Her feet are cut by flints risen to the surface by the sifting motion of water through silt-rich soil. Jack had explained it to her: long ago, this was all sea, and even just two thousand years ago it looked nothing like it does now. It was an estuary where sea and river intertwined, with this raised land a kind of peaty promontory. Standing here – they'd been standing on the brow of the hill over which she's now passed; it was the furthest they ever went – we would probably have been standing at the shoreline.

Ahead of her, though not by far, her husband's figure has come to a halt. She approaches him quickly. The air is thick and now there is a growl of thunder, unmistakable, but still no rain although the air is no longer dry. It feels like lukewarm steam. If she could see it, she is sure that that's what it would appear to be. She has the fleet thought that perhaps that's what it is. As a child, she saw a photograph in a textbook of a volcano, the eruption, if she remembers this right, of Etna. Geysers of steam shot out of the earth as though a giant subway rumbled underneath.

'My God, was there any need to come out this far?' She had not meant to sound so frightened, and only when she speaks does she realise that it's true, that she is deeply afraid, and that her earlier thoughts of no longer minding about the dangers that might come to herself have gone. She does care still. She does want more of life now she has seen what life can be. She wants to go off like a child and shine her torch about it, make her own tracks through it, dream its maps into existence.

At this moment, she forsakes everything but that. She wants more time to live. She forsakes land and history and even family, and have I done wrong? She wants only the gift of time's unfolding, so that when her love returns, she will be there to meet him. She is happy to wait for ever if it means that that moment will come again.

She takes a pace backwards and wants to run. Her husband's silence is terrifying to her. She knows that to talk now would be superfluous, that at this point there will be only actions. As though we are two beasts, she thinks, and the music of language has no power to touch us. She takes another pace back, he follows her in ragged tandem.

He does not speak, but there is a noise that seems to be stuck in his throat like an animal's call of warning. It reminds her of something she has heard only once before, when she was very small, too small to be properly afraid, and with some reason. Her father carried her on his shoulders. He made her titanic. He held her clear of danger.

—

They were in the forests around Munich. She, and her mother and father. The forests were good for ceps: well tended, composed of beech trees mainly, so that the forest floor was coppery – gold where the light caught it, bronze where there were only shadows. There was a noise suddenly from very far off and she felt her father jump, cursing softly, turning to her mother and saying in a rapid whisper that they should turn back to the road. Her mother's breath was sharply withdrawn, and she said, 'Hush!' to Elena when she started humming as they turned about. There were wild boar in the forest. She heard them grumble and scuff the air with their bristled breath.

They walked from the forest in silence. When they met the road it seemed to pick them up like a bright river, carrying them clear of harm; then her parents explained to her the dangers of the boar.

That was the sound she heard just now: her husband's call of anger and possession. She tries to back away but Harry grips her by her wrists and holds her so she cannot move. It has started to rain. Water falls on her face and the boom of summer thunder comes louder now so she can barely hear him, or herself. He pulls her hard towards him, shaking her. 'I heard you go out last night. You were with him for hours. Did you think you could get away with it? Take me for a fool? You couldn't even wait until I'd left.'

She tries to struggle free but he holds her fast. 'No, Harry, it wasn't like that at all. I wasn't with him.'

His hands dig into the flesh of her shoulders and she squirms backwards in fear that he will hit her. Instead, he grapples her tight against him, his rage become the anguish of a child. 'How could you?' And for the first time, she recognises his voice: his mask falls, and he is shut out alongside her in a wild place, two people pitted stark against each other – too-conscious, uncomprehending. 'It isn't right,' he shouts at her. 'You had no right to do this to me.'

Even without being able to see his face, she can tell that he is crying, his chest bowed with anguish. They stand together, their bodies buckled in struggle. 'But I can't change what's happened.' He suddenly lets go of her hands and she stumbles backwards. The night seems to draw its breath, as though the storm is all worn through. Steadying herself, she watches him start to stagger away, directionless, but then he stoops to pick something up and is back beside her in one stride, taking hold of her wrists behind her back with one hand, and pushing her ahead of him to where the peaty ground grows wet, so that she thinks her feet might break through its crust and find deep water. The way ahead is pitch, and there seems to be nothing there at all, as though the land has split open to reveal a cave that has no end.

In her fear she calls out Jack's name, and her husband bellows so loud behind her that when she says his name again the sound is lost. She is twisted round, half turned back towards him, when she sees his right hand raised, holding something that cuts the wetness of the rain like flint. He brings it down clumsily on her skull. In the same movement, he pushes her forward and she falls into the darkness.

Harry Greenwood wipes his face on his sleeve, tasting mud and the salt of his own perspiration. He rubs his breastbone with the flat of his hand. Still his breath will not be steady. He breathes deeply outwards but some obstruction remains in his windpipe, the physical manifestation of his fear grown palpable as a tumour.

He sees himself with her on the blackened hillside, the way his hands felt like a weapon he had never held before, suddenly set there in his palms. It was as though a small black part of him had become monstrous, matching him limb for limb, an ancient hatred seizing him with narcotic trickery, so that he was both conscious and unconscious of what he was doing. How was such a thing possible? He could not cite that in defence of what had happened. But even as he struck her, pushing her from him, his heart's reflex was to grasp hold of her and shake some love for him back into her. And yet the love he sought did not exist. To hold her was to clutch at an illusion. She loved another. So he struck out at that other man and saw, too late, that it was she who crumpled into darkness, and then he ran, fast and directionless as a blind quarry pursued across the moor.

Now Harry bends down to clean his hands on the verge and the pure scent of grass rises through his fingertips. His black evening suit is wet through. He loosens his tie. Unless someone touches him, they will not be able to see that his clothes are wet. He looks up at the hillside. He half expects to see a track of light streaming out behind him, a trail of evidence leading straight back to where he left her. But there is nothing, only the unbroken darkness.

How far he has run he does not know. His chest hurts with effort and his neck feels thick with panic and exertion. He rejoined the road almost a mile outside town. He could see the small cluster of lights between the two elevated points of the land, and realised that he must have run in a horseshoe-shaped curve, doubling back on himself to meet the road higher up where it meandered in a loose zigzag towards the hilltop. The distance back gave him the chance to think. And yet when he reached the outskirts of the town, his mind drew a blank, as though his thoughts had been erased with every footfall.

His shoes are covered with mud. He carefully removes them so that he can clean them on the verge, crouching down to undo the laces outside the main gates of the hotel. He hears voices on the road behind him. Someone singing. Laughter. A woman's soft sigh nestled in her throat, a man's gentle reply. The footsteps slow down, mingle and stop. They must be kissing.

The rain has ceased now, and the thunder has cleared. It is a different night entirely from the one it was only a few hours ago. Instead of growing darker, now that the clouds have emptied the sky has become lighter, almost blue again, as though the hours have unravelled back to day. The moon is visible now, too. It is half full, perhaps a little less than half full. Harry squints up at it, assessing it.

The voices begin again on the road behind him. He does not wish to be seen. Shoeless, he forces his way between a gap in the rhododendrons and the dark fir trees. He hears the two lovers come up the steep hill, both of them softly singing now, though neither seems to know all the words, Harry thinks as he listens to them. They must be drunk. From inside the cover of the bushes, he watches the flicker of their bodies as they pass. He can see the flash of the woman's dress. He hears the sound of her heels on the tarmac of the road, the wet press of leather made sharper by the rainfall. The man's shoes have nailed soles, and his pace, even drunk, is smart and regular. Harry supposes that he is in the army. He saw a number of uniforms this evening in the hotel bar.

He holds his breath as they seem to linger at the gateway. He thinks of his shoes. Perhaps they are visible beneath the bushes. The couple passes out of sight and hearing up the driveway. Harry wipes his shoes clean on the grass verge, puts them back on. He touches his collar, sets his shirt straight, pats his breast pocket. Thank God. He has remembered a comb. He takes it out and smooths down his hair. Its wetness gives the illusion of fresh Brylcreem.

Approaching the hotel, he can see someone waiting inside the doorway. He follows the lead of the couple who just passed him on the road and tries to hum. By humming, he hopes to appear drunk. But the noise that comes out of his throat is tremulous, and he coughs, hesitates, feels his heart jump against his ribcage. He lingers on the driveway, feels inside his jacket pocket for a cigarette. When he draws out the packet it crumples damply in his fist and he replaces it. It could simply have been empty. If he is being watched, then that could have been the explanation, he tells himself, cursing under his breath.

If anyone asks, he will say that he has been for a walk to clear his head after spending rather too long at a bar in the town. He does not stand out in crowds; he is always being mistaken for someone else; people often say that they have seen him when he was not even there. He will mention, directly, that he supposes his wife has already gone up to her room, so can he have some warm milk to take up to her himself?

'Your wife, sir, already in her room?'

'She came with me into the town. We decided to get out of the hotel, pardon me for that, but it was so noisy and crowded, and I haven't seen her for a little while, so, well, forgive me, we wanted to have a quiet drink, a tête-à-tête, you understand I'm sure.'

It's an explanation that will sound perfectly natural, he tells himself. A man's claim on his wife's affection demanding just such exclusivity, naturally enough, to wish for a drink *à deux* – not wishing for any other number. He feels his jaw stiffen to think this.

He notices the figure moving in the doorway, hesitant, as though looking out for someone. He guards his movements. There is no reason not to believe me, he reassures himself, no reason to suspect me of any wrongdoing.

Harry slows his pace, kicks gravel as he walks. His mind is stifled with images risen from the past, scenes that have not entered his thoughts for years but which, inexplicably, have now resurfaced so that he can think of nothing else.

He remembers – but how long ago this seems – after an impersonation he once laughingly did of Primo Carnera, how Elena's face cleared suddenly in surprise. 'You should have been an actor,' she said, only half joking, shooting him nervous glances all that evening – where had they been? Yes, he recalls, it was with the Bergdorfs out in Malibu; he'd gone fishing with Sam Bergdorf, and his wife Sally had forced pink gins on poor Elena all that afternoon. 'Keep pace, honey' was her way of saying 'cheers'. He remembers Elena's relief when he'd come in from the boat. By then the deal was done. Sam would put up the ten thousand that Harry needed. It was a good day. She had been so glad just to see him then. Her eyes seemed to change colour when she was happy – you couldn't act that.

But he cannot think of such things now. If he thinks of them he will be lost. He turns his back on the hotel and looks out over the garden, the ornamental yew hedges gleaming phosphorescent in the light from inside the building. He straightens his back. His spine feels cold, and fragile as though it has been replaced with a stick of ice. A fast prayer runs through his head. I am weak, yes. But I am not a bad man. Now I will carry on as before. See that her family is safe. Do what I can for others. Not stray from the general good. It was just this personal wrong I was not able to tolerate. Like a spat between neighbours: an eye for an eye. We had a bargain. She broke it. That's where I stopped being my wife's keeper.

He breathes out quickly, trying not to flinch at the sound of a gate creaking on its hinges somewhere out of sight in the far recesses of the garden. He blows his nose. He can see the way she looked the other night, her dress a sheath of gold that only reinforced his understanding of her guilt: the way the faint pattern in the fabric's weave had reminded him of a snake – a Mojave diamond-back; and it had put him in mind of a day out filming in the desert when one of the cameramen had brought the sloughed-off skin of a snake to show to Elena. She had covered her face in horror. But the skin was beautiful, fragile as a new-formed shell, catching the sunlight. She had looked just like that when she followed after him the other day: they argued; he left the room in anger; he turned round to see the falseness of her beauty and it seemed to break his heart. How could she have done this to him? Now he could trust no one. She had spoiled that innocence of trust.

He rubs his jaw; it is locked with tension. What has happened has happened. No law says a man must endure harm, regardless of what harm is done against him. Now everything has been balanced. He can carry on as before, without this wrong set against him, pulling him down with it. That is what he could not stand: the taint, the personal outrage weighing against his sense of right and wrong.

And what man would not do likewise? He glances up at the hillside behind the hotel. His neck stiffens at the impression he just had of someone calling to him. But it was nothing. He was mistaken. And yet life is not like that, he tells himself. Certain convictions are set in stone and can be read from any angle, just the same. They are not liable to be overthrown by being misheard.

He peers up at the hillside. Is there a light up there? Perhaps it is just a car passing. And that sound? It must've been someone playing music in an unlit house concealed by a fold in the land. He shakes himself. Common sense says that I heard nothing, and so I did not hear a thing. There are some absolutes derived from common sense. Just as certain lies are entirely permissible. After all, what is a lie but someone's aiming for a greater truth, a greater happiness or good?

Just as it was better for me to tell her that it must be she who couldn't conceive, not I who could not make her pregnant. That was a lie to serve a purpose that later she would have thanked me for. Stars grow dull, their lights dimmed with the distraction of children. It was better for her to end with herself, not to dilute herself by continuing after she had gone, through all the attenuations of a family. She must have known that, even just in secret.

But he falters momentarily, and corrects himself. No, he must be honest on this point. She did not know that. He cannot speak for her in this. He takes out his handkerchief and wipes his brow where along the hairline small beads of sweat have formed.

He clears his throat and turns towards the main door of the hotel. It cannot be so hard to see this through, he tells himself. I must simply jump tracks, behave as though a parallel reality were true. I must act according to the logic of a different world that could, very easily, be real. He tries to visualise the naturalness of his return and all that he will say. He runs the alternative script through his mind: 'Well, we were just leaving the hotel, about to go into the town to have a drink at the George, when she says, "Darling, actually I feel a bit peaky" – she was here for her health, you know, just a little rest, and, well, the other reasons you'll understand are too important to tell everyone. Oh, if you insist. There may be a movie. She will be the star. Anyway. She said she was feeling a little bit off-colour, but that that shouldn't stop me. "And do you mind?" I asked her. "Just a nightcap."

'Well, it was a few more, but she will understand – she will have fallen asleep now anyway, as she said she would. "I'll stay here at the hotel, don't worry," she said, and I imagine went straight back up to her room. Perhaps she stayed a while downstairs in the drawing room, reading a magazine. And you might have noticed her there? Yes, I expect you will have seen her. She is quite heartbreakingly lovely, and I don't mind – no, why should I? – if you have noticed this about her.

It is to be expected. You probably knew her from the pictures. You remember the face but not the movie. The story of my life.'

Harry will shrug then, having no admissible reason yet to worry. 'She must have come back without your noticing her, loveliness and all, my dear fellow.' He will smile at the bellboy as he goes upstairs to find her.

GHOST MUSIC

The woman is half covered with water. But the rain has stopped, and the earth over her head will be dry again tomorrow.

She is in a secret place, near the flowering of an underground spring that once showed on the surface of the sea like a cauldron's broiling roll – a constant upwards fountain of hot springwater forcing its way up to the air. Now the sea has withdrawn, an island has been made, forests of hazel have risen and fallen to peat, and the heat of the spring has cooled; its force is almost spent. But rising through Cretaceous chalks, the water tastes like wine it is so rich in minerals and traces of spent elements.

The land belongs to a man called John Andersen. Generations from now, his granddaughter – a clever business mind – will have the source tested, and realise that she is 'sitting on a goldmine', as her husband puts it. She will name her mineral water 'Water from the Well'. It will be sold in Waitrose and certain of the larger branches of Sainsbury's, although it is a cause of regret to her that it will never be sold for export: it fails to meet the numerous standards for purity.

The woman rises, falls. The motion of water turns her. Shine a light into the crevice where she is lodged no more than five feet from the surface, and her body would seem already ancient. Mud-covered and dark with peat. Her green dress clings to her. Green turned black wraps slick about her limbs. She might almost be a mermaid: her thighs seem bound together by the weight of wet silk, strong as scaly skin. Her blonde hair is coloured auburn – a shade closer to her natural walnut brown. It has fallen from its hidden clasps to spread out like a stain around her face. She is a

265

different woman, as though she has been pushed through layers of a different life.

Shine a torch very close, and you'd see the mark on her throat, hidden beneath a necklace of gold filigree, dropping seven small garnets like beads of blood – although in fact what blood was spilt has flowed away from her downhill, where the streamwater scatters it beneath the peat. It is invisible. It would be impossible to detect. Now, it belongs less to her than to the silence that has absorbed it. And with its effects unfelt, its cause also is hidden: a crack to the back of her skull with a stone – even this violence is already muffled by the intervention of duration, a finger pressed to the hushed mouth of trouble.

At one time, the two sides of the crevice were far apart. The landscape was remade by ice, then heat and the weight of endless oppositions. New boundaries were drawn up, broken down by forgotten wars far beneath the surface of the land, which none the less still breathes, rising and falling as it will rise and fall again. But still, there was a time – exactly when or how the land divided at this exact point it is impossible to say, but there must have been a moment, a pin stuck in time's map, a before and after nestled either side of the transfigured second – when one side of the land edged away from the other, the chalky Downs breaking slightly from the shale and marble quarried to make floors and pediments and art, and to create the blank façades of certain of the smarter buildings around the country, concealing the too-bright red of brick beneath.

Between this division, the land was full of holes. The valley was really a crack in a larger mass of land. The crevice was a needle-eye into the water table miles beneath. She might have fallen further. But inside it was like a honey-comb. To find your way further down would be to navigate a labyrinth.

The body lifts and falls, shifted by an unseen movement of water. In the upper air, a gull cuts the night with moonlight on its wing. It dips close to the surface of the moor, dreaming in its hunger of a vast, lost sea, beaking only at pink chaffweed.

It might all, so easily, have resembled nothing like this. Time might have been packed differently. Different moments might have been crammed with different things or, just as potently, left empty of all circumstance and residue.

One degree of temperature higher or lower, a different concoction of gases, a tectonic struggle differently resolved, and the landscape would have been unrecognisable. A woman not met by a man called Jacob Leeman in November 1908 in a Düsseldorf coffee house; a novel not written, or set down differently; a train not taken one day in late June 1938 to a small provincial town in England. All that has happened might, just as easily, not have occurred.

The same notes might have been touched, the same points in time met on the clockface, but strike them differently, and time itself is changed. This woman in particular might have liked that idea. It would have reminded her of her mother's piano playing: she could tell jokes with the keys just like Chico Marx, making the family howl with laughter at the way she'd colour in the keyboard's black and white with stories.

Still the walnut grandfather ticks on, its labours of wound metal offering no sign of the significance concealed in minutes: the storms of love, of birth and death, all hidden as open secrets within the emptying clockface.

When she wakes, she is quite sure that she is dead. She cannot move. She has been broken, irreparably. She has vomited often, and is heavily concussed, although by now the sickness might have come anyway, and for a different reason. Her lover's almost-child is snug inside her, living in faint tandem with its mother. She will never know this. How could she even suspect such a thing?

'You must be infertile, my dear': this is what her husband had told her, his head tilted in an angle of regret that, secretly, somewhere so deep inside herself that she could not quite catch sight of it, she did not absolutely trust. The lie, insisted on, did not quite ring true; it had a timbre only certain people heard, like the sharpness of hearing that only a dog might snap at. But she did not have the courage to insist on any contradictory truth, and so she let the lie alone.

Now she is suffering two kinds of death: herself, and their child; the third death would come with her love's forgetting.

She is aware of her breath blowing bubbles where half of her mouth is in water. She knows this only because of the noise the bubbles make when they break: a muffled crack like rainfall, or like the pop of cigarette smoke expelled into a summer's evening, or pine-needles splintering to softness beneath her skin weighed down by another's body – sounds which woke her once before from just such depths of unknowing.

Beyond this she is conscious of nothing. She does not know her name or where she is. She has an idea that is wrapped up in itself so tightly that to phrase it is to stretch it out beyond its actual length, as though it's best suited to a symbolic form of logic, not a sentence, although that's all she has: I want to live because I love.

It is all she has, and as such it is everything at this moment. It approaches and retreats in a gentle ebb and flow, and when it comes back to her it is rearranged by that tidal motion, though still it means the same thing. I love because I want to live. It falls away, comes back broken and reduced, but is the same still, for all that. I love to live. And, I live to love. And when she herself falls from the sentence beneath the waves, love and life are left there still, unheard but intertwined.

He had not meant to stay so long, waiting once more by the river. But each time he stands up to go, something keeps him there. Most often, it would be a sound on the road, a car engine humming from far off, approaching the bridge. He'd hear the driver change down a gear to take the corner. The engine would lag and labour as though on the point of stopping. To let a passenger out? By 'a passenger', of course, he meant only her.

Or else it would be a noise in the undergrowth that would send his eyes swivelling into the darkness, peering behind him beneath the willows. Is it her? She must have seen his note and come at last to find him. There'd be a crack of dry twigs, or a slither as the long grass parted, and then nothing. No, it was not Elena; it was no one at all.

Or there might be a noise out on the water, as though someone's foot had slipped into the shallows as they came towards him along the banks from further up. Perhaps she has walked in plimsoles along the road, he imagines, holding his breath, and isn't sure how to find the exact spot I described, so she has worked her way down by the side of the bridge and then, very carefully – which is why she makes so little noise – is even now tightroping her way along the narrow limits of the riverbank. The sedge and wild watercress make the edge slippery. That splash just then might have been her foot slipping on the mud.

No, again, it is not her. He sits back down. It is like looking out for ghosts.

A duck passes him, faintly churning the water. That was what had made the noise. That cracked twig behind him was just a bird, disturbed by his presence here. He breathes again, rubs his eyes.

But it is the thought that these noises might mean her that keeps him here. It is as though their similarity to the possible sound of her arrival colours the moments almost the exact shade they'd be if, in fact, they were filled with her. So he stays, and waits. Her arrival would harmonise with the sounds already all about this place. In that way, he tells himself, it is almost to be expected.

He remembers the way she slipped into the seat beside him in the rose-garden. What had she said? 'I knew you'd want proof.' So she must know it now, more than ever. His thinking like this is a kind of prayer. He shuts his eyes just as they had been shut that evening. He had opened them then to find her head resting against his shoulder. Her presence had completed him. He had not felt like himself until that moment. He had not seen how full a person could be and still not break, or come apart at the edges. He made a transition then through ages of his and so many other people's lives. He realised how much he depended on that extension of himself into the world, into the new place their love had created there.

The shock of that moment remade his memory, and he saw how lonely he had been until he met her. He'd mistaken his moderate happiness for the limits of his life. She broke the banks of his credulity, made him reel at the mediocrity of his vision. I had no idea, he remembers thinking when she left him, disappearing back inside the hotel, that life could be so huge and still containable in a single instant. Just a woman, unexpected, in a young man's arms. It spelt out all his understanding, all his dreams; the impossibility of anything's being as it is for longer than that moment of illumination, with everything else composed of either longing or regret – and how much that is a tiny price to pay. In return: the sum of life.

But how much distance does a man need to see the significance of a single moment? He felt as though he needed thousands of years before he'd be able to stare square at the brightness they had made.

He looks down at the river's surface, twisting in the moonlight. The water flows swift and inexplicable. There has been only one fall of rain in the last week – that same night – and Jack cannot understand how it should run so full. The countryside whispers yellow with summer's heat. The earth at the roadside is baked hard and sounded hollow to walk on when he came here. People talked about the need for new pipes to be laid so the town could have more water. Now, it is close to drought. The rainfall has been too brief. The river's fullness is a puzzle, as though the rest of the island is beneath a cloud.

Jack peers at his watch-face in the gloom. It is almost one o'clock. His father will wonder where he is. When he left the car at home, and was on the point of going straight back out on foot, his father had taken hold of him by the shoulder. 'I thought you said it was over?'

His grip had been hard and Jack swung round, shaking his hand away. 'And if it is? Would that satisfy you?' His father's face paled, and Jack knew that he had gone too far. 'Nothing will be enough for you now.' Jack's voice was broken as he turned away. 'You know as well as I that nothing can finish something like this. It isn't over for you and Mother, even after—' He heard the door shut quiet behind him as his father left the room. At what point had he stopped listening to him? He could not hear his footsteps, and could tell that he was standing motionless behind the door, impatient for Jack to leave.

Jack had felt the rage gather and swell in his fingertips as though he had physically struck his father. He felt hateful and ashamed. He strode from the house, cursing as he scribbled a note for her and pinned it to the gatepost at the head of the driveway. It gave instructions how to find him. He felt absurd pinning it there, like a child in hope of Santa Claus. He damned his father for his disbelief and censure. At least now if she looked for him again, this time she would find him. His eyes smarted with tears as he ran downhill, through the quiet town.

Now he thinks of how that bellboy's face had appeared to contain a warning, when earlier that evening he told Jack that she had gone. He had seemed to want to tell him something, and Jack is sure he knows just what it was: she went away with another man. For a moment, he had made himself believe that she wasn't there because perhaps she had gone in search of him. But secretly he knew it was not true. Give up hope, don't be a fool – the boy might as well have said that.

Jack stretches his neck. His head aches with waiting. It is as painful as though someone had punched him on the back of his skull. Even if I wanted to, I couldn't give up hope. He looks through the rustling canopy of trees, so much taller than they were when he first came here as a boy. He imagines the seasons unfolding, and the years, and how easy it would be to wait for any length of time if he could be certain that at some future moment she would return to him. He shuts his eyes to the alternative. He tells himself that this is what he must perfect: waiting and silence. If he can do that—

He goes down to the water and crouches beside it. It smells of peat, although even in the darkness he can see that it runs clear, and when he dips his fingers into it, it is icy cold. He cups his hands and drinks from it. It tastes almost sweet, as though someone has scented it with flowers, or crushed ripe grapes into it higher upstream. He takes off his shoes and socks, and hesitates, feeling the damp mud curl up through his toes.

Without thinking, he strips off his shirt and trousers, and then, glancing about him in the darkness – to hell with anyone seeing me – he stands there naked beside the water. The air is warmish on his skin. He looks at the surface sliding past as though made of whorled plates of ice. It is impossible to guess at its depth. But he knows the river well. He has seen it dried up often enough to know all the shapes along its bed, the places where the earth is raised, and where the hollows are.

He glances up through the trees where the willows shine silver in the night, and the branches form a lattice overhead as though he stands inside a shrine. Grasshoppers rub their wings, though no rain comes.

—

273

He pauses, readying himself for the right moment, waiting for the river to bring the right moment to him, and then he dives in. He stays underwater for a long while and opens his eyes in the double-handed harmony of darkness. There are flashes of light beneath the surface of the river. He wonders if it is just starlight that makes so much brightness pass before his eyes, as though without sound his sight had struck a perfect chord. Or perhaps it is just a car passing. But for a few seconds he swims in beauty in the river, and he would later swear on his life, in private, to himself, that he saw her, swimming alongside him there.

12

Jack is drying himself with his shirt when he hears the sound of someone approaching along the riverbank. This time there is no doubt. A nesting duck skitters across the water, and the twigs break loud underfoot. 'Elena?' He is caught in the flashlight's unsteady beam, his heart seeming to shrink and stop at the thought that it is her. His naked skin prickles with imagining her nearness. Instinctively, he reaches out his arms towards her.

The torch snaps off to darkness and suddenly he feels a man's weight rushing against him, half falling into him, half seizing hold of him by the upper arms, strong hands digging into his uncovered flesh. The man repeats her name, his voice ground low and full of anger. In his mouth the word is corrupted, spat out like a curse. Jack cannot see his face. He lashes out at him, wrestling himself free, and only then, when the faint moonlight falls upon him, can he see that it is his father, panting out of breath in front of him, a hand raised to his head where Jack just struck him.

He starts to back away, but his father takes hold of him again. 'For God's sake, Jack, what are you thinking of?' His strength is a shock that makes Jack wince as he shakes him. 'Look at yourself.'

The older man abruptly lets go his hold of Jack's arms so that they fall back heavy to his sides. 'What have you done?' He turns from him, cursing, as though finding his nakedness unbearable. 'Where is she?'

Jack can feel his face burn with humiliation as he dresses. 'She isn't here, if that's what you're thinking.'

'No?' His father sweeps the water with the flashlight. 'I found the note you left for her, just as anyone else might have done.' Jack fastens his shirt, looks away when the light falls upon him. His father takes hold of his face by the chin as though he were a child, his voice accusing. 'What's this?' He touches his cheek, holds his hands inside the circle of light. A daub of blood is visible on his fingertips.

'What do you think? You must've cut me just now.' He pushes himself free.

'My God, Jack.' His father's voice comes out no louder than an outbreath, as though the last few minutes have exhausted him and he can go no further.

They stand together for a moment in silence. A car passes on the bridge and his father hides the torch against his body so that no light will be visible from the road. They can hear the river hiss through the reeds lined along the banks and through the willows trailing in the swollen water. When his father speaks at last, Jack feels the lightness of the river-sounds seem to run through him, diminishing him as though he were unravelling to nothing. 'The police have been at the house, asking for you. She's disappeared. Her husband reported her missing just after twelve.'

Jack tries to speak but can say nothing. He opens his mouth and a noise escapes that he does not recognise as his own. Disappeared? It does not make sense. He covers his face. 'Disappeared' is the shadow forewarning death. The darkness seems to fall around him like a rain of fine coal dust constantly descending. The ground seems soft enough for him to fall to without harm. And that man was her husband? He staggers backwards, blundering into a tree, 'I must find her,' but his father takes hold of his wrist, explaining something that Jack cannot understand. His voice seems abstracted, harmless. Certain words rise to the surface, most are lost. Jack cocks his head, trying to shut out that other sound, the static hush and rumble, as though with one step he might walk into the river and be swallowed whole, these moments unconscripted, disowned to memory.

His father takes his arm and tries to lead him away. 'The police could be back any moment, come on.'

Jack cannot move. His body aches. 'No, I must go to find her.' He sees himself at the hotel earlier that evening. What had the bellboy said – that he had just missed her? As though he might have turned round at that moment and caught hold of her before she vanished from sight. Instead, he raged blind inside his jealousy, imagining her going off with another man, and drove away, came down here to wait as though waiting was a test of her affection.

He leans over to stop the dizziness, the blood running to his head. 'But I was there.'

'The car was seen, not who was driving.' His father's voice is impatient. 'We have to get back before they come again.'

Jack thinks of the boy's expression, the fear that he had read as a kind of warning. 'Someone did see me there.'

His father is already trying to work his way back along the riverbank to the road. 'Perhaps they just saw the car and assumed it was me. It's an easy mistake to make.'

'It wasn't a mistake. The bellboy knows who I am. We spoke.' His father turns back to him. The night is very still, with no kind of disturbance or noise, no sirens, fast cars or trains hurtling to disaster, just the emphatic stillness of late summer when a storm has broken, passed away.

'But he didn't mention it to the police. Does he know about you and her?'

Jack sees himself standing beside her on the station platform on the first day, the way that even before he spoke to her he was conscious of a kind of tide of sound seeming to propel him towards her. It would have been obvious even to a stranger, even then, that he was in love with her. And he thinks of the messages that that boy passed between them, naming the times and places where they would meet. 'He knows, yes,' Jack whispers.

He hears his father curse, kick out at the ground. 'So when that boy remembers, and changes his story, what then? You're going to let your life rest on whether or not he keeps your secret?' He takes Jack's arm and pushes him forward along the path. 'Your word against his isn't good enough.'

They reach the road, and his father cuts the torchlight. 'You need proof.'

'But I've done nothing. I was here alone.' His father does not answer him and in the darkness he can feel his accusation and is defenceless against it. His father is right to think him guilty. He is to blame for whatever harm has come to her, but not for the reason his father thinks. He waited when he should have done anything but that. He feels his hands bunch to fists in sudden anger – at himself, at the mistrustful world, at her for disappearing, and at his father for his blame. He wants to kill someone for what has happened. He would be a killer if it would make any difference. His father touches his arm and he jumps back as though he had drawn a knife on him.

'It's not enough to have things hanging on a word.' His voice is quiet now, and Jack feels like a child dragged from groggy sleep, his thoughts jumbling into one another, making no sense. His father is right. Everything hangs on a word, and he can see his whole life dangling there. He staggers backwards and his father takes his arm. 'Come on, I have an idea.'

Apart from their hurrying footsteps the town is silent. When they reach the station house, he notices that the clouds have now entirely lifted, and moonlight is falling on the tracks and on the white gravel of the driveway.

'This way, outside.' His father nods his head towards the back door that opens on to the yard. The fire shifts in the grate, the coals settling to embers. The night outside is very still and the panes of glass at the window are black and unrevealing. 'We'll have to be quick in case the police come here again.'

Jack lets him lead him out into the darkness. The air is hot against his face, as though the trees were charcoal, smouldering, and not dark with night at all. Their feet are almost noiseless on the York stone flagging of the yard. The waterbutt gleams a dish of light back up to the sky where already the moon is fading into dawn.

He can smell the water's stillness. He goes over to it and looks down into it as into a well. He dreams of wishing – an act remote as time-travel now. But his own face is all that's there, with no chance of any other. He can see the magnitude of pain already colouring his features. He feels monstrous, like someone else's creation. I cannot suffer this much pain. It will remake me, and there'll be nothing left. *What has happened to her?* He forces his head beneath the water to stop the shout of anguish he feels rising through his veins.

He spits water and bile when he comes up for air. The night is so warm it seems to dry his face in moments. He steadies himself against the wall.

'Over here.' His father leads him to the woodpile. 'Listen. This is your story. You just got home, directly after working on the tracks. You're late because you fell, some way out of town, and damaged your leg. You waited in case someone passed, but no one came. You struggled back, but it was hard, and took hours. I will lie for you. And I'll say it was me at the hotel. You were never there. How could you have driven with a damaged leg?' He holds his son by the shoulders and Jack registers the thought that not since he was a small child has he felt his father hold him quite so tenderly. 'That will be your proof. You'll be right again soon.'

Jack shakes his head, tries to take hold of his father's arm and make him understand his innocence. But he has no strength in his grip and his hand feels like a paw. He has failed everyone. He himself does not feel innocent now. If he hadn't met her, this would not have happened. And if he had tried to find her this evening, rather than waiting for her to look for him, then he might be holding her right now. He clutches his chest. His heart seems to shudder and jump, as though winding down towards standing still for ever. He is to blame for everything. It is right that he should fabricate false proofs.

When his father stands back a pace, bending to lift one of the broken sleepers, Jack can see how his face is shining, as though the skin were made from fine metal. Tears streaming down his cheeks have turned them precious. 'They could be here any moment.' His father's voice is weak-sounding and full of fear. Jack feels sick to have caused him this much grief and worry.

'Here, let me.' Jack helps him lift the heavy wood, arranging it beneath his legs. 'Like this.' His father demonstrates, as though he were a carpenter, showing him how to construct something of great seriousness and elegance.

'Yes, I see.' Jack helps him arrange things so that his legs are sandwiched between the sleepers and some smaller pieces of wood.

'Hold them steady.' His father raises his left hand in caution. Tears fall from his face on to the flagstones.

He takes the mallet in his right hand and swings a demi-arc of iron down on to the thin part of the wood. It splinters, fracturing the bone beneath, much as though this evening, on his way back across the fields, Jack had stumbled in the dusk and fallen, perhaps on the rocky bed of a stream where the stones had been loosened by rain, and had tumbled down to trap his legs beneath the heavy flints. How else could he have hurt himself this way? The thought of a father deliberately hurting his son, or of a son sacrificing himself for dubious proof of his goodness, is a story few would believe. The lie is a far more plausible story. It will serve him as his proof.

From the other side of the house, Jack can hear a freight train's sudden thunder. The sound does not diminish but seems to be held there, perfected, as though it has run right though the building, filling up each room like a high storm-tide.

'Messy breaks.' The doctor shakes his head the next day. 'You should have got me out sooner. What were you thinking of, leaving it this late?'

It is early morning, around half past six. Jack hadn't been able to stand it any longer. He fell in and out of consciousness with pain.

The doctor tapped his watch and frowned. He had already called for an ambulance to take the young man to the cottage hospital in the next town. He put it down to pride and stubborn deference that they hadn't called him sooner. In an obscure way, it flattered him. He imagined their deliberations: we shouldn't trouble him; the doctor has more important business than this.

When the ambulance arrived, the bells made father and son look up in shock, their faces drawn. The noise appeared to stun them, as though they didn't quite know what it would mean. On seeing that it was the ambulance, they seemed relieved.

The doctor thought nothing more of the entire episode, until months later the legs still hadn't properly mended, and then he cursed the lad's father for his stupidity. His son would never walk again unaided. When war came, he would have no chance to fight. In later life, he'd probably have to use a wheelchair. A few hours would have made all the difference.

The doctor told this story to his wife, who nodded and frowned and poured him another cup of tea. She confessed that it mystified her how he could take such things upon himself, dishing out life and death, the secrets of mortality inside a black leather bag that she polished for him after church with saddle wax. She handed him a slice of Victoria sponge. 'There was nothing more you could have done.'

Her hand upon his brow reminded him of his mother's touch and he turned to look at her in gratitude. 'The things people do.' He sighed as he put his arm around her waist. But she was right. For his part, he had done what he could. His conscience was clear. Though it was a pity, all the same.

When he smelt smoke, Jack thought that he was still inside his nightmare. But his father enters his room with a tray of breakfast, waking him. He opens the curtains, and they look together out of the window. 'The first time for almost a hundred years.' His father glances at him. 'It's stopped their searching in its tracks.'

Jack has seen the heather burning before, and the bracken smouldering in autumn, with the land left dark red afterwards beneath. But he has never seen anything like this. It looks as though the horizon is on fire, with the hillside blazing and the sky above it black as though someone has shaken soot across clear water.

'The shale beds have caught in the heat.' His father shuts the sash window. From a mile away, traces of smoke have slipped through the inch-wide gap at the top. 'They'll have to wait till it's burnt itself out. The fire's so deep all they can do now is wait.'

On the table by the bed, a piece of metal catches the light. His father breathes in sharply: his son's razor, the steel blade uncovered. He clears away a dirty mug and plate on to the breakfast tray, placing the razor alongside them. He puts a hand on Jack's shoulder. They do not meet one another's eye. 'Hedgerows, heather, trees, all fallen overnight to ash. It'll mean everything up there will be destroyed. It's too late now to try to find anything – it'll all be gone.'

His father leaves the room. Jack can hear him moving about downstairs. The sound of crockery being set down, a plate put in the sink. He can hear the front door opening, and the scuffling sound as his father puts on his boots. When the door closes behind him, a faint vibration runs through the walls.

Holding a sheaf of paper in his hand, he had told Jack yesterday, 'She's all over town.' And then he saw what the papers were: 'Have you seen this woman?' Notices declaring that she was missing, asking for any information to be reported to the police. His father had been asked to put them up around the station. Leaning out of the window,

Jack could see that one had been pinned to the gatepost at the front of the house. Of course, he could not see from that distance what it was. But when the wind caught it, he could hear the paper slapping against the wood as he tried to sleep. He thinks of his own note pinned there before – *Come and find me. I'm waiting for you by the river* – the intimacy of his plea obliterated by a public demand that she be found.

His legs are in plaster. He has lain all night beneath a single sheet, sleeping only for a couple of minutes at a time. Each time he slept, he fell back into nightmares. It is the second morning after she went missing. He refuses to believe his father – that it's too late. And without evidence, he will not believe that she is dead. He dodges the thought like a blow; he knows that he will not survive it if it falls.

He shuts his eyes. He can visualise perfectly the moment when he will hear of her or see her. He does not think that she will return here, or to him. He reasons that since it was her husband he saw her with, and not another lover, her disappearance was the result of some kind of ultimatum. Perhaps her husband wanted a sign of her affection that she could not deliver, and so she gave him the slip, just as she did to me. He imagines her even now some miles from here, already fixing herself up with a different name. And was she really 'Leeman' before 'Greenwood'? Had anything she told him about herself been true?

The vision of her ingenuity, her instinct for self-preservation, touches him with pleasure and he wishes that he had some way of conveying this to her. That he loves her, will be in love with her always, for he has understood what love can only mean – a gift. Something given without hope of anything in return, and without conditions laced about it to do with pride and saving face and a person's standing in the world. None of these things matters, he knows this now, and reels at his stupidity of recent days – his demands for ownership, and petulance that she was free. Free to leave him; free to die. He shuts his eyes. No. That much he cannot bear. He retracts that ounce of freedom and curses himself for having allowed the thought to stray beyond the limits of what he can contain.

He visualises the moment when he will catch sight of her in a crowd with such force and exactitude that it amounts to a feeling of expectation. And if I see her with another man? He flinches at this vision. But the feeling of pain quickly subsides: *alive*. As long as she lives. I'll take that pain of seeing her with someone else, anything, just so long as she lives. He can no longer believe in her illness. Who would kill a dying woman? The question is phrased at the back of his mind before he can stop it, and again he shuts his eyes.

No, neither ill nor dead, but just gone. Disappeared but still alive. And what had she said? 'I knew you'd want proof.' He imagines receiving a sign from her. A letter or long-distance phone call. Perhaps even a musical postcard, unsigned, sent to him from some far-flung place, and on it, a tune that played one time when they were together – just enough of a clue to let him know that she still lives. But he cannot remember the melodies any more. His heart feels deaf to music.

He raises himself up so that he can watch the flames. He is exhausted. His blood feels ancient in his veins, as though grief is an old man's transfusion. The day comes slowly, delayed by the darkness of smoke.

The fires rage for three days and destroy the surface of moorland for around twelve miles square. The story of this natural phenomenon knocks her off the front page of the regional newspaper. He'd asked his father to bring him the papers every day. Complaining, his father did this, and watched as Jack cut out all mentions of her to keep in his painted Coronation tin. Jack knew that his father was afraid for him, seeing him compile his mad archive, cataloguing the unhealthiness of his heart. But what was the alternative? To pretend he saw no hope.

When the police had stopped by after Jack returned from hospital, they did not question him about the previous night: his father's lie about driving to the hotel was believed; the bellboy kept his silence; and Jack's broken legs were ample proof that he could not possibly have been there. Instead, they wanted to know about the fact that Jack had been seen talking to her one time, a couple of weeks ago, at the hotel. Perhaps he knew something that might be useful.

His palms sweated, his hands trembling, as he cleared his throat to talk. He glanced at his father, who was fussing with the sugar bowl, his rigid back turned towards him. He could see that he was too nervous even to draw breath. But the policemen merely smiled when he told them, 'I wanted her autograph. She wouldn't let me have it,' as though they had received the same response a hundred times that day. 'It was stupid, really, I'm not even sure what pictures she's in. But I recognised her face, so——' One of them held up his hand as though there was no need to explain. He felt sick as he spoke the words, not from any fear at being discovered, but through the desire to tell them everything. It seemed to lodge in his throat, as though to speak another word would be to cough it up – a large ball of love for her that would fall to the floor, be undeniable.

After they had gone, he listened to them talking together outside, their voices lowered. 'I'll bet' – he could imagine the younger one taking out his pocketbook as he spoke, fingering the notes for a wager – 'she's just gone and scarpered. That kind do. We'll be hearing from her husband when he gets word of her, you'll see.'

Jack listened to them and his heart raced. It's true, of course, they must already have a clue to justify saying something like that, some kind of evidence. People of her 'kind', as they put it, don't just disappear. They're right, of course they are. But as their footsteps faded on the gravel of the driveway, he heard one of them laugh to the other, as though the entire conversation had been a stunt, done only to torment him. He covered his mouth with his hands to stop himself from crying out. They would have heard him, and realised he had been lying. His palms were wet with sweat.

His father came back into the room and stared at him, as though he had visualised so clearly the way the policemen would come to take away his son that he was shocked to see him still there. 'Don't worry now, it's over.' He leant down to take Jack in an awkward embrace, his thin frame trembling.

The day the fires subsided, with his father's help, Jack made it down the stairs so that he could sit out at the front of the house in a wheelchair. From there, he could see the hillside and the road, and watch people coming and going towards the station.

It is early evening and, from time to time, he falls into a light sleep. He is woken by infrequent cars, and by sudden crescendos of sound from the radio playing behind him in the house. There is little wind, and the trees are almost silent.

He is just stretching himself awake, when he notices a man walking in his direction along the road, as though about to come up towards the station house. He seems so out of place in the town that Jack cannot help but stare. The man is rapt in thought, and does not seem to notice that he is being watched until he is just at the bend in the road. He looks up to see Jack sitting about ten yards away from him with his legs in plaster. Perhaps this is what catches his eye. Jack watches him. The man does not smile.

He thinks that he seems familiar, but cannot say where he has seen him before, as though the new context has changed him, or as though, before, he has only seen him at a great distance, or high speed. From his clothes, he supposes he might have seen him at the hotel. He is late middle-aged, quite tanned, and with very dark hair. He is dressed in a fine tweed suit, cut double-breasted in the style that Americans like to wear.

The man's pace slows, and he looks up suddenly at the sound of an approaching train so that the light from the house falls for the first time upon his face. Jack has seen him before. Twice, on two quite separate occasions. Seeing him this third time is like taking off dark glasses. Three images fit together, like three faint shadows running into one, only then becoming clear. He can feel his heart seem to slow down with the hugeness of understanding. Both times he saw that man before, he was with her.

The first time was at the hotel. The man she danced with. Her husband. The second time comes down on his mind like a thunderbolt, locking the three impressions tight in place. Yes, he has seen him on three separate occasions: that evening in the garden, now, and at the gate of the hotel on the day he drove up there to look for her, the day she disappeared. 'You've just missed her.' He'd been driving so fast to try to find her that he nearly knocked the man into the bush – and is that why he is looking oddly at me now? Jack thinks, trying not to stare; no, he cannot have seen me then. But the sensation he had had that someone was with him. That flash of green – her dress? – that he had thought must be no more than undergrowth disturbed by wind.

The man seems to hesitate, though only for a brief moment, before passing away and out of sight. His footsteps make no noise on the warm road.

Jack watches the branches of the fir tree at the gate lift and fall in a shadowed hush of breeze – exactly how they looked that day. He stares at the empty road, and from the kitchen behind him he hears the radio playing a tune that brings her close beside him, as though she were singing it softly in his ear – although he does not know its name. Would she have known? She hummed it to him once, he's sure. He presses his forehead, feels a kind of dizziness as after drugs or deep sleep.

'You resting?' His father leans out of a first-floor window. 'Eight o'clock news is on in a moment. Been asleep long?'

He rubs his eyes. So was that sleep, just then? That can't have been a dream. It revealed too much. It seemed too near not to be real.

'Dad, can you see if there's anyone on the road from up there?' He twists round in his chair, calling up to his father. The blood pounds in his head.

'What? No, there's nothing to see.' He hears the window close, a voice announcing the news on the radio inside the house.

He notices a few large spots of rain starting to fall. Too late. He tilts his head up to the sky. This rain should've come three days ago and stopped the fire.

'You must try to stop worrying. Nothing will happen now. You're not part of the picture.' It was some months after she had disappeared, and his father had meant to reassure him, but this fact was a knife's pressure against Jack's heart. His father was right. He wasn't even in the picture. He did not exist. But he was stunned by the magnitude of this equation, for he saw that it was true, in every respect that mattered to him now.

He pondered on this the way he would have examined a flint, found in a new-ploughed field – rubbing it free of mud, weighing it in his palm, looking at it from every angle to guess at its past purpose. There was no evidence to link him to her, as though 'they' had existed only in his mind.

Apart from the boy at the Grand, no one had witnessed his involvement with her; he was not her husband; he was not even a guest at the hotel. Not belonging to her world, he had no substance in it because he had made no noise there – that had been the price. He had remained silent. To speak out now would be absurd. It would mean confessing everything – which was what, exactly? That she was the love of his life. Who would care? There were hundreds who might say the same, gawping at her screen double. Besides, who would listen to him, against her husband? That was something she understood too well – people carry different weights in the world; they are not numerically equivalent. She counted for so many more than herself.

His father is right. He is not even in the picture. It is too late to try to enter it now. That time has passed. He has delayed too long. It would be like cursing in the tail-fumes of a vanished train. It was never his intention to seize her from her world, but to wait for her to step outside it. He waited for that moment still, like waiting for a rock to rise from beneath an ebbing tide when already the sand has buried it too deep to be revealed.

With the fire, the search subsided. Nothing was exposed. She did not return, and her body was not found. No one needed to articulate the reason for this. It was one unspoken thing that everyone could hear. Any evidence there might have been would've been destroyed by fire. There would be no traces and no clues. Perhaps something might be found among the ashes. It would not be conclusive. And when the rain fell, almost uninterrupted for a week, everything was thrown off-course. The embered crust of the moor grew spongy and came away in pieces. The river turned black. Ashes ran through the town. Bits of burnt wood floated beneath the bridge. Looking at the skyline, Jack thought it seemed changed. Hawthorn hedgerows had fallen in the flames; the Scots pines were broken by the heat, as though struck down by reverse forks of lightning. When people went up to take a look, they saw that the stumps were burnt from the bottom up.

'There's a chance I saw her buying a ticket for the seven forty-two,' Jack's father had told the police on the first day, when they had handed him a photograph of her. 'Of course, I can't swear to it. But it could have been her.' The search took up in London. There was a possible sighting late that same night at Paddington station although, pursued, it came to nothing. A woman's body turned up in the Serpentine, but that was found to be a seamstress from Woking – although 'the similarity was remarkable', in the words of Harry Greenwood, who had stayed in London, at the deferential request of the police, for over a month. But with no evidence or known motive, there was nothing about the man to arouse suspicion. He took a flight back to America to break the news that there'd be no movie, not this time.

Most suspicion lay on the men who, around the time of her disappearance, had been hired to clear the tracks. They worked up and down the country, few had fixed addresses, they took what jobs they could, and this gloss of vagrant unpredictability made them a focus of people's suspicion. But everything came to nothing. All leads dissolved. She remained a 'missing person', just a young woman who disappeared.

The hotel was not touched by the fire. But it was not the same – nothing like the same place, or so Jack heard. The town, too, seemed to fade back into its former self, as though for the years of its celebrity it had been overreaching itself like a rubber band stretched, snapped back. The scandal of her disappearance, the foreignness of such an event, seemed to make the townspeople close ranks, and by leaning back on silence and good manners, their character seemed to have withered about a root it could not quite own, or confess to – as though they'd all been discovered to go about in contraband silk underwear and had to live down that reputation with pursed lips and stiff serge suits that itched beneath the armpits, or places that they'd never dare to scratch.

It made Jack hate them, the English. But he set aside his hate very carefully. He was one of them. He, too, had kept his voice down when he should have bellowed and made havoc with a silence that did nothing but exclude him. I belong here too, he should have raged, taking her by the hand to show them just what belonging really looked like. Because although love had exiled him, it planted him for ever in a world he knew was more real by far than any he might have found by breaking through that silence.

But he watched the way people stepped off the train with a slightly hunted air, or so he thought, as though they were embarrassed by something they could not quite name, and their embarrassment, becoming habit, had made them mean. Perhaps 'mean' was too strong. Perhaps it was a meanness of spirit, or a mistrust of exuberance that had turned to instinct. It littered their character, Jack thought, and made them seem unclear, as though now there would never come a time when, like him, they would throw off their clothes and jump naked into the river.

Waiting for the right moment might be a form of deference, or politeness, Jack supposed, and such a knack for appeasement might even mean that they were able to endure and, by enduring, stay the course. But it would engender no triumph. Waiting for the river to bring along the right moment would bring only *this*. By 'this', he meant himself, for he too had waited – for something that had almost once happened. His nearness to it, to her, had been enough. The strawberry plants reseeded themselves, the vine grew, the honeysuckle flowered, scenting the evenings with its bee-loud hoard, and on still nights in autumn, when there had been rain, he could still hear the river running high and full – even from here.

In the months following her disappearance, the town itself appeared smaller than before. It seemed defeated, but its defeat became a point of pride. Make do and mend. Red lipstick looked to Jack like a badge of warning, or a sign of membership of a club. Our lips are sealed. Soon enough, uniforms replaced the station platform's pinstriped blue. The one restaurant in town closed down for want of custom. Strangers were noticed. Foreign cars were frowned upon, openly. One time, Jack's father reported an American couple being publicly denounced for playing 'All God's Chillen Got Rhythm' on a transistor radio. The woman had worn real nylon stockings. Her husband drove a Ford coupé. They had motored here from London with the roof down. How such showiness was even possible. Could they not foresee the consequences?

But they were not 'trying to stay in town', as his father reported it. They had merely been sightseeing, following the trail of an out-of-date Baedeker guide. The woman had laughed when the café told her that they didn't serve Coke. Homemade lemonade, but not Coke. Her nose had wrinkled and she had ordered, 'OK, coffee, hold the cream.'

Hold it? How?

'She doesn't want milk,' the younger waitress whispered.

The hotel ran on a diminished staff. Bookings were cancelled. There was talk of closure. Descriptions of peeling paintwork and the sandstone darkening with unblasted age, the ravages of just one winter. By springtime, the garden had already started to 'run riot', according to the station cleaner, who did odd jobs there still, although he was seldom in demand. The box and yew had lost their shape. The rose-garden had not been pruned, so that by summer, 'It'll show,' he warned; although by then it no longer mattered. There were fieldmice in the laundry room, the tennis-courts had not been limed, and the pool stood empty.

Jack never went there again. Physically, it would have been too hard, at first: it took him almost a year to get used to the wheelchair. And after that, what was the point? He had it in his mind already. He didn't need to go back there to ogle along with all the others. To have done so would have been to dislodge the truer image. So he stayed away, and kept his image safe.

When war came at last, the hotel was temporarily saved, the sickness of its recent memory erased: it was reconnoitred as an army barracks, and with this new purpose it flourished once again.

Sometimes, on very still nights – even from the station house – it was possible to hear music, filtering through the trees. Jack would shut his eyes and imagine her running across the lawn to find him, 'I knew you'd want proof.' Or when night came, he'd see himself driving like a madman through the town and up the hotel driveway to be told, 'You just missed her,' and his heart would seem to stop, his fingers trembling as though at that moment he might have reached out, stretched just a little further into the quick-flowing tide that she was running with and meet her there, just before she left. He saw himself walking one pace faster into the hotel lobby and catching the tail of her perfume, so that if he turned round he would hear her footsteps on the marble, see the flicker of her white-hemmed dress, her shadow on the window-blind as she strolled by outside.

When people first met Jack, they would think that perhaps he was slightly deaf. Inadvertently, with time, his body fell to adopting a posture of listening, with his head cocked to one side. He felt that if he listened hard enough, he could sometimes almost hear her. It was not madness, or simple wishfulness, that made him think this. It was as though he could bend his ear to tune in to a different wave of time.

He would not hear her directly. When he heard certain melodies that they had listened to, or that had been playing when they were together, he would have her before him again too vividly – the vision would glare with a falsity of public possession, and he would feel like a man at a movie, gloating. It would be when everyone else had left the cinema, when the music stopped, after he'd put away the newspaper clippings, when the fullness of her had been whittled away almost to nothing – perhaps he'd be working, or tinkering in the greenhouse, or talking with a friend or stranger – that suddenly he'd catch a pure sound of her, and he'd tilt his head as though to gather it up like a raindrop in a lupin leaf. She would tremble there and he'd hold his breath for fear of anything that might dislodge her.

'I'll repeat myself, sorry.' People would mistake his gesture for the attentiveness of deafness, and clear their throats, start to shout at him. He let them. By then she would be gone.

But he had felt the edge of her dress against his hand. The heat of her sun-warmed hair had brushed his face and he had breathed her scent. It was what he saw when he opened his eyes that he disbelieved. She was not there? Of course, that could not be true. How could it? She was there in everything.

'They just managed to save her in time.' David returns to the room to tell Anna the reason for the rumbling noises and the flashes of light she had seen in the night. There was a fire up on the moor, close by the dig. They had worried that it might damage the body, but the fire had been put out after a few hours. A helicopter sprayed water, fire-engines had been called in, there was a hydrant a mile or so out of town on the moorland road, put there for just that purpose.

'Something a bit like this happened some time before the war, according to the guy downstairs, though then it was the shale beds, and much more serious. This was just on the surface. Only the heather caught, probably someone out walking, careless with a match. It was easily containable.' He hands her a cup of coffee, then takes it away again and sets it down on the table so that he can take her in his arms and kiss her. 'This first.'

Her hair smells of lavender, and he remembers their walk back from the pub last night, the way he'd stolen sprigs of it from someone's garden and knotted her a crown. 'Queen of Midsummer.' He'd smiled at the way she gave a little skip when he crowned her.

They have breakfast and then go out 'to look at the damage'. It's a clear day and the ground is damp, the air humid. It must have rained shortly before dawn. When they walk together through the long grass of the meadow, up towards the hilltop, their legs are quickly drenched in water as though they'd been wading through a river. They don't mind. The high sun dries them. They are happy.

At the ridge of the hill, David looks back down at the town. He can see the station house, and the signs of where the tracks once ran along the crook of the valley. The trees still grow tall there, where they would have crowded the trains as they passed by through the tunnel of green, the fronds of willow and aspen flickering along the metal carriages. To arrive at the station then, he imagines, must've been to seem to break out from beneath shallow water, or to wake from sleep. The town would not be visible until you were right at its centre. It was screened from view by the depth of green and the height of the embankments either side of the tracks.

Looking down at the station house, David points it out to Anna. She screens her eyes from the sun. 'It's derelict, surely?' She mentions to him how, on the first day she arrived here, she had looked down from a similar point, and thought she could see smashed panes of glass in the shed and the greenhouse, which anyway seemed to be overgrown, and that there were no lights on, or signs that anyone might still live there. 'Odd,' she looks down at it now, 'that anyone should live in the place when it's no longer actually a station. Think they're waiting for a train?' She laughs and turns away.

David tells her how he knows that someone lives there, because he used their telephone on the day he found the body. 'And look, there he is.' He points.

They can see a man sitting in what appears to be a wheelchair just outside the greenhouse. David wishes they were closer, so that he could shout down to him and thank him for letting him use his telephone. 'He can't have any idea how important it was. I'm not sure he even registered when I said there was a body.' David smiles to think of this. But they are too far away to shout to him. He would not hear them from this distance.

David waves, thinking that if the man looks up that maybe he will recognise him. But he shows no sign of having seen him.

'Perhaps he's sleeping.' David lowers his hand, puts it around Anna's shoulders and they turn to head off across the moor.

'Or dreaming,' Anna whispers, drawing his arm closer about her.

They cut down below the line of the hilltop and watch the high clouds cast shadows across the moor. The smoke has vanished and the air is pure and fresh, as though the fires have razed it clean.

'Look,' David follows where she points, 'it's true, on a clear day you really can see the sea.'

Three days have passed since the boy ran down the hillside in the late afternoon and asked to use Jack's phone. He has heard nothing more, and has not seen the boy again. A false alarm, he supposes. If there is news, if they have found something after all these years, he will hear about it soon enough.

He wheels himself out of the greenhouse. He had fallen asleep, as is his habit. He had taken a novel there to read. But he didn't even open it. It made a good head-rest, wedged behind him against the back of his neck. He often goes in there to read. He enjoys the sensation of looking at the world through glass and words. He likes the humid atmosphere and the smell of the plants. Whenever he has mentioned this to visitors, they peer about the greenhouse in confusion, looking for hothouse blooms – orchids and fleshy-petalled lilies, cacti that flower and fade in a single day. Ridiculous plants. It's the smell of tomato leaves running through his hands that he loves most. Convolvulus, and the creeping progress of the vine. The swell of an aubergine from its flower sinister as deadly nightshade – this is the kind of thing he prefers. Or strawberry leaves tipped up to reveal the shock of red beneath.

While he sits outside, late sunlight falls upon his face. The sky is a pink-blue wash of colour around the sun, but lower down along the horizon the clouds are gathering, and he knows that later there will most likely be a storm. This has been June. Heat and rain cutting up the month so that now, just past the solstice, the season seems divided and unnerved, as though liable to fall down on either side of the weather with massive emphasis. Jack wonders which way it will fall, and whether it will be properly summer, before the summer ends.

He listens to the last sounds of the day. The thin high whistle of nesting swallows; cars driving down into the town; voices passing by on the road. Just outside the greenhouse door, he hesitates, breathing in deeply the scents of the ending day. It is only then that he notices the smell of burning, although he can see no plume of smoke. The wrong time of year for household fires. He supposes it must be a garden bonfire from down in the town, or someone burning compost on one of the allotments. The smell seems to fade even as he tries to catch it. He gives it no more thought.

He touches his breast pocket and feels her image there. By the time he reaches the front door of the house, the first rain has fallen. Large drops, widely spaced. Heavy enough to make the dust rise. He glances up at the sky to hear the start of thunder.

No lights are on when he goes inside. The hallway is greenish with shadows. A thunderclap makes him look back suddenly at the rain falling thickly now, and when he does this, his wheelchair knocks hard against the table in the hall where the telephone is kept. Jack knows his way through the hallway to the last centimetre. How had the table come to be sticking out like that? Perhaps that boy ran into it when he was in such a hurry to use the phone the other day. Jack frowns in puzzlement. He leans over to straighten the table and notices a scrap of paper that must have fallen down behind it when it came loose from the wall. The dry plaster has crumbled, perished with age, and one of the nails has fallen out.

He has to stretch to reach the piece of paper. It almost knocks him off-balance, and the arm of his chair digs into his chest. Perhaps he should leave it for Mary to clear up on Friday. He stretches again and just manages to pick it up.

There is no light in the hallway to read by and he backs up so that he can look at it in the light cast by the gathering storm. He has never seen the paper before, but he recognises her handwriting instantly. His breath stops fast in his chest as though someone just ran into him. He has to swallow hard to breathe again. He twists round, peering into the falling rain, half expecting to see her there. Was that the sound of a car on the road? He thought he heard something, as though she might have just left the note for him only minutes earlier, then vanished once more into the evening. He stares into the darkness but can see nothing. That car sound was just the hiss of rain on stone, the wind gusting through leaf-heavy trees.

He stares at the piece of folded paper in his hands. He dares not open it straight away. It seems too light in his hands, like the skeleton of a leaf that he could make disappear by crushing in his palm. He stares at it, and rubs his eyes, which feel suddenly sore. The paper is yellowed with time, and the dust it has gathered in its folds makes his nose start to itch. Very carefully, he unfolds it.

It is just a small piece of embossed paper. Hotel stationery. There are few words on the page. The hand-writing is hurried yet deliberate, emphatic-seeming, even though the black ink has faded to pale brown. It is undated. It simply asks him to wait and to keep faith, and not to doubt her because she'll come to him any moment now, and if he can do this then she promises all will be well, and that he is her one and only, and that she loves him more each second.

Instead of an initial at the end of the note, for the first time, she has written out her full name, and in a swift PS, at the very bottom right-hand corner of the page, in slightly heavier, clearer script, she has written out and underlined the words 'I love you'. She knew that he would want proof.

He stares down at the note in his hands until his vision blurs with tears and he can no longer read it; then he refolds it very carefully and places it on the table. His hands are trembling and something seems to be racing, quicksilver-fast, through his blood. A sort of fear, is it? It feels like the panic said to accompany a heart-attack, or as though his life has grown light inside him, so that with one more breath it might finally dissolve, as though his hold on existence has been too fragile for too long – ever since he first lost her. His neck is stiff with repressed grief. He is overwhelmed by the urge to get away and clear from himself, and from everything he now knows.

He backs his chair out of the house into the evening, and turns downhill towards the town. The rain is falling fast and the clouds are the colour of polished lead, shining most where the rain has gathered.

After only a few yards, he is wet through to his skin. By the time he reaches the bridge, he feels as though he has swum the entire distance. He is exhausted. His ribcage burns, and his arms ache as after a mile of paddling through choppy water. He has never come this far unaided. But now that he is here he can stop.

He is at the exact point where, before, he would have ducked beneath the willow and pushed his way through the tall undergrowth to get to his place beside the water. He would have been able to sit there beneath the dripping trees on the slab of sandstone and watch the river glide by in all its dimpled fullness. It is little changed since then. There are different road signs on the humpbacked bridge. But he can still hear the sound of the river in full spate, churning by the stanchions, the hiss along the banks that sounds like a long-drawn in-breath, unreleased.

He goes over to the other side, and notices that there is a possible way down. He supposes that it has only recently been made – a narrow concrete slope down to the towpath. If he goes down there, he will not be able to get back up. This does not concern him. A car is approaching on the road. He will be in its way if he does not move. He works his way down until he is at the river's edge.

From this position, he can look across at the far bank, about five metres distant, and for the first time see the place where a lifetime ago he used to sit and watch the river, and where one time he stood and without hesitation jumped in to find her swimming alongside him, her hair flickering across her lips as she turned to smile at him. His breath feels broken inside his chest. He shuts his eyes, leaning forward so that he can hear the beating of the raindrops on the silvered surface of the water. And if I jump back in, will I find that she has kept her promise and is waiting for me when I break the surface?

He watches the river's slow boiling roll, and feels it run through him now, torrential.

A noise on the road makes him look up. Someone is walking down the towpath towards him. He cannot make out who it is. The rain is too dense, and night has already covered the riverbank in shadow. His breath stops as he watches the figure approaching, hesitating just out of view before walking swiftly towards him.

'I saw you from the road.' The man's voice is kind and reflective. 'You're never going to get back up unless I give you a hand.' Jack has the impression that he must have watched him all the time he's been here, anticipating the right moment to say something.

He looks up at the man, but he cannot speak. He does not want to leave. How can he, now that she has given him this sign? Any second, surely, she will appear. He feels sure that she is somewhere very near, as though she is watching him from the far riverbank.

He peers into the darkness and can see nothing there. But he can feel her in the rainfall, the fast air between the drops like the prelude to a train. He can see her everywhere, before and after and shot through every aspect of this present moment – though still he cannot hold her. But it makes no difference, he understands this now: she is here, has always been inside his heart, and that is everything. She kept her promise. She was his proof.

His body shakes with released emotion, and the man puts a hand on his shoulder to quieten him. He lets himself be pushed back up the incline. He would never have made it up that slope alone. His arms are worn out and he has no strength left.

'I'll take you home,' the man tells him. Jack thanks him, the words half hidden by his tears. He starts to explain where he lives when the man puts a hand on his shoulder. 'I know,' he murmurs, 'I'm Ted Andersen. We've met before. My uncle used to own the meadow behind your house. I work at the Grand. I was bellboy there before the war.'

His voice is so soft that Jack can barely catch the sound of his words against the hush of rain. 'I'll take you home,' he says again, almost as though he has not already spoken, not told him who he is: the one who kept their secret for them, their only witness.

Jack thanks him, and they go together through the town.

Acknowledgements

With many thanks, as always, to Jonny Geller. Also, with gratitude to Charlotte Mendelson, Amy Philip, Jane Morpeth and Hazel Orme, at Headline. I am also indebted, in particular, to Seamus Heaney's *Bog Queen*; Hilaire Belloc's *Hills and the Sea*; *A Land*, by Jacquetta Hawkes, with drawings by Henry Moore; Liam de Paor's *Archaeology*; *The English Countryside*, with an introduction by H.J. Massingham; and *Bog Bodies*, ed. R.C. Turner and R.G. Scaife (British Museum Press), though all factual errors I claim as my own. Thanks also to my mother, for taking me to digs, and my sister, for digging with me.